Don't Let Go

Harlan Coben

CENTURY

1 3 5 7 9 10 8 6 4 2

Century
20 Vauxhall Bridge Road
London SW1V 2SA

Century is part of the Penguin Random House group of companies
whose addresses can be found at global.penguinrandomhouse.com.

Penguin
Random House
UK

First published in Great Britain by Century in 2017

www.penguin.co.uk

A CIP catalogue record for this book is available from the British Library.

ISBN 9781780894232 (Hardback)
ISBN 9781780894249 (Trade Paperback)

Printed and bound by Clays Ltd., St Ives plc

Penguin Random House is committed to a sustainable future
for our business, our readers and our planet. This book is made
from Forest Stewardship Council® certified paper.

Pour Anne
A Ma Vie de Coer Entier

Author's Note

When I was growing up in suburban New Jersey, there were two common legends about my hometown.

One was that a notorious Mafia leader lived in a baronial mansion protected by an iron gate and armed guards and that there was an incinerator in the back that may have been used as a makeshift crematorium.

The second legend—the legend that inspired this book—was that adjacent to his property and near an elementary school, behind barbed-wire fencing and official NO TRESPASSING signs, there stood a Nike missile control center with nuclear capabilities.

Years later, I learned that both legends were true.

Don't Let Go

Daisy wore a clingy black dress with a neckline so deep it could tutor philosophy.

She spotted the mark sitting at the end of the bar, wearing a pinstripe gray suit. Hmm. The guy was old enough to be her dad. That might make it more difficult for her to make her play, but then again, it might not. You never knew with the old guys. Some of them, especially the recent divorcés, were all too ready to preen and prove they still had it, even if they'd never had it in the first place.

Especially if they'd never had it in the first place.

As Daisy sauntered across the room, she could feel the eyes of the male patrons crawling down her bare legs like earthworms. When she reached the end of the bar, she made a mild production of lowering herself onto the stool next to him.

The mark peered into the glass of whiskey in front of him as though he were a gypsy with a crystal ball. She waited for him to turn toward her. He didn't. Daisy studied his profile for a moment. His beard was heavy and gray. His nose was bulbous and putty-like, almost as though it were a Hollywood silicone special effect. His hair was long, straggly, mop-like.

Second marriage, Daisy figured. Second divorce in all probability.

Dale Miller—that was the mark's name—picked up his whiskey gently. He cradled it in both hands as though it were an injured bird.

"Hi," Daisy said with a much-practiced hair toss.

Miller's head turned toward her. He looked her straight in the eyes. She waited for his gaze to dip down the neckline— heck, even women did it with this dress—but it stayed on hers.

"Hello," he replied. Then he turned back to his whiskey.

Daisy usually let the mark hit on her. That was her go-to technique. She said hi like this, she smiled, the guy asked whether he could buy her a drink. You know the deal. But Miller didn't look to be in the mood to flirt. He took a deep swallow from his whiskey glass, then another.

That was good. The heavy drinking. That would make this easier.

"Is there something I can do for you?" he asked her.

Burly, Daisy thought. That was the word to describe him. Even in that pinstripe suit, Miller had that burly-biker-Vietnam-vet thing going on, his voice a low rasp. He was the kind of older guy Daisy found oddly sexy, though that was probably her legendary daddy issues rearing their insecure heads. Daisy liked men who made her feel safe.

It had been too long since she'd known one.

Time to try another angle, Daisy thought.

"Do you mind if I just sit here with you?" Daisy leaned a little closer, working the cleavage a bit, and whispered, "There's this guy . . ."

"Is he bothering you?"

Sweet. He didn't say it all macho poseur, like so many of the d-bags she had met along the way. Dale Miller said it calmly, matter-of-factly, chivalrously, even—like a man who wanted to protect her.

"No, no . . . not really."

He started looking around the bar. "Which one is he?"

Daisy put a hand on his arm.

"It's not a big deal. Really. I just . . . I feel safe here with you, okay?"

Miller met her eyes again. The bulbous nose didn't go with the face, but you almost didn't notice it with those piercing blue eyes. "Of course," he said, but in a cautious voice. "Can I buy you a drink?"

That was pretty much all the opening Daisy needed. She was good with conversation, and men—married, single, getting divorced, whatever—never minded opening up to her. It took Dale Miller a little more time than usual—drink 4, if her count was correct—but eventually he got to the impending divorce from Clara, his, yup, second wife, who was eighteen years his junior. ("Should've known, right? I'm such a fool.") A drink later, he told her about the two kids, Ryan and Simone, the custody battle, his job in finance.

She had to open up too. That was how this worked. Prime the pump. She had a story at the ready for just such occasions—a completely fictional one, of course—but something about the way Miller carried himself made her add shades of candor. Still, she would never tell him the truth. No one knew that, except Rex. And even Rex didn't know it all.

He drank whiskey. She drank vodka. She tried to imbibe at a slower pace. Twice she took her full glass to the bathroom, dumped it into the sink, filled it with water. Still, Daisy was feeling a little buzzed when the text came in from Rex.

R?

R for "Ready."

"Everything okay?" Miller asked her.

"Sure. Just a friend."

She texted back a *Y* for "Yes" and turned back to him. This was the part where she would normally suggest that they go someplace quieter. Most men jumped at the chance—men were nothing if not predictable on that score—but she wasn't sure that the direct route would work with Dale Miller. It wasn't that he didn't seem interested. He just seemed to be somehow—she wasn't sure how to put it—above it.

"Can I ask you something?" she began.

Miller smiled. "You've been asking me things all night."

There was a slight slur in his voice. Good.

"Do you have a car?" she asked.

"I do. Why?"

She glanced about the bar. "Could I, uh, ask you for a ride home? I don't live far."

"Sure, no problem." Then: "I may need a little time to sober up—"

Daisy hopped off the stool. "Oh, that's okay. I'll walk, then."

Miller sat upright. "Wait, what?"

"I kinda need to get home now, but if you can't drive—"

"No, no," he said, managing to stand. "I'll take you now."

"If it's trouble . . ."

"No trouble, Daisy."

Bingo. As they started for the door, Daisy quickly texted Rex:

OOW

Code for "On Our Way."

Some might call it a con or a swindle, but Rex insisted that it was "righteous" money. Daisy wasn't sure about righteous, but she didn't feel a lot of guilt about it either. The plan was simple in execution, if not motive. A man and a woman are getting divorced. The custody battle turns nasty. Both sides get desperate. The wife—technically speaking, the husband could use their services too, though so far it had always been the wife—hired Rex to help her win this bloodiest of battles. How did he do it?

Nail the husband on a DUI.

What better way to show the man is an unfit parent?

So that was how it worked. Daisy's job was twofold: Make sure the mark was legally drunk, and then get him behind the wheel. Rex, who was a cop, pulled them over and arrested the mark for driving under the influence, and boom, their client gets a big boost in the court proceedings. Right then, Rex was waiting in a squad car two blocks away. He always found an abandoned spot very close to whatever bar the mark would be drinking in that evening. The fewer witnesses, the better. They didn't want questions.

Pull the guy over, arrest him, move on.

They both stumbled out the door and into the lot.

"This way," Miller said. "I parked over here."

The lot's surface was made up of loose pebbles. Miller kicked them up as he led her to a gray Toyota Corolla. He hit the key fob. The car gave a muted double honk. When Miller headed toward the passenger door, Daisy was confused. Did he want her to drive? God, she hoped not. Was he more wasted than she thought? That seemed more likely. But she quickly realized it was neither of those things.

Dale Miller was opening the door for her. Like a real gentleman. That was how long it had been since Daisy had known a real gentleman. She hadn't even realized what he was doing.

He held the door. Daisy slid into the car. Dale Miller waited until she was all the way in and properly situated before he carefully closed the door behind her.

She felt a pang of guilt.

Rex had pointed out many times that they weren't doing anything illegal or even ethically dubious. For one thing, the plan didn't always work. Some guys don't hang out in bars. "If that's the case," Rex had told her, "then he's in the clear. Our guy is already out drinking, right? You're just giving him a little push, that's all. But he doesn't have to drink and drive. That's his choice in the end. You're not putting a gun to his head."

Daisy put on her seat belt. Dale Miller did the same. He started the car and put it in reverse. The tires crunched the pebbles. When he was clear of the spot, Miller stopped the car and looked at Daisy for a long moment. She tried to smile, but it wouldn't hold.

"What are you hiding, Daisy?" he asked.

She felt a chill but didn't reply.

"Something happened to you. I can see it in your face."

Not sure what else to do, Daisy tried to laugh it off. "I told you my life story in that bar, Dale."

Miller waited another second, maybe two, though it felt to her like an hour. Finally, he looked forward and put the car in drive. He didn't say another word as they made their way out of the parking lot.

"Take a left," Daisy said, hearing the tension in her own voice. "And then it's the second right."

Dale Miller was silent then, making the turns deliberately, the way you do when you've had too much to drink but don't want to get pulled over. The Toyota Corolla was clean and impersonal and smelled a little too strongly of deodorizer. When Miller took the second right, Daisy held her breath and waited for Rex's blue lights and siren to come on.

This was always the scary part for Daisy, because she never knew how someone was going to react. One guy tried to make a run for it, though he realized the futility before he reached the next corner. Some guys started cursing. Some guys—too many of them—started sobbing. That was the worst. Grown men, coolly hitting on her moments earlier, some still with their hand sliding up her dress, suddenly starting to blubber like preschoolers.

They realized the severity in an instant. That realization crushed them.

Daisy didn't know what to expect with Dale Miller.

Rex had the timing down to a science, and as though on cue, the spinning blue light came to life, followed immediately by the squad-car siren. Daisy pivoted and studied Dale Miller's face to gauge his reaction. If Miller was distraught or surprised, neither emotion was showing on his face. He was composed, determined, even. He used his blinker to signal before carefully veering to a proper stop by the curb as Rex pulled up behind him.

The siren was off now, the blue light still circling.

Dale Miller put the car in park and turned to her. She wasn't sure what expression to go with here. Surprise? Sympathy? A "What can you do?" sigh?

"Well, well," Miller said. "It looks like the past has caught up with us, eh?"

His words, his tone, his expression unnerved her. She wanted to yell for Rex to hurry, but he was taking his time the way a cop does. Dale Miller kept his eyes on her, even after Rex did a knuckle knock on his window. Miller slowly turned away and slid open the window.

"Is there a problem, Officer?"

"License and registration, please."

Dale Miller handed them over.

"Have you been drinking tonight, Mr. Miller?"

"Maybe one," he said.

With that answer, at least, he was the same as every other mark. They always lied.

"Do you mind stepping out of the car for a moment?"

Miller turned back toward Daisy. Daisy tried not to cringe under his gaze. She stared straight ahead, avoiding eye contact.

Rex said, "Sir? I asked you—"

"Of course, Officer."

Dale Miller pulled the handle. When the interior car light

came on, Daisy closed her eyes for a moment. Miller rolled out with a grunt. He left the door open, but Rex reached past him and slammed it closed. The window was still cracked, so Daisy could hear.

"Sir, I would like to run a series of field sobriety tests on you."

"We could skip that," Dale Miller said.

"Pardon me?"

"Why don't we go right to the Breathalyzer, if that would be easier?"

That offer surprised Rex. He glanced past Miller for a moment and caught her eye. Daisy gave a small shrug.

"I assume you have a field Breathalyzer in your squad car?" Miller asked.

"I do, yes."

"So let's not waste your time or mine or the lovely lady's."

Rex hesitated. Then he said, "Okay, please wait here."

"Sure."

When Rex turned to go back to his squad car, Dale Miller pulled out a gun and shot Rex twice in the back of the head. Rex crumpled to the ground.

Then Dale Miller turned the gun toward Daisy.

They're back, she thought.

After all these years, they found me.

Chapter One

hide the baseball bat behind my leg, so Trey—at least, I assume it is Trey—won't see.

The Maybe-Trey bebops toward me with the fake tan and the emo fringe do and the meaningless tribal tattoos lassoing bloated biceps. Ellie has described Trey as a "purebred twat waffle." This guy fits the bill.

Still, I have to be sure.

Over the years, I have developed a really cool deductive technique to tell if I have the right guy. Watch and learn:

"Trey?"

The choadwank stops, gives me his best Cro-Magnon forehead furrow, and says, "Who wants to know?"

"Am I supposed to say, 'I do'?"

"Huh?"

I sigh. See what kind of morons I have to deal with, Leo?

"You replied, 'Who wants to know?'" I continue. "Like you're being cagey. Like if I called out, 'Mike?' you wouldn't have said, 'You got the wrong guy, pal.' By answering 'Who wants to know?' you've already told me you're Trey."

You should see the perplexed look on this guy's face.

I take a step closer, keeping the bat out of sight.

Trey is all faux gangsta, but I feel the fear coming off him in hot waves now. Not surprising. I am a respectable-sized guy, not a five-foot woman he could slap around to feel big.

"What do you want?" Trey asks me.

Another step closer.

"To talk."

"What about?"

I swing one-handed because that's fastest. The bat lands whiplike on Trey's knee. He screams, but he doesn't fall. Now I grip the bat with both hands. Remember how Coach Jauss taught us to hit in Little League, Leo? Bat back, elbow up. That was his mantra. How old were we? Nine, ten? Doesn't matter. I do just what Coach taught us. I pull the bat all the way back, elbow up, and step into my swing.

The meat of the wood lands flush on the same knee.

Trey goes down like I shot him. "Please . . ."

This time, I lift the bat high overhead, ax-chop-style, and, putting all my weight and leverage into it, I again aim for the same knee. I can feel something splinter when the blow lands. Trey howls. I lift the bat again. By now Trey has both hands on the knee, trying to protect it. What the hell. Might as well be sure, right?

I go for the ankle. When the bat crash-lands, the ankle gives way and spreads under the onslaught. There is a crunching sound like a boot stepping on dried twigs.

"You never saw my face," I tell him. "You say a word, I come back and kill you."

I don't wait for the reply.

Do you remember when Dad took us to our first Major League Baseball game, Leo? Yankee Stadium. We sat in that box down the third-base line. We wore our baseball gloves the whole game, hoping a foul ball would come our way. It didn't, of course. I remember the way Dad tilted his face toward the sun, those Wayfarers on his eyes, that slow smile on his face. How cool was Dad? Being French, he didn't know the rules—it was his first baseball game too—but he didn't care, did he? It was a day out with his twin boys.

That was always enough for him.

Three blocks away, I drop the bat into a 7-Eleven Dumpster. I'd worn gloves so there would be no fingerprints. I had bought the bat years ago at a garage sale near Atlantic City. There is no way you could track it back to me. Not that I was worried. The cops wouldn't bother Dumpster diving into cherry Slurpees to help out the likes of a professional asshat like Trey. On TV, they might. In reality, they would chalk it up to a local beef or drug deal gone wrong or gambling debt or something else that made it well and truly deserved.

I cut through the lot and take a circuitous route back to where I parked. I am wearing a black Brooklyn Nets cap—very street—and I keep my head down. Again, I don't think anyone would take the case seriously, but you might meet up with an overzealous rookie who pulls CCTV or something.

It costs me nothing to be careful.

I get into my car, hit Interstate 280, and drive straight back to Westbridge. My mobile phone rings—a call from Ellie. Like she knows what I'm up to. Ms. Conscience. I ignore it for now.

Westbridge is the kind of American Dream suburb the media might call "family-friendly," maybe "well-to-do" or even "upscale," but it wouldn't reach the level of "tony." There are Rotary Club barbecues, July Fourth parades, Kiwanis Club carnivals, Saturday morning organic farmers' markets. Kids still ride their bikes to school. The high school football games are well attended, especially when we play our rival, Livingston. Little League is still a big deal. Coach Jauss died a few years ago, but they named one of the fields after him.

I still stop by that field, though now in a police car. Yep, I'm *that* cop. I think of you, Leo, stuck out in right field. You didn't want to play—I know that now—but you realized that I might not have joined without you. Some of the old-timers still talk about the no-hitter I pitched in the state semifinals. You weren't good enough to make that team, so the Little League powers that be put you on as a statistician. I guess they did that to keep me happy. I don't think I saw that at the time.

You were always wiser, Leo, more mature, so you probably did.

I pull up to the house and park in the driveway. Tammy and Ned Walsh from next door—in my head he's Ned Flanders because he's got the pornstache and the too-folksy manner—are cleaning their gutters. They both give me a wave.

"Hey, Nap," Ned says.

"Hey, Ned," I say. "Hey, Tammy."

14

I'm friendly like that. Mr. Nice Neighbor. See, I am the rarest of creatures in suburban towns—a straight, single, childless male is about as common out here as a cigarette in a health club—and so I work hard to come across as normal, boring, reliable.

Nonthreatening.

Dad died five years ago, so now I guess some of the neighbors perceive me as *that* single guy, the one who still lives at home and skulks around like Boo Radley. That's why I try to keep the house well maintained. That's why I try to make sure I bring my appropriate female dates back to the house during daylight hours, even when I know said date won't last.

There was a time when a guy like me would be considered charmingly eccentric, a confirmed bachelor. Now I think the neighbors worry that I'm a pedophile or something along those lines. So I do all I can to alleviate that fear.

Most of the neighbors also know our story, and so my staying here makes sense.

I'm still waving to Ned and Tammy.

"How is Brody's team doing?" I ask.

I don't care, but again, appearances.

"Eight and one," Tammy says.

"That's terrific."

"You have to come to the game next Wednesday."

"I'd like that," I say.

I'd also like to have my kidney removed with a grapefruit spoon.

I smile some more, wave again like an idiot, and head into the house. I moved out of our old room, Leo. After that night—I always refer to it as "that night" because I can't accept "double suicide" or "accidental death" or even, though no one really thinks it is, "murder"—I couldn't stand the sight of our old bunk bed. I started sleeping downstairs in the room we called the "little den" on the first floor. One of us probably should have done that years earlier, Leo. Our bedroom was okay for two boys, but it was cramped for two teenage males.

I never minded, though. I don't think you did either.

When Dad died, I moved upstairs into his master bedroom. Ellie helped me convert our old room into a home office with these white built-ins in a style she calls "Modern Urban Farmhouse." I still don't know what that means.

I head up to the bedroom now and start to shed my shirt, when the doorbell rings. I figure it's the UPS or FedEx guys. They're the only ones who stop by without calling first. So I don't bother going down. When the doorbell rings again, I wonder whether I ordered something that would need a signature. Can't think of anything. I look out the bedroom window.

Cops.

They are dressed in plain clothes, but I always know. I don't know if it's the bearing or the outfit or just some intangible, but I don't think it is strictly because I am one—a one-cop-to-another kind of thing. One of the cops is male, the other female. For a second, I think that it might be connected to Trey—logical deduction, right?—but a quick glance at their unmarked police car, which is so obviously an unmarked police car it might as well have the words "unmarked police car" spray-painted on both sides, reveals a Pennsylvania license plate.

I quickly throw on a pair of gray sweats and check my look

in the mirror. The only word that comes to mind is "dashing." Well, that isn't the only word, but let's go with it. I hurry down the steps and reach for the doorknob.

I had no idea what opening that door would do to me.

I had no idea, Leo, that it would bring me back to you.

Chapter Two

Like I said, two cops—one a man, one a woman.

The woman is older, probably midfifties, and sports a blue blazer, jeans, and practical shoes. I can see the hip bulge from her weapon ruining the line of the blazer, but she doesn't hit me as the kind to care. The guy is probably forty and wears a suit of dead-leaf brown usually favored by your nattier vice principals.

She gives me a tight smile and says, "Detective Dumas?"

She pronounces my name *Doo-mass*. It's French, actually, *Doo-MAH*, like the famed author. Leo and I were born in Marseilles. When we first moved to the USA and the town of Westbridge at age eight, our new "friends" thought it was ridiculously clever to pronounce Dumas as "Dumb Ass." Some adults still do, but we, uh, don't vote for the same candidates, if you get my drift.

I don't bother correcting her.

"What can I do for you?"

"I'm Lieutenant Stacy Reynolds," she says. "This is Detective Bates."

I don't like the vibe I'm getting here. I suspect that they are here to deliver bad news of some sort, like someone close to me has died. I had done the condolence bit many times in my official capacity. It's not my forte. But pitiful as it may sound, I couldn't even imagine who in my life meant enough to me for anyone to send out a squad car. The only person is Ellie, and she's in Westbridge, New Jersey, too, not Pennsylvania.

I skip the "Nice to meet you" and head straight for the "So what's this all about?"

"Do you mind if we come in?" Reynolds says with a weary smile. "It's been a long drive."

"I could use the bathroom," Bates adds.

"Hit the head later," I say. "Why are you here?"

"No need to be testy," Bates says.

"No need to be coy either. I'm a cop, you've come a long way, let's not draw this out."

Bates glares at me. I don't give a rat's buttock. Reynolds puts a hand on his arm to defuse the situation. I still don't give a rat's buttock.

"You're right," Reynolds says to me. "I'm afraid we have some bad news."

I wait.

"There's been a murder in our district," she continues.

"A cop killing," Bates adds.

That gets my attention. There is murder. And there is a cop killing. You don't want those to be two separate things, one being worse than the other, but you don't want a lot of things.

"Who?" I ask.

"Rex Canton."

They wait to see if I show anything. I don't, but I'm trying to work the angles.

"You knew Sergeant Canton?" she asks.

"I did," I say. "A lifetime ago."

"When was the last time you saw him?"

I am still trying to figure out why they are here. "I don't remember. High school graduation maybe."

"Not since then?"

"Not that I remember."

"But you might have?"

I shrug. "He might have come for a homecoming or something."

"But you're not sure."

"No, I'm not sure."

"You don't seem broken up about his murder," Bates says.

"On the inside I'm dying," I say. "I'm just supertough."

"No need for sarcasm," Bates says. "A fellow officer is dead."

"No need to waste our time either. I knew him in high school. That's it. I haven't seen him since. I didn't know he lived in Pennsylvania. I didn't even know he was on the job. How was he killed?"

"Gunned down during a traffic stop," Reynolds says.

Rex Canton. I knew him back in the day, of course, but he was more your friend, Leo. Part of your high school posse. I remember the goofy picture of you all dressed up as some mock rock band for the school talent show. Rex played the drums. He had a gap between his two front teeth. He seemed like a nice enough kid.

"Can we cut to it?" I ask.

"Cut to what?"

I am so not in the mood. "What do you want with me?"

Reynolds looks up at me, and maybe there's a hint of a smile on her face. "Any guesses?"

"None."

"Let me use your toilet before I pee on your stoop. Then we'll talk."

I move out of the doorway to usher them in. Reynolds goes first. Bates waits, hopping up and down a bit. My mobile rings. Ellie again. I hit ignore and send her a text that I'll call her back as soon as I can. I hear the water running as Reynolds washes her hands. She comes out; Bates goes in. He is, uh, loud. As the old saying goes, he needed to pee like a racehorse.

We move into the living room and settle in. Ellie fixed up this room, too. She aimed for "woman-friendly man cave"— wood paneling and huge-screen TV, but the bar is acrylic and the leatherette loungers are an odd shade of mauve.

"So?" I say.

Reynolds looks at Bates. He nods. Then she turns back to me. "We found fingerprints."

"Where?" I ask.

"Pardon?"

"You said Rex was gunned down during a traffic stop."

"That's right."

"So where was his body found? His squad car? The street?"

"The street."

"So you found fingerprints where exactly? On the street?"

"The where isn't important," Reynolds tells me. "The who is."

I wait. Neither speaks. So I say, "Who do the prints belong to?"

"Well, that's part of the problem," she says. "See, the fingerprints got no hits on any criminal database. The person has no record. But you see, they were still in the system."

I have always heard the expression "the hairs on my neck stood up," but I don't think I ever quite got it until now. Reynolds waits, but I won't give her the satisfaction. She's carrying this ball now. I'll let her take it to the goal line.

"The prints got a hit," she continues, "because ten years ago, you, Detective Dumas, put them in the database, describing her as a 'person of interest.' Ten years ago, when you first joined the force, you asked to be notified if there was ever a hit."

I try not to show the shock, but I don't think I'm doing too good a job. I'm flashing back, Leo. I'm flashing back fifteen years. I'm flashing back to those summer nights when she and I would walk by moonlight to that clearing on Riker Hill and lay out a blanket. I flash back to that heat, of course, the exquisiteness and purity of that lust, but mostly I flash back to the "after," me flat on my back, still catching my breath, staring up into the night sky, her head on my chest, her hand on my stomach, and for the first few minutes we would be silent, and then we would start talking in a way that made me know—*know*—I would never get tired of talking to her.

You would have been the best man.

You know me. I never needed a lot of friends. I had you, Leo. And I had her. Then I lost you. And then I lost her.

Reynolds and Bates are studying my face now. "Detective Dumas?"

I snap out of it. "Are you telling me the prints belong to Maura?"

"They do, yes."

"But you haven't found her yet."

"No, not yet," Reynolds says. "Do you want to explain?"

I grab my wallet and house keys. "I'll do it on the ride. Let's go."

Chapter Three

Reynolds and Bates naturally want to question me right now.

"In the car," I insist. "I want to see the scene."

We are all heading down the brick walkway my father put in himself twenty years ago. I take the lead. They hurry to catch up.

"Suppose we don't want to take you with us," Reynolds says.

I stop walking and do a toodle-oo finger wave. "Buh-bye, then. Safe ride back."

Bates really doesn't like me. "We can compel you to answer."

"You think? Okay." I turn to head back inside. "Let me know how that turns out."

Reynolds gets up in my face. "We are trying to find a cop killer here."

"Me too."

I'm a very good investigator—I just am, no reason for false modesty here—but I need to see the scene myself. I know the players. I may be able to help. Either way, if Maura is back, there is no way I'm letting this go.

I don't really want to explain all this to Reynolds and Bates.

"How long is the ride?" I ask.

"Two hours if we speed."

I spread my arms, welcoming-like. "You'll have me alone in a car for all that time. Imagine all the questions you can ask."

Bates frowns. He doesn't like it, or maybe he's so used to playing bad cop to Reynolds's reasonable one that he is set on automatic. They will cave. We all know this. It is just a question of how and when.

Reynolds asks, "How will you get back here?"

"Because we ain't Uber," Bates adds.

"Yeah, return transportation," I say. "That's what we should all be concentrating on."

They frown some more, but this is done now. Reynolds gets in on the driver's side, Bates the passenger.

"No one is going to open a door for me?" I say.

Needless needling, but what the hell. Before I get in, I take out my phone and go to my Favorites. From the driver's seat, Reynolds gives me a WTF look. I hold up a finger to tell her this will only take a moment.

Ellie answers, "Hey."

"I have to cancel tonight."

Every Sunday night I volunteer at Ellie's shelter for battered women.

"What's up?" she asks.

"Do you remember Rex Canton?"

"From high school? Sure."

Ellie is happily married with two girls. I'm godfather to both, which is odd, but it works. Ellie is the best person I know.

"He was a cop in Pennsylvania," I say.

"I think I heard something about that."

"You never mentioned it to me."

"Why would I?"

"Good point."

"So what about him?"

"Rex was killed on the job. Someone shot him during a traffic stop."

"Oh, that's awful. I'm sorry to hear that."

With some people, it's just words. With Ellie, you could feel the empathy.

"What's that have to do with you?" she asks.

"I'll let you know later."

Ellie didn't waste time with asking why or for more details. She got that if I wanted to say more, I would have.

"Okay, call me if you need anything."

"Take care of Brenda for me," I say.

There is a brief pause here. Brenda is a mother of two and one of the battered women at the shelter. Her life has been made a living nightmare by a violent douchenozzle. Two weeks ago, Brenda fled to Ellie's shelter in the thick of night with a concussion, broken ribs, and nothing else. Since then, Brenda has been too frightened to go outside, not even to get some air in the shelter's isolated courtyard. She left everything other than her children behind. She shakes a lot. She constantly winces and cringes as if awaiting a blow.

I want to tell Ellie that Brenda could go home tonight and finally pack her belongings, that her abuser—a cretin dubbed Trey—wouldn't be home for a few days, but there is a certain discretion even between Ellie and me here.

They'd figure it out. They always do.

"Tell Brenda I'll be back," I say.

"I will," Ellie says, and then she hangs up.

I sit alone in the back of the squad car. It smells like squad car, which is to say of perspiration and desperation and fear. Reynolds and Bates are up front, like they're my parents. They don't start asking me questions right away. They are completely silent. I roll my eyes. Really? Did they forget I'm a cop too? They are trying to get me to talk, to reveal something, wait me out. This is the vehicular equivalent to sweating a perp in the interrogation room, intentionally making him wait.

I'm not playing. I close my eyes and try to sleep.

Reynolds wakes me up. "Is your first name really Napoleon?"

"It is," I say.

My French father hated the name, but my mother, the American in Paris, insisted.

"Napoleon Dumas?"

"Everyone calls me Nap."

"Queer-ass name," Bates says.

"Bates," I say. "Instead of Mister, do they call you Master?"

"Huh?"

Reynolds holds back a chuckle. I can't believe Bates has never heard this one before. He actually tries it out, saying softly to himself, "Master Bates," before he figures it out.

"You're an asshole, Dumas."

He pronounces my last name correctly this time.

"So you want to get to it, Nap?" Reynolds says.

"Ask away."

"You're the one who put Maura Wells into the AFIS, correct?"

AFIS. Automated Fingerprint Identification System.

"Let's pretend the answer is yes."

"When?"

They know this already. "Ten years ago."

"Why?"

"She vanished."

"We checked," Bates says. "Her family never reported that she was missing."

I don't reply. We let the silence linger a bit. Reynolds breaks it.

"Nap?"

It won't look good. I know that, but it can't be helped. "Maura Wells was my girlfriend in high school. When we were seniors, she broke up with me via a text. Cut off all contact. Moved away. I looked for her, but I could never find her."

Reynolds and Bates exchange a glance.

"You talked to her parents?" Reynolds asks.

"Her mom, yeah."

"And?"

"And she said Maura's whereabouts were none of my business and I should move on with my life."

"Good advice," Bates says.

I don't take the bait.

Reynolds asks, "So how old were you?"

"Eighteen."

"So you looked for Maura, you didn't find her . . ."

"Right."

"So then what did you do?"

I don't want to say it, but Rex is dead and Maura may be back and you have to give a little to get a little. "When I joined the force I put her prints into the AFIS. Filed a report saying she was missing."

"You really didn't have any standing to do that," Bates says.

"Debatable," I say, "but are you here to bust me over a protocol issue?"

"No," Reynolds says. "We are not."

"I don't know," Bates says, feigning dubious. "A girl dumps you. Five years later, you break procedure by putting her in the system, so you can, what, try to hook up with her again?" He shrugs. "Sounds stalkerish."

"Pretty creepy behavior, Nap," Reynolds adds.

They know some of my past, I bet. They don't know enough.

"I assume you looked for Maura Wells on your own?" Reynolds asks.

"Some."

"And I assume you didn't find her."

"Correct."

"Any thoughts on where Maura's been the past fifteen years?"

We are on the highway now, heading west. I am still trying to put this together. I try to place my memories of Maura in terms of Rex. I think about you now, Leo. You were friends with them both. Does that mean anything? Maybe, maybe not. We were all

29

in the same graduating class, so we all knew one another. But how close was Maura to Rex? Had Rex perhaps recognized her by chance? And if so, does that mean she killed him?

"No," I say. "No thoughts."

"It's odd," Reynolds says. "There has been no recent activity for Maura Wells. No credit cards, no bank accounts, no IRS filings. We're still checking the paper trail—"

"You won't find anything," I say.

"You've been checking."

It's not a question.

"When did Maura Wells fall off the radar?" she asks me.

"Far as I can tell," I say, "fifteen years ago."

Chapter Four

The murder scene is a small stretch of the kind of quiet back road you might find near an airport or train depot. No residences. An industrial park that has seen better days. A sprinkling of what were either abandoned warehouses or ones on the way out.

We step out of the squad car. A few makeshift wooden horses block off the murder scene, but a vehicle could drive around them. So far I have seen none do so. I keep that in mind—the lack of traffic. The blood hasn't been cleaned up yet. Someone did a chalk outline of where Rex fell. I can't remember the last time I saw one of those—an actual chalk outline.

"Walk me through it," I say.

"You aren't here as an investigator," Bates snaps.

"You want to have a pissing contest," I ask, "or you want to catch a cop killer?"

Bates gives me the narrow eyes. "Even if the cop killer is your old flame?"

Especially if. But I don't say that out loud.

They take another minute to pretend to be difficult, and then Reynolds starts in. "Officer Rex Canton pulls over a Toyota Corolla in this area at approximately one fifteen A.M., purportedly for a DUI."

"I assume Rex radioed it in?"

"He did, yes."

That is protocol. If you stop a car, you radio in or look up the license plate number, see if the car is stolen, if there are any priors, that kind of thing. You also get the name of the car owner.

"So who owned the car?" I ask.

"It was a rental."

That bothers me, but a lot about this bothers me.

I say, "It wasn't one of the big chains, was it?"

"Pardon?"

"The rental company. It wasn't, like, Hertz or Avis."

"No, it was a small place called Sal's."

"Let me guess," I say. "It was near an airport. No advance reservation."

Reynolds and Bates share a glance. Bates says, "How do you know that?"

I ignore him and look at Reynolds.

"It was rented by a guy named Dale Miller from Portland, Maine," Reynolds says.

"The ID," I ask. "Was it fake or stolen?"

Another glance exchanged. "Stolen."

I touch the blood. It's dry. "CCTV cameras at the rental agency?"

"We should be getting the footage soon, but the guy working the desk said Dale Miller was an older man, sixties, maybe seventy."

"Where was the rental car found?" I ask.

"Half mile from Philadelphia airport."

"How many sets of fingerprints?"

"In the front seat? Just Maura Wells's. The rental agency does a pretty thorough cleaning between customers."

I nod. A truck makes the turn and cruises past us. This is the first vehicle I've seen on this road.

"Front seat," I repeat.

"Pardon?"

"You said fingerprints in the front seat. Which side— passenger side or driver's?"

Yet another glance exchanged.

"Both."

I study the road, the position of the fallen body in chalk, try to piece it together. Then I turn and face them. "Theories?" I ask.

"Two people, a man and your ex, Maura, are in the car," Reynolds says. "Officer Canton pulls them over for a DUI. Something spooks them. They panic, shoot Officer Canton twice in the back of the head, take off."

"The man probably does the shooting," Bates adds. "He's out of the car. He fires, your ex slides to the driver's side, he jumps in as a passenger. That would explain her fingerprints as both a passenger and a driver."

"As we said before, the car was rented with a stolen ID,"

Reynolds continues. "So we assume the man at the very least had something to hide. Canton pulls them over, figures something isn't right—and it gets him killed."

I nod as though I admire their handiwork. Their theory is wrong, but since I don't yet have a better answer, there is no reason to antagonize them. They are holding out on me. I would probably do the same if the roles were reversed. I need to find out exactly what they aren't telling me, and the only way to do that is to be nice.

I force up my most charming smile and say, "May I see the dash cam?"

That would be the key, of course. They don't often show everything, but in this case, it would show enough. I wait for them to answer—they would have every right to stop cooperating now—but this time when they do the exchange-a-glance thing I sense something different.

They appear uncomfortable.

Bates says, "Why don't you stop jerking us around first?"

So much for the charming smile.

"I was eighteen," I say. "A senior in high school. Maura was my girlfriend."

"And she broke up with you," Bates says. "You told us this."

Reynolds shushes him with a hand gesture. "What happened, Nap?"

"Maura's mother," I say. "You must have tracked her down. What did she say?"

"We're asking the questions, Dumas," Bates replies.

But again Reynolds gets that I want to help. "We found the mother, yes."

"And?"

"And she claims she hasn't spoken to her daughter in years. That she has no idea where she is."

"You talked to Mrs. Wells directly?"

Reynolds shakes her head. "She refused to speak with us. She issued this statement via counsel."

So Mrs. Wells hired an attorney. "You buy her story?" I ask.

"Do you?"

"No."

I'm not ready to tell them this part yet. After Maura dumped me, I broke into her house. Yep, stupid, impulsive. Or maybe not. I was feeling lost and confused with the double whammy of losing a brother and then the love of my life. So maybe that explains it.

Why did I break in? I was searching for clues to Maura's whereabouts. Me, an eighteen-year-old kid, playing detective. I didn't find much, but I stole two things from her bathroom: a toothbrush and a glass. I had no inkling I was going to become a cop at the time, but I saved them, just in case. Don't ask me why. But that's how I got Maura's prints and DNA into the system when I could.

Oh, and I got caught.

By the police nonetheless. Specifically, Captain Augie Styles.

You liked Augie, didn't you, Leo?

Augie became something of a mentor to me after that night. He's the reason I'm a cop now. He and Dad became friends too. Drinking buddies, I guess you'd call them. We all bonded in tragedy. It makes you grow close—someone else who gets what you're going through—and yet pain is always there. A carrot-stick relationship, the pure definition of bittersweet.

"Why don't you believe the mom?" Reynolds says.

"I kept tabs."

"On your ex's mother?" Bates is incredulous. "Christ, Dumas, you're a full-fledged, card-carrying stalker."

I pretend Bates isn't here. "The mother gets calls from throwaway phones. Or at least, she used to."

"And you know this how?" Bates asks.

I don't reply.

"Did you have a warrant for checking her phone records?"

I don't reply. I stare at Reynolds.

Reynolds says, "You figure it's Maura calling her?"

I shrug.

"So why is your ex working so hard to stay hidden?"

I shrug again.

"You must have a thought," Reynolds says.

I do. But I'm not ready to go there quite yet. The thought is, at first blush, both obvious and impossible. It took me a long time to accept it. I have run it by two people—Augie and Ellie—and both think I'm nuts.

"Show me the dash cam," I say to her.

"We're still asking questions," Bates says.

"Show me the dash cam," I say again, "and I think I can get to the bottom of this."

Reynolds and Bates share another uncomfortable glance.

Reynolds steps toward me. "There is none."

This surprises me. I can see that it surprises them too.

"It wasn't on," Bates says, like that explains it. "Canton was off duty."

"We assume Officer Canton switched it off," Reynolds says, "because he was heading back to the station."

"What time does he get off?" I ask.

"Midnight."

"How far is the station from here?"

"Three miles."

"So what was Rex doing from midnight until one fifteen?"

"We are still trying to put his last hours together," Reynolds says. "Near as we can tell, he just kept the cruiser out late."

"That's not unusual," Bates adds quickly. "You know the deal. If you have a day shift, you just take the squad car home."

"And while turning off the dash cam is not protocol," Reynolds says, "it's done."

I'm not buying it, but they aren't selling it hard either.

The phone clipped to Bates's belt rings. He reaches for it and steps away. Two seconds later, he says, "Where?" There is a pause. Then he hangs up and turns to Reynolds. There is an edge in his voice. "We need to go."

They drop me at a bus depot so barren I wait for a tumbleweed to blow through it. No one is working the ticket counter. I don't even think they have a ticket counter.

Two blocks down the road I find a "no-tell motel" that promises all the glamour and amenities of a herpes sore, which in this case is a logical metaphor on several levels. The sign advertises hourly rates, "color TV" (do some motels still offer black-and-white?), and "theme rooms."

"I'll take the gonorrhea suite," I say.

The guy behind the desk tosses me a key so fast I fear that I may be getting the suite I requested. The color scheme for the room could most generously be dubbed "faded yellow," though it seems suspiciously close to the urine family. I strip off the bedspread, remind myself that I'm up-to-date on my tetanus shots, and risk lying down.

Captain Augie didn't come to our house after I broke into Maura's.

I think he was afraid Dad would have a seizure if he saw that squad car pull into our driveway again. I'll never let go of that image—the squad car making the turn as though in slow motion, Augie opening the driver's-side door, his world-weary steps up our walk. Augie's own life had already been blown apart hours before—and now there he was, knowing his visit would do the same to ours.

Anyway, that's why Augie cornered me heading to school about my breaking into Maura's house, instead of going to my dad.

"I don't want to get you in trouble," Augie told me, "but you can't do stuff like that."

"She knows something," I said.

"She doesn't," Augie told me. "Maura's just a scared kid."

"You talked to her?"

"Trust me, son. You have to let her go."

I did—still do—trust him. I didn't—still haven't—let her go.

I put my hands behind my head and stare at the stains on the ceiling. I try not to speculate on how the stains might have gotten there. Augie is on the beach at the Sea Pine Resort in Hilton Head right now with a woman he met on some senior online-dating site. No way I want to interrupt that. Augie divorced eight years ago. His marriage to Audrey took a fatal hit "that night," but it limped along for another seven years before mercifully being put to sleep. It took Augie a long time to start dating again, so why blow it up with speculation?

Augie would be home in a day or two. It could wait.

I debate calling Ellie and bouncing my insane hypotheses off her, but suddenly there is a heavy, insistent knock. I throw my feet off the bed. Two uniformed cops are at the door. They both wear scowls. They say that sometimes you start looking like your spouse. It applies to police partners too, I guess. In this case, both are white and overmuscled and have prominent foreheads. If I met them again, it would be hard to remember which was which.

"Mind if we come in?" Cop One sneers.

"You got a warrant?" I ask.

"No."

"Yes," I say.

"Yes, what?"

"Yes, I mind if you come in."

"Too bad."

Cop Two pushes by me. I let him. They both come in and close the door.

Cop One offers up another sneer. "Nice dump you got here."

This, I assume, is supposed to be some kind of clever insult. Like I'd personally worked on the décor.

"We hear you're holding out on us," Cop One says.

"Rex was our friend."

"And a cop."

"And you're holding out on us."

I don't really have the patience for this, so I pull out my gun and aim it between the two of them. Their mouths make surprised Os.

"What the hell . . . ?"

"You entered my motel room without a warrant," I say.

I point the gun at one, then the other, then back to the middle.

"It would be easy to shoot you both, stick your pieces in your hands, claim the shooting was justified."

"Are you out of your mind?" Cop One asks.

I hear the fear in his voice, so I move toward him. I give him my best crazy eyes. I'm good at the crazy eyes. You know this, Leo.

"You want to have an ear fight with me?" I ask him.

"A what?"

"Your brah"—I gesture with my head toward Cop Two—"leaves. We lock the door. We put down our weapons. One of us walks out of this room with the other's ear in his mouth. What do you say?"

I lean closer and make a biting motion.

"You're fucking nuts," Cop One says.

"You got no idea." And now I'm so into it, I almost hope he'll take me up on it. "You in, big guy? What do you say?"

There is a knock on the door. Cop One practically leaps toward the knob to open it.

It's Stacy Reynolds. I hide the gun behind my leg. Reynolds is clearly not happy to see her colleagues. She glares at them. They both lower their heads like chastened school bullies.

"What the hell are you two clowns doing here?"

Cop Two says, "Just . . . ," and then he actually shrugs.

"He knows stuff," Cop One says. "We were just doing some legwork for you."

"Get out. Now."

They do. Reynolds now notices my piece against my leg. "What the fuck, Nap?"

I holster the gun. "Don't worry about it."

She shakes her head. "Cops would be better at their jobs if God gave them bigger dicks."

"You're a cop," I remind her.

"Me especially. Come on. I need to show you something."

Chapter Five

Hal, the bartender at Larry and Craig's Bar and Grille, has a wistful look on his face.

"She was smoking hot," Hal says. A small frown begins to surface. "Too hot for that old dude, that's for sure."

Larry and Craig's Bar and Grille clearly has a bar and clearly has no grille. It's that kind of place. The sticky floor is coated in sawdust and peanut shells. That combo stench of stale beer and vomit wafts from said floor and fills all nostrils. I don't need to take a piss, but if I do, I know the urinal won't flush but will be overflowing with ice cubes.

Reynolds nods at me to take the lead.

"What did she look like?" I ask.

Hal is still frowning. "What part of 'hot' isn't good English?"

"Redhead, brunette, blonde?"

"Brunette is brown, right?"

I glance at Reynolds. "Yeah, Hal. Brunette is brown."

"Brunette."

"Anything else?"

"Hot."

"Yeah, we got that."

"Built," Hal says.

Reynolds sighs. "And she was with a guy, right?"

"She was out of his league, that I can tell you."

"And you have," I remind him. "Did they come in together?"

"No."

"Who came in first?" Reynolds asks.

"The geezer did." Hal gestures toward me. "Sat right where you are now."

"What did he look like?" I ask.

"Midsixties, long hair, raggedy beard, big nose. Looked like a guy who rode a hog, but he was dressed in a gray suit, white shirt, blue tie."

"He you remember," I say.

"Huh?"

"He you remember. But her?"

"If you saw the way she wore that black dress, you wouldn't remember much else either."

"So he's sitting here alone drinking," Reynolds says, getting us back on track. "How long before the woman came in?"

"I don't know. Twenty, thirty minutes."

"Then she comes in and . . . ?"

"She makes an entrance, you know what I'm saying?"

"We do," I say.

"She goes right over to him." Hal says this wide-eyed, as though he's describing a UFO landing. "Starts hitting on the guy."

"Any chance they knew each other before?"

"Don't think so. Not the vibe I got."

"What vibe did you get?"

Hal shrugs. "Figured that she was a pro. That was my take, you want to know the truth."

"You get a lot of pros in here?" I ask.

Hal gets wary. Reynolds says, "We don't give a shit about solicitation, Hal. This is a cop killing."

"Sometimes, yeah. I mean, there are two strip clubs within a mile. Sometimes the girls from there want to do a little business off-site."

I look at Reynolds, but she's already nodding in my direction. "I got Bates working that angle."

"You ever see her in here before?" I ask.

"Twice."

"You remember?"

Hal spreads his hands. "How many times I gotta tell you?"

"Hot," I say for him. I am good at denial. This "hot" might not be Maura, though, uh, the description, vague as it is, does indeed fit.

"Those other two times," I continue, "she leave with guys?"

"Yep."

I picture it. Three times at this dump. Three times leaving with guys. Maura. I swallow back the ache.

Hal rubs his chin. "Come to think of it, she might not be a pro."

"What makes you say that?"

"Not the type."

"What's the type?"

"It's like that judge said about porn: You know it when you see it. I mean, she could be. Probably is. But it could be something else. She could just be a freak, you know? We get these MILFs that come in sometimes, happily married, three kids at home. They come in here and they bed guys and, I don't know. Freaks. Maybe she's one of those."

How reassuring.

Reynolds taps her foot. She brought me here for a specific reason, and it isn't to follow this line of questioning.

Enough putting it off. I nod at her. It's time.

"Okay," Reynolds says to Hal. "Show him the videotape."

The TV is an old console. Hal has it propped up on the bar. There are two customers at the bar now, but both seem enamored of the glasses in front of them and nothing else. Hal hits the switch. The screen comes alive, first as a blue dot and then, thirty seconds later, as angry static.

Hal checks the back of the TV. "Cord's loose," he says. He jams it back in. The other end of the fraying cord is plugged into a Zenith VCR player. The door is broken, so I can look into the slot and see the old cassette.

The play button descends with an audible click. The video quality sucks—yellow, filmy, unfocused. The camera is set up high above the parking lot so as to cover everything, and yet because of that, it pretty much covers nothing. I can make out car types maybe and some colors, but there's no way to read license plates.

"Boss just tapes over and over until the tape rips," Hal explains.

I know the deal. Insurance company probably requires a CCTV presence, so the boss complies in the cheapest way possible. The tape trudges forward. Reynolds points to a car on the upper right. "We think that's the rental."

I nod. "Can we hit the fast-forward?"

Hal does so. It speeds up old-school, so you can see everything happening faster. He releases the button when two people exit. Their backs are toward us. They are at a distance, shot from behind, blurry with the camera set too far away.

But then I see the woman walk.

Time stops. There is a slow, steady tick-tick-ticking in my chest. Then I can feel the ka-boom right as my heart explodes into a million pieces.

I remember the first time I saw that walk. There was a song Dad loved by Alejandro Escovedo called "Castanets." Do you remember it, Leo? Of course you do. There's that line where he sings about this impossibly sexy woman: "I like her better when she walks away." I never concurred—I preferred when Maura walked right toward me, shoulders back, eyes boring into me—but boy, did I get it.

Senior year, the Dumas twins both fell in love. I introduced you to Diana Styles, Augie and Audrey's daughter, and a week later, you hooked me up with Maura Wells. Even in this—dating, girls, falling in love—we had to be in sync, right, Leo? Maura was the beautiful outsider who hung with your geek squad. Diana was the good-girl cheerleader and student council vice president. Her father, Augie, was captain of the police and my football coach. I remember him making a joke at practice about his daughter dating the "better Dumas."

At least, I think it was a joke.

Dumb, I know, but I still wonder about the what-ifs. We never talked specifics about life after high school, did we? Would you and I have gone to the same college? Would I have stayed with Maura? Would you and Diana . . . ?

Dumb.

Reynolds says, "Well?"

"That's Maura," I say.

"You sure?"

I don't bother replying. I'm still watching the tape. The gray-haired guy opens the car door, and Maura slips into the passenger seat. I watch him circle back around and get into the driver's seat. The car reverses out of the spot and starts cruising toward the exit. I watch carefully until the car is gone from view.

"How much did they drink?" I ask Hal.

Hal is wary again.

Reynolds reminds him of the severity in the same way: "We don't give a crap about overserving, Hal. This is a cop killing."

"Yeah, they were drinking pretty good."

I think about it, try to get it to make sense.

"Oh, one other thing," Hal says. "Her name wasn't Maura. I mean, that's not the name she used."

"What name did she use?" Reynolds asks.

"Daisy."

Reynolds looks at me with a concern I find oddly touching. "You okay?"

I know what she's thinking. My great love, whom I've spent the past fifteen years obsessing over, was hanging out in this toilet, using a fake name, leaving with strange men. The stench of this place is starting to get to me. I stand, thank Hal, and hurry to the front door. I open it and step into the same lot I just saw on the video. I gulp some fresh air. But that's not why I'm here.

I look toward where the rental car had been parked.

Reynolds comes up behind me. "Thoughts?"

"The guy opened the car door for her."

"So?"

"He didn't stagger. Didn't fumble with his keys. Didn't forget his manners."

"And again I say: So?"

"Did you watch him drive out of here?"

"I did."

"No swerving, no quick stops or starts."

"Meaningless."

I start walking down the road.

"Where are you going?" she asks.

I keep walking. Reynolds follows. "How far is the turn?"

She hesitates because I think she now sees where I'm going with this. "Second right."

That's about what I'd figured. The entire walk from the bar to the murder scene takes us less than five minutes. When I get to it, I look back at the bar and then down to the spot where Rex fell.

It isn't making sense. Not yet. But I'm getting closer.

"Rex pulled them over awfully fast," I say.

"He was probably staking out the bar."

"I bet if we watch that video we'll see a lot of drunker guys stumbling out," I say. "So why them?"

Reynolds shrugs. "Maybe the rest were local. This guy had a rental plate."

"Nail the out-of-towner?"

"Sure."

"Who happens to be driving in a car with a girl Rex knew in high school?"

The wind has picked up. A few strands of hair get in Reynolds's face. She pushes them away. "I've seen bigger coincidences."

"So have I," I say.

But this isn't one of them. I try to picture it. I start with what I know—Maura and the old man in the bar, coming out, he holds the door for her, they drive off, Rex pulls them over.

"Nap?"

"I need you to look something up for me," I say.

Chapter Six

The security feed at Sal's Rent-A-Vehicle is of better quality. I watch the video in silence. As is too often the case with security footage, this camera is also set up high. Every bad guy knows about this, and so they do the simple things to beat it. Here, the guy with the stolen ID in the name of Dale Miller is wearing a baseball cap pulled low. He keeps his head down so that it's impossible to see his features with any sort of clarity. I can maybe make out the start of a beard. He limps.

"A pro," I tell Reynolds.

"Meaning?"

"Cap pulled low, head down, fake limp."

"How do you know the limp is fake?"

"The same way I knew Maura's walk. A walk can be distinctive. What's the best way to hide that and get you to focus on something meaningless?"

"Fake a limp," Reynolds says.

We head outside Sal's shack of a rental office and into the cool night air. In the distance, I see a man light up a cigarette. He lifts his head and breathes out a long smoke plume, just like Dad used to do. I took up smoking after Dad died and kept at it for more than a year. I know how nuts that is. Dad died of lung cancer after a lifetime of smoking, and yet my reaction to his horrible death was to smoke. I liked stepping outside alone with a cigarette like this guy is doing. Maybe that was the appeal for me—when I lit up, people stayed away from me.

"We can't rely on the age thing either," I say. "The long hair, the beard—he could be wearing a disguise. Lots of times a guy will pretend to be old so you underestimate him. Rex pulls over an old man for a DUI, he may let his guard down."

Reynolds nods. "I'll still have an expert comb through the surveillance tape frame by frame. Maybe they'll get something more distinct."

"Sure."

"You have a theory, Nap?"

"Not really."

"But?"

I watch the guy take a deep drag and let it out through his nose. I'm a Francophile now—wine, cheese, fluency in the language, the whole kit 'n' caboodle, which may also explain my short-lived smoking. The French smoke. A lot. Of course, I came by my Francophilism, to invent a word, honestly, what with being born in Marseilles and spending the first eight years of my life in Lyon. It isn't a show thing for me like it is with those pretentious twat waffles who know nothing about wine but suddenly need a special carrying case and treat the pulled cork like a lover's tongue.

"Nap?"

"Do you believe in hunches, Reynolds? Do you believe in cop intuition?"

"Fuck no," Reynolds says. "Every stupid mistake I've seen a cop make stems from their reliance on"—she makes quote marks with her fingers—"'hunches' and 'intuition.'"

I like Reynolds. I like her a lot. "Exactly my point."

It's been a long day. It feels like I whacked Trey with the bat a month ago. I've been working off adrenaline, and now I'm tapped out. But like I said before, I like Reynolds. Maybe I owe her too. So I figure, why not?

"I had a twin brother. His name was Leo."

She waits.

"You know anything about this?" I ask.

"No; should I?"

I shake my head. "Leo had this girlfriend named Diana Styles. We all grew up in Westbridge, where you picked me up."

"Nice town," Reynolds says.

"It is, yeah." I don't know how to tell this. It makes no sense, so I just keep rambling. "So our senior year, my brother, Leo, is dating Diana. One night, they go out. I'm not around. I have a hockey game in another town. We were playing Parsippany Hills. Funny what you remember. I had two goals and two assists."

"Impressive."

I half smile at my old life. If I close my eyes, I can still recall every moment of that game. My second goal was the game winner. Shorthanded. I stole the puck right before the blue line, flew down the left side, juked the goalie, lifted the backhander over his shoulder. Life before, life after.

An airport shuttle van marked with the words "Sal's Rent-A-Vehicle" pulls up to the front of the little hut. Weary travelers—everyone looks weary when they're renting a car—fall out and get in line.

"So you had a hockey game in another town," Reynolds prompted.

"And that night, Leo and Diana were hit by a train. They died instantly."

Reynolds's hand goes to her mouth. "I'm so sorry."

I say nothing.

"Was it an accident? Suicide?"

I shrug. "No one knows. Or at least I don't."

The last guy off the shuttle is an overweight businessman dragging an oversized suitcase with a broken wheel. His face is neon red from exertion.

"Was there an official finding?" Reynolds asks.

"Accidental deaths," I say. "Two high school kids, plenty of booze in their system, some drugs too. People used to walk on those railroad tracks, sometimes doing stupid dares. Another kid died up there in the seventies trying to jump the track. Anyway, the entire school freaked out, went into mourning. The deaths got plenty of sanctimonious media coverage as a warning to others: young, attractive, drugs, drinking, what is wrong with our society, you know the deal."

"I do," Reynolds says. Then: "You said senior year."

I nod.

"That was when you were dating Maura Wells."

She's good.

"So when exactly did Maura run off?"

I nod again. Reynolds gets it.

"Shit," she says. "How soon after?"

"A few days later. Her mother claimed I was a bad influence. She wanted her daughter out of this terrible town with teens who got stoned and drunk and walked in front of trains. Maura supposedly transferred to a boarding school."

"Happens," Reynolds says.

"Yep."

"But you didn't buy it?"

"Nope."

"Where was Maura the night your brother and his girlfriend died?"

"I don't know."

Reynolds sees it now. "That's why you're still searching for her. It's not just her spellbinding cleavage."

"Though we shouldn't just discount that."

"Men," Reynolds says. She moves toward me. "You think—what?—Maura knows something about your brother's death?"

I say nothing.

"Why do you think that, Nap?"

I make quote marks with my fingers. "'Hunch,'" I say. "'Intuition.'"

Chapter Seven

have a life and a job, so I get a car service to drive me home.

Ellie calls me and asks for an update, but I tell her it can wait. We plan a breakfast at the Armstrong Diner for the morning. I turn off my phone, close my eyes, and sleep the rest of the ride. I pay the driver and offer to add more so he can find a motel for the night.

"Nah, I gotta get back," the driver tells me.

I overtip. For a cop, I'm fairly rich. Why wouldn't I be? I'm Dad's sole heir. Some people claim that money is the root of all evil. Could be. Others say that money can't buy you happiness. That may be true. But if you handle it right, money buys you freedom and time, and those are a lot more tangible than happiness.

It's past midnight, but I still get in my car and head to Clara Maass Medical Center in Belleville. I flash my ID and find Trey's floor. I peek in his room. Trey is asleep, his leg in the air wrapped in an enormous cast. No visitors. I flash my ID at a nurse and tell her I'm investigating his assault. She tells me that Trey won't be walking on his own for at least six months. I thank her and leave.

I go home to the empty house, get in bed, stare at the ceiling. Sometimes I forget how odd it is for a single guy to be living in a house in this kind of neighborhood, but I'm used to it by now. I think about how that night started with such promise. I'd come home from that win against Parsippany Hills so fired up. Ivy League scouts were there that night. Two made me offers on the spot. I couldn't wait to tell you about it, Leo. I sat in the kitchen with Dad and waited for you to get home. Good news was never yet good news until I shared it with you. So Dad and I talked and waited, but we were both listening with half an ear for your car to pull into the driveway. Most kids in town had a curfew, but Dad never gave us one. Some parents in town saw that as lazy parenting, but Dad shrugged and said he trusted us.

So you didn't come home at ten, Leo, or eleven or midnight. And when a car finally did pull into the driveway at nearly 2:00 A.M., I ran to the door.

Only it wasn't you, of course. It was Augie in a squad car.

I wake up the next morning and take a long, hot shower. I try to keep my mind clear for now. No new facts had come in overnight on Rex, and I don't want to waste more time on speculation. I get in the car and head to the Armstrong Diner. If you want to know the best diners in town, always ask a cop. The Armstrong is a hybrid of sorts. The physical is pure New Jersey diner retro—a chrome-and-neon exterior, big red letters spelling out DINER on the roof, a soda-fountain bar with handwritten specials on a board, faux leather booths. The cuisine, however, is hip and socially conscious. The coffee is referred to as "fair trade." The food is "farm to table," though when you order eggs, I'm not sure what other route they'd go.

Ellie is waiting for me at the corner table. No matter what time I tell her, she is always there first. I slide in across from her.

"Good morning!" Ellie says with her customary over-the-top cheer.

I wince. She loves that.

Ellie slides one foot under her butt to sit up a little higher. She is coiled energy. Ellie looks like she's moving even when she's sitting still. I've never taken her pulse, but I bet her resting heart rate is over a hundred.

"Who should we start with?" Ellie asks. "Rex or Trey?"

"Who?"

Ellie frowns at me. "Trey."

My face is blank.

"Trey is Brenda's abusive boyfriend."

"Oh, right. What about him?"

"Someone attacked him with a baseball bat. He won't be able to walk for a long time."

"Ah, that's a shame," I say.

"Yeah, I can see you're crushed."

I almost say, *Crushed like Trey's leg,* but I hold back.

"On the positive side," Ellie continues, "Brenda was able to go back to his place. She got her stuff and the kids' stuff and she was finally able to sleep. So we are all grateful for that."

Ellie looks at me a second too long.

I nod. Then I say, "Rex."

"What?"

"You asked if I wanted to start with Rex or Trey."

"We covered Trey," she says.

Now I look at her. "So we're done talking about him?"

"We are."

"Good," I say.

Bunny, the old-school server with a pencil in her over-bleached hair, comes over and pours the fair-trade coffee.

"Usuals, hons?" Bunny asks.

I nod. So does Ellie. We come here a lot. Most of the time, we get the broken-yolk sandwiches. Ellie prefers the "simple"—two runny eggs on sourdough with white cheddar and avocado. I go for the same but also with bacon.

"So tell me about Rex," Ellie says.

"They found fingerprints at the murder scene," I say. "They belong to Maura."

Ellie's eyes blink to wide. I have had my share of bad breaks in life, I guess. I have no family, no girlfriend, no good prospects, not a lot of friends. But this magnificent person, this woman whose pure goodness is so blindingly obvious in the darkest of nights, is my best friend. Think about that. Ellie chose *me* for that role—best friend—and that means, no matter how much of a mess I may be, I do some things right.

I tell her everything.

When I get to the part about Maura with the guys in the bar, Ellie's face crumples. "Ah, Nap."

"I'm fine with it."

She gives me the look of skepticism I normally deserve.

"I don't think she was hooking or picking up men," I say.

"What, then?"

"Might be worse in some ways."

"How?"

I shake it off. It makes no sense to speculate until Reynolds gets back to me with the information.

"When we spoke yesterday," Ellie says, "you knew about Maura's fingerprints, didn't you?"

I nod.

"I could hear it in your voice. I mean, one of our old high school friends dying, sure, that's big, but you sounded . . . anyway, I took a little initiative." Ellie reaches down into a pocketbook the size of an army duffel and pulls out a large book. "I found something."

"What is that?"

"Your high school yearbook."

She drops it on the Formica table.

"You ordered one in the beginning of our senior year, but you never picked it up, for obvious reasons. So I held on to it for you."

"For fifteen years?" I ask.

Now it's Ellie's turn to shrug. "I was head of the yearbook committee."

"Of course you were."

High School Ellie was prim and proper and wore sweaters

and pearls. She was our class valedictorian, that girl who always whined she was going to fail a test and then she would be first to finish, with a straight A, and spend the rest of class doing her homework. She carried several perfectly sharpened number two pencils at all times, just in case, and her notebook always looked like yours did on the first day of school.

"Why are you giving it to me now?" I ask.

"I need to show you something."

I notice now that certain pages are marked off with pink Post-it notes.

Ellie licks her finger and flips to a page toward the back. "Did you ever wonder how we handled Leo and Diana?"

"Handled them how?"

"In the yearbook. The committee was divided. Do we just leave their photos in their normal place, in alphabetical order with the class, just like every other graduating senior—or do we pull them out and give them some kind of 'in memoriam' in the back?"

I take a sip of water. "You guys really discussed this?"

"You probably don't remember—we didn't know each other all that well—but I asked you what you thought."

"I remember," I say.

I had snapped at her that I didn't care, though my language may have been more colorful. Leo was dead. Who gave two shits about how the yearbook handled that?

"In the end, the committee decided to pull them out and create an in memoriam section. The class secretary. . . . Do you remember Cindy Monroe?"

"Yes."

"She could be kind of anal."

"You mean an asshole."

Ellie leans forward. "Isn't that what anal means? Anyway, Cindy Monroe reminded us that technically speaking, the main listing pages were for graduating seniors."

"And Leo and Diana died before graduating."

"Right."

"Ellie?"

"Yes."

"Can we get to the point now?"

"Two broken-yolk sandwiches," Bunny says. She drops the plates in front of us. "Enjoy."

The smell wafts up, travels through my nostrils, and grabs hold of my stomach. I reach for the sandwich, carefully grab it with both hands, and take a bite. The yolk breaks and starts to seep into the bread.

Ambrosia. Manna. Nectar of the gods. You choose the terminology.

"I don't want to ruin your breakfast," she says.

"Ellie."

"Fine." She opens the yearbook to a page toward the back.

And there you are, Leo.

You're wearing my hand-me-down blazer because though we were twins, I was always bigger. I think I bought that jacket in eighth grade. The tie is Dad's. You were terrible at making a knot. Dad always did it for you, and with a flourish. Someone has tried to slick down your unruly hair, but it just isn't happening. You're smiling, Leo, and I can't help but smile back.

I'm not the first person to lose a sibling prematurely. I'm not the first to lose a twin. Your death was catastrophic, no question, but it wasn't the end of my life. I recuperated. I was back in school two weeks after "that night." I even played in a hockey game the following Saturday against Morris Knolls—the distraction was good for me, though maybe I played with too much fury. Got a ten-minute major for nearly putting a kid through the glass. You'd have loved it. Sure, I was a bit morose in school. For a few weeks everyone showered me with attention, but they got over that. When my history grade slipped, I remember Mrs. Freedman kindly but firmly telling me that your death was no excuse. She was right. Life goes on, as it should, though it's also an outrage. When you have grief, at least you have something. But when grief ebbs away, what's left? You go on, and I didn't want to go on.

Augie says that's why I obsess over the details and won't accept what is so obvious to others.

I stare at your face. When I speak, my voice is a little funny. "Why are you showing me this?"

"Look at Leo's lapel."

Ellie reaches across the table and points with her finger to a small silver pin. I smile again.

"It's crossed Cs," I say.

"Crossed Cs?"

I'm still smiling, remembering your dorkiness. "It was called the Conspiracy Club."

"Westbridge High didn't have a conspiracy club."

"Not officially, no. It was supposed to be some kind of secret society kinda thing."

"So you knew about it?"

"Sure."

Ellie takes hold of the yearbook. She flips toward a page in the front and spins the book so I can see. It's my photo now.

My posture is ramrod, my smile tight. God, I look like a frigging tool. Ellie points to my empty lapel.

"I wasn't a member," I say.

"Who else was?"

"Like I said, it was supposed to be a secret society. No one was supposed to know. It was just this goofball group of like-minded nerds . . ."

My voice trails off as she flips the page again.

It's Rex Canton's picture. He's sporting a crew cut and a gapped-tooth smile. His head is tilted to the side like someone just surprised him.

"So here's the thing," Ellie says. "When you mentioned Rex, I looked him up in the yearbook first. And I saw this."

She points again. Rex has the tiny *CC* on his lapel.

"Did you know he was a member?"

I shake my head. "But I never asked. Like I said, it was supposed to be their little secret society. I didn't pay much attention."

"Do you know any other members?"

"They weren't supposed to talk about it, but . . ." I meet her eyes. "Is Maura in the yearbook?"

"No. When she transferred, we pulled her picture out. Was she a member . . . ?"

I nod. Maura moved to town toward the end of our junior year. She was a mystery to all of us, this superhot aloof girl who seemed to have no interest in any of the high school conventions. She liked to go to Manhattan on weekends. She backpacked through Europe. She was dark and mysterious and drawn to danger, the kind of girl you figured dated college guys or teachers. We were all too parochial for her. How did you get to be friends with her, Leo? You never told me that. I remember coming home one day, and you two were doing homework at the kitchen table. I couldn't believe it. You with Maura Wells.

"I, uh, checked Diana's picture," Ellie says. There's a catch in her throat here. Ellie was Diana's best friend since second grade. That's how Ellie and I formed a bond too—in grief. I lost you, Leo. She lost Diana. "Diana doesn't have the pin. I think she would have told me about this club if she was in it."

"She wouldn't have been a member," I say, "unless maybe she joined after she started dating Leo."

Ellie grabs hold of her sandwich. "Okay, so what's the Conspiracy Club?"

"You have a few minutes when we're done with breakfast?"

"Yes."

"Let's take a walk then. It might make it easier to explain."

Ellie takes a bite, gets yolk on her hands, wipes her hands and face. "You think there's any connection between this and . . . ?"

"What happened to Leo and Diana? Maybe. You?"

Ellie picks up a fork and spears her yolk. "I always thought Leo and Diana died in an accident." She looks up at me. "I thought your other explanations were, uh, far-fetched."

"You never told me that."

She shrugs. "I also thought you could use an ally instead of someone else saying you were crazy."

I am not sure how to respond to that so I just say, "Thank you."

"But now . . ." Ellie scrunches up her face in deep thought.

"Now what?"

"We know the fate of at least three members of the club."

I nod. "Leo and Rex are dead."

"And Maura, who disappeared fifteen years ago, happened to be at Rex's murder scene."

"Plus," I add, "Diana may have been a member too after the school picture was taken. Who knows?"

"That would make three dead. Either way, to believe it's a coincidence—to believe that their fates aren't somehow connected—well, *that's* far-fetched."

I pick up my sandwich and take another bite. I keep my eyes down but I know Ellie is watching me.

"Nap?"

"What?"

"I went through the entire yearbook with a magnifying glass. I checked every single lapel for that pin."

"Did you find any others?" I ask.

Ellie nods. "Two more. Two more of our classmates were wearing that pin."

Chapter Eight

We start up the old path behind Benjamin Franklin Middle School. When we were students, this path was called the Path. Clever, right?

"I can't believe the Path is still here," Ellie says.

I arch an eyebrow. "You used to come up here?"

"Me? Never. This was for the rowdy kids."

"Rowdy?"

"I didn't want to say 'bad' or 'rebellious.'" She puts her hand on my arm. "You used to come up here, right?"

"Senior year mostly."

"Drinking? Drugs? Sex?"

"All three," I say. Then with a sad smile, I add something I would add only when talking to her. "But I wasn't much for drinking or drugs."

"Maura."

I don't have to reply.

The wooded area behind the middle school is the place kids went to smoke, drink, get high, or hook up. Every town has one. Westbridge is no different on the surface. We start climbing up the hill. The woods are windy and long rather than deep. You feel as though you are miles from civilization, but in fact, you're never more than a few hundred yards from a suburban street.

"Our town's make-out point," Ellie says.

"Yep."

"Except more than making out."

No need to reply. I don't like being here. I haven't been here since "that night," Leo. It isn't about you. Not really. You were killed on those train tracks on the other side of town. Westbridge is pretty big. We have thirty thousand residents. Six elementary schools feed two middle schools, which feed one high school. The town is almost fifteen square miles. It would take me at least ten minutes to drive from here to the spot where you and Diana died, and that's only if I got lucky with the lights.

But this wooded area makes me think of Maura. It makes me remember the way she made me feel. It makes me remember that no one since her—and, yeah, I know how this sounds— has ever made me feel that way.

Am I talking about the physical?

Yep.

Label me a pig; I don't care. My only defense is that I believe the physical is entangled with the emotional, that the ridiculous sexual heights that this eighteen-year-old boy reached with her weren't just about technique or newness or experimentation or nostalgia but about something deeper and more profound.

But I'm also savvy enough to admit that could be bullshit.

"I didn't really know Maura," Ellie says. "She moved in, what, end of junior year?"

"That summer, yeah."

"She kinda intimidated me."

I nod. Like I said, Ellie was our class valedictorian. There is a photograph in that yearbook of Ellie and me because we were voted "Most Likely to Succeed." Funny, no? We knew each other a little before posing for that picture, but I'd always figured that Ellie was a Little Miss Priss. What would we have in common? I could probably go through a mental timeline and figure out the steps that led to Ellie and me being friends after that photo was taken, how we grew closer after losing Leo and Diana, how we stayed friends as she went off to Princeton University and I stayed home, all of that. But off the top of my head, I don't remember the details, what we saw in each other outside of grief, where the signposts lay. I'm just grateful.

"She seemed older," Ellie says. "Maura, I mean. More experienced. Sort of, I don't know, sexy."

Hard for me to argue.

"Some girls just have that, you know? Like everything they do, like it or not, is a double entendre. That sounds sexist, doesn't it?"

"A little."

"But you understand what I mean."

"Oh, I do."

"So the other two members of the Conspiracy Club," she says, "were Beth Lashley and Hank Stroud. You remember them?"

I do. "They were friends with Leo. Did you know them?"

"Hank was a math genius," she says. "I remember he was in my calculus class freshman year and then they had to make up his own curriculum for him. Went to MIT, I think."

"He did," I say.

Ellie's voice turns grave. "Do you know what happened to him?"

"Some of it. Last I heard, he's still around town. He plays pickup basketball by the oval."

"I saw him, what, six months ago near the train station," Ellie says with a shake of her head. "Talking to himself, ranting. It was awful. Such a sad story, don't you think?"

"I do."

She stops walking and leans against a tree. "Let's just go through the members of the club for a second. For the sake of this discussion let's assume Diana became a member, okay?"

"Okay," I say.

"So we then have six members in total. Leo, Diana, Maura, Rex, Hank, and Beth."

I start walking again. Ellie joins me and keeps talking.

"Leo is dead. Diana is dead. Rex is dead. Maura is missing. Hank, well, he's . . . what should we call him? Homeless?"

"No," I say. "He's an outpatient at Essex Pines."

"So he's, what, mentally ill?"

"Let's go with that."

"And that leaves Beth."

"What do you know about her?"

"Nothing. She left for college and never came back. As our alumni coordinator, I've reached out, tried to get a mailing address, you know, to invite her to the reunions and homecomings. Nothing."

"Her parents?"

"They moved to Florida last I heard. I wrote to them too, but there was no reply."

Hank and Beth. I would need to talk to them. And say what exactly?

"Where are we going, Nap?"

"Not far," I say.

I want to show her—or maybe I want to see for myself. I'm visiting old ghosts. The smell of pinecones fills the air. Every once in a while, we see a broken liquor bottle or an empty pack of cigarettes.

We are getting close now. It's my imagination—I know that—but the air seems suddenly still. It feels as though someone is out there, watching us, holding their breath. I stop at a tree and run my hand across the bark. I find an old rusty nail. I move to the next tree, run my hand down it, find another rusty nail. I hesitate.

"What?" Ellie asks.

"I've never walked past here."

"Why?"

"It was restricted. These nails? There used to be signs all along here."

"Like, No Trespassing signs?"

"The signs read, 'Restricted Area Warning' in large red letters," I say. "Underneath was a ton of scary smaller print about the area being declared restricted in accordance with some code number and that anything can be confiscated, no photography, you'll be searched, blah blah blah. It ended with the following words italicized: '*Deadly Force Is Authorized.*'"

"It really said that? About deadly force?"

I nod.

"You have a good memory," she says.

I smile. "Maura stole one of the signs and hung it in her bedroom."

"You're kidding."

I shrug.

Ellie nudges me. "You liked the bad girls."

"Maybe."

"Still do. That's your problem."

We keep walking. It feels odd going past where the signs hung, as though some invisible force field has finally dropped and allowed us to move forward. In fifty yards we are able to see the remnants of a barbed-wire fence. When we get closer, we can start to make out the ruins of shacks poking through the underbrush and overgrowth.

"I did a school report on this junior year," Ellie says.

"On what?"

"You know what was out here, right?"

I do, but I want her to tell it.

"A Nike missile base," she says. "A lot of people don't believe that, but that's what these were originally. During the Cold War—I'm talking about the 1950s—the army hid these bases in suburban towns like ours. They stuck them on farms or in wooded areas like this. People thought it was just an old wives' tale, but they were real."

There is a hush in the air. We move closer. I can make out what must have been old barracks. I try to imagine the scene—the soldiers, the vehicles, the launchpads.

"Forty-foot-high Nike missiles with nuclear warheads could have been launched from right here." Ellie shades her eyes and stares up as though she can still see them. "This spot is probably less than a hundred yards from the Carlino house over on Downing Road. The Nikes were supposed to protect New York City from a Soviet missile or airplane attack."

It's good for me to hear this refresher. "Do you know when the Nike missile program was dropped?" I ask.

"Early 1970s, I think."

I nod. "This one closed down in 1974."

"A quarter century before we were in high school."

"Right."

"So?"

"So most people, well, if you ask the old-timers, most will tell you that if these bases were secret, they were the worst-kept secret in northern New Jersey. They all knew about them. One guy said they actually put one of the missiles on a float in the July Fourth parade. I don't know if that's true or not."

We keep walking. I want to get inside the old base—I don't know why—but the rusted fence is still holding firm like an old soldier refusing to step down. We stand and look through the chain link.

"The Nike base in Livingston," Ellie says. "It's a park now. For artists. The old army barracks have been converted to artist studios. The launcher base in East Hanover was torn down to make room for a housing development. There's another base down in Sandy Hook where you can take a Cold War tour."

We lean forward. The woods are completely still. No birds coo. No leaves rustle. I can hear only the sound of my own breathing. The past does not simply die away. Whatever happened here still haunts these grounds. You can feel that sometimes—when you visit ancient ruins or old estates or when you are alone in the woods like this. The echoes quiet, fade away, but they never go completely silent.

"So what happened to this Nike base after it closed?" Ellie asks me.

"That," I say, "is what the Conspiracy Club wanted to find out."

Chapter Nine

We walk back to Ellie's car. She stops by the driver's-side door and cups my face in her hands. It's a maternal touch, something I don't recall experiencing with anyone other than Ellie, and, yes, I know how odd that sounds. She looks at me with genuine concern.

"I'm not sure what to say here, Nap."

"I'm fine."

"This may be the best thing for you."

"How's that?"

"Not to sound melodramatic, but the ghosts from that night linger in you. Maybe the truth will set them free."

I nod and close the door for her. I watch her drive away. As I head to my own car, my mobile rings. It's Reynolds.

"How did you know?" she asks.

I wait.

"On three other occasions, Officer Rex Canton stopped drunk drivers in that same spot."

I wait some more. Reynolds could have found that out in minutes. There is more to tell here, and I'm pretty sure I know what it is.

"Nap?"

She wants to play it this way, so I say, "All the DUIs were for men, correct?"

"Correct."

"And all were going through either a divorce or child custody hearing?"

"Custody hearings," Reynolds says. "All three."

"I doubt it was just those three," I say. "He probably used other spots."

"I'm going through all of Rex's DUIs. It may take some time."

I get in my car and start it up.

"How did you know?" Reynolds asks. "And don't tell me hunch or intuition."

"I didn't know for sure, but Rex stopped that car very quickly after it left that bar."

"He could have just been scouting the place."

"But we saw the tape. Even with the crappy quality, you could tell the driver didn't sway or drive erratically. So why would Rex pick on him? And by coincidence the woman in the car went to high school with Rex—it was all too much. It had to be a setup."

"I still don't get it," Reynolds says. "Did this guy fly in to execute Rex?"

"Probably."

"Did your ex help him?"

"I don't think so," I say.

"Is that love talking?"

"No, logic."

"Explain."

"You heard the bartender," I say. "She came in, had drinks with him, got him liquored up, got him in the car. She wouldn't have had to go through all those stages if she and the hit man were working together."

"Could have just been part of the act."

"Could have been," I say.

"But your way makes sense. So you think Maura was working with Rex?"

"I do."

"Doesn't mean she didn't set Rex up too."

"Right."

"But if she wasn't involved in the murder, where is she now?"

"I don't know."

"The hit man could have turned the gun on her. Could have forced her into the driver's seat. Could have made her drive him to an airport or something."

"Possible."

"And then what?"

"We're getting ahead of ourselves," I tell her. "We need to do some more legwork. I doubt the wives in these custody cases just walked up to Rex and said, 'Hey, I need to damage my husband's rep.'"

"Right, so how did they hire him?"

"My guess would be through a divorce attorney. That's our

first move, Reynolds. The three women probably had the same lawyer. Find out who it is and we can ask him about Rex and Maura."

"He—or she, let's not get sexist—will claim it's work product."

"One step at a time."

"Okay," Reynolds says. "So maybe the killer was one of the targeted husbands who wanted revenge?"

That makes the most sense, but I remind her that we don't know enough yet. I don't get into the Conspiracy Club because her findings seem to cut against all that. I'm still hanging on to my silly little hope that somehow Rex's murder will circle back to you, Leo. No reason not to, I guess. Reynolds will take the lead on this DUI angle. I can still work on the Conspiracy Club angle. That means locating Hank Stroud and Beth Lashley.

But more than that, it means bringing in Augie.

I could still wait on it. There is no reason to tear open this wound again, especially if Augie is in the midst of making some strides in his personal life. But keeping something from Augie isn't my style. I wouldn't want him deciding what I could and could not take. I need to show him the same respect.

Still, Augie is Diana's father. This won't be easy.

As I hit Route 80, I press the button on my steering wheel and tell my phone to call Augie. He answers on the third ring.

"Hey, Nap." Augie is a big guy with a barrel chest. His voice is comfortingly gruff.

"You back from Hilton Head?"

"We got in late last night."

"So you're home?"

"Yeah, I'm home. What's up?"

"Can I stop by after my shift?"

He hesitates. "Yeah, sure."

"Right. So how was the trip?"

"See you later," Augie says.

He hangs up. I wonder whether he was alone as we spoke or if his new lady friend is still with him. That would be nice, I think, at the same moment I also think that it's none of my business.

Augie lives in a brick garden apartment on Oak Street in a development that might aptly be called Divorced Dads Mews. He moved in "temporarily" eight years ago, leaving Audrey, Diana's mother, the house where they had raised their only child. A few months later, Audrey sold the house without first informing Augie.

Audrey did that, she once told me, for Augie's sake more than hers.

When Augie answers the door, I can see his golf clubs in the foyer behind him.

"So how was Hilton Head?" I ask.

"Nice."

I point behind him. "You brought your clubs?"

"Wow, you're quite the detective."

"I don't like to brag."

"I brought them," Augie says. "But I didn't play."

That makes me smile. "So it went well with . . . ?"

"Yvonne."

"Yvonne," I repeat, arching an eyebrow. "Great name."

He moves away so as to let me in and says, "I don't think it's going to work out between us."

My heart sinks. I've never met Yvonne, but for some reason I picture her as this confident woman with a big, throaty laugh, an easy way, fun, grateful, who liked to thread her arm through Augie's as they walked the beach near their hotel. I feel a loss for someone I never met.

I look at him. He shrugs.

"There'll be another," he says.

"Plenty more fish in the sea," I agree.

You'd expect the apartment interior to be on the generic-read-dumpy side, but it's not. Augie loves going to local art fairs and buying paintings. He rotates them, never keeping them in the same spot for more than a month or two. The oak bookshelves with glass fronts are jammed with books. Augie is the most voracious reader I know. He's divided the books into two simple categories—fiction and nonfiction—but he hasn't alphabetized them by author or anything like that.

I take a seat.

"You off duty?" Augie asks.

"I am. You?"

"Same."

Augie is still captain of the Westbridge Police Department. He retires in a year. I became a cop because of what happened to you, Leo, but I'm not sure it would have happened without Augie's guidance. I sit in the same plush chair I always take when I'm here. He uses the trophy from the high school state championship football team—the one I played on, the one he coached—as a bookend. Other than that there is nothing personal in this room—no photographs, no certificates, no awards, nothing like that.

He hands me a bottle of wine. It's Chateau Haut-Bailly 2009. Retails for about two hundred dollars.

"Nice," I say.

"Open it."

"You should save it for a special occasion."

Augie takes the bottle from my hand and jams the corkscrew into the top. "Is that what your father would tell us?"

I smile. "No."

My great-grandfather, Dad often told us, saved his best wines for special occasions. He was killed when the Nazis invaded Paris. The Nazis ended up drinking his wine. Lesson: You never wait. When I was growing up, we used only the good plates. We used the best linens. We drank out of Waterford crystal. When my father died, his wine cellar was nearly empty.

"Your dad used fancier words," Augie tells me. "I prefer a line from Groucho Marx."

"That being?"

"'I shall drink no wine before its time. Okay, it's time.'"

Augie pours the wine into one glass, then the other. He hands one to me. We clink glasses. I twirl the wine a bit and smell. Nothing too showy.

I get a gorgeous nose of blackberry, plum, crème de cassis, and—go with me on this—lead pencil shavings. I take a sip—succulent, ripe fruit, fresh, lively, you get the deal. The finish lasts a solid minute. Spectacular.

Augie waits for my reaction. My nod tells all. We both look to the spot where Dad would be sitting if he were with us. The longing vibrates deep in my chest. He would have loved this moment. He'd have savored both this wine and this company.

Dad was the pure definition of what the French label joie de vivre, which roughly translated means "exuberant enjoyment of life." I'm not sure about that definition. My own experience is that the French love to *feel*. They take in the full experience of great loves and great tragedies without backing down or crouching into some sort of defensive stance. If life is going to punch them in the face, they stick their chins out and savor the moment. That is living life to the fullest.

Dad was like that.

And that's why I would be a great disappointment to him, Leo.

So maybe in the important things, I'm not a Francophile at all.

"So what's on your mind, Nap?"

I start with Rex's murder and then hit him with Maura's fingerprints. Augie drinks his wine with a little too much care. I finish the story.

I wait. He waits. Cops know how to wait.

Finally, I say, "So what do you make of it?"

Augie rises from his seat. "Not my case. Ergo not my job to make something out of it. But at least you know now."

"Know what?"

"Something about Maura."

"Not much," I say.

"No, not much."

I say nothing, take a sip.

"Let me take a wild guess," Augie says to me. "Somehow

you think this murder has something to do with Diana and Leo."

"I don't know if I'm willing to go that far yet," I say.

Augie sighs. "What have you got?"

"Rex knew Leo."

"He probably knew Diana too. You were all in the same class, right? It's not that big a town."

"There's more to it."

I reach into my bag and pull out the yearbook. Augie takes it from my hand.

"Pink Post-it notes?"

"Ellie," I say.

"Should have known. So why are you showing me this?"

As I explain about the pins and the Conspiracy Club, an amused smile comes to his lips. When I finish he says, "So what's your theory, Nap?"

I say nothing. His smile grows.

"Do you think that this Conspiracy Club uncovered a great big scary secret about a secret military base?" he asks. He starts waving his fingers around like he's casting a spell. "A secret so terrible that, what, Diana and Leo had to be silenced? Is that how your theory goes, Nap?"

I take another sip of wine. He starts to pace, flipping to the pages marked off with the Post-it notes.

"And now, fifteen years later, Rex for some odd reason needs to be silenced too. Odd he didn't have to be silenced back then, but whatever. Suddenly, secret agents are dispatched to take him out."

Augie stops and stares at me.

"Are you enjoying this?" I ask.

"A little, I guess."

He opens up to another page with a pink Post-it note. "Beth Lashley. Is she dead too?"

"No, I don't think so. I haven't found anything on her yet."

Augie frantically flips to another page. "Oh, and Hank Stroud. Well, we know he's still in town. Not all there, I admit, but the bogeymen haven't taken him out yet."

He flips the page once again, but this time he freezes. The room is silent now. I look at his eyes and I wonder whether coming here was wise. I can't see the exact page he's looking at, but I can tell that it's a page toward the back. So I know. His expression doesn't change, but everything else does. Pain creases his face. There is a small shake in his hand now. I want to say something comforting, but I know that this is one of the moments when words would be like an appendix—superfluous or harmful.

So I shut up.

I wait as Augie stares at the photograph of his seventeen-year-old daughter, who never came home that night. When he finally speaks again, it's like something heavy is sitting on his chest.

"They were just kids, Nap."

I can feel my grip on the glass tighten.

"Stupid, inexperienced kids. They drank too much. They mixed pills with the alcohol. It was dark. It was late. Were they just standing on the tracks? Were they running down them, laughing and high, and never knew? Were they playing chicken with the train, trying to jump across the tracks, the same game that killed Jimmy Riccio back in 1973? I don't know, Nap. I wish I did. I wish I knew exactly what happened. I want to know if Diana suffered—or was it quick? I want to know if she turned at the last second and knew that her life was about to end or if she was oblivious when she died. See, my one job, my only job, was to protect her, and I let her go out that night, and so I wonder if she was scared that night. I wonder if she knew that she was going to die—and if she did, did she call out my name? Did she yell for her father? Did she hope that somehow maybe I'd be able to save her?"

I don't move. I can't move.

"You're going to look into this, aren't you?"

I manage to nod. Then I'm able to say, "Yeah."

He hands me the yearbook and starts out of the room. "Maybe you should do it on your own."

Chapter Ten

So I start to look into it on my own.

I call Essex Pines Medical Center and get one of Hank's doctors on the line surprisingly fast. He says, "You know about HIPAA and patient confidentiality, right?"

"Right."

"So I can't tell you anything about his condition."

"I just want to talk to him," I say.

"He's an outpatient."

"I'm aware of that."

"Then you're aware that means he doesn't live here."

Everyone's a wiseass. "Doctor . . . I'm sorry I missed your name."

"Bauer. Why?"

"Just so I know who's jerking me around."

Silence.

"I'm a police officer and I'm trying to find Hank. Do you have any idea where he might be?"

"None."

"Do you have an address for him?"

"He's only given us a PO box in Westbridge. And before you ask, there are rules that prevent me from telling you that Hank usually comes to Essex Pines three to five days a week, but he hasn't been here in over two weeks."

Two weeks. Dr. Bauer hangs up. I let him. I have another idea.

I stand by the basketball courts located off the oval in front of Westbridge High School and listen to the sweet echo of a ball against asphalt at twilight. What is in front of me is a thing of beauty called "pickup basketball." There are no uniforms, no coaches, no set teams, no referees. Sometimes the white line is out-of-bounds on the baselines, sometimes it's the chain-link fence. You start the game with a check at the top of the key. Winners stay on, you call your own fouls. Some of these people are friends, some strangers. Some have important jobs, some are barely getting by. Tall, short, fat, thin, all races, creeds, religions. One guy is wearing a turban. None of that matters here. It's all about how you ball. Some trash talk, some stay quiet. You know about planned playdates. You know about adult leagues. This—pickup basketball—is the wonderfully anarchistic and archaic opposite.

I hear the grunts, the guys calling out picks, the staccato

shuffling of sneakers. Ten guys are playing—five on five. There are three guys on the sidelines waiting. A fourth approaches and asks, "You got next?" The guys nod.

I recognize about half the players. Some I know from high school. Some are neighbors. The guy who runs the town lacrosse program is out there. Many of these guys work in the financial community, but I also spot two high school teachers.

I don't see Hank.

As the game comes to an end—they are playing to ten by ones—a tall man I know parks and gets out of his car. One of the four waiting quickly points and calls out, "We got Myron!" The other guys start hooting and hollering at Myron. Myron smiles back sheepishly.

"Look who's back," one guy calls out.

The others join in: "How was the honeymoon, Romeo?" "You're not supposed to be tan, dude." "Yeah, you're supposed to stay indoors, if you catch my drift," to which Myron says, "Yeah, I didn't get that at first, but once you added 'if you catch my drift,' it became clear to me."

Lots of good-natured laughing and congrats to the groom.

Remember Myron Bolitar, Leo? How Dad would take us to watch him play high school basketball in Livingston, just to show us what greatness was? Myron used to be a confirmed old bachelor. Or so I thought. He got married recently to a cable-news anchorwoman. I can still remember Dad's voice in the stands: "Seeing greatness," he would tell us, "is always worth it." That was Dad's philosophy. Myron ended up being great—a huge superstar at Duke University and a first-round NBA draft pick. Then, boom, he had a freak injury and never made it in the pros.

There's a lesson there too, I guess.

But here on these courts he's still treated like a hero. I don't know if that's due to nostalgia or what, but I get it. He's still something special to me too. We are both adults now, but some part of me still feels a little intimidated and even uplifted when he shows me attention.

I blend into the group greeting him. When Myron gets to me, I shake his hand and say, "Congrats on the nuptials."

"Thanks, Nap."

"But you're a bastard for abandoning me."

"On the positive side, you're now the hottest bachelor in the area." Then, spotting something on my face, Myron pulls me aside. "What's up?"

"I'm looking for Hank."

"He do something wrong?"

"No, I don't think. I just need to talk to him. Hank usually plays Monday nights, right?"

"Always," Myron tells me. "Of course, you never know what Hank you're going to get."

"Meaning?"

"Meaning Hank, uh, fluctuates. Behaviorally."

"Meds?"

"Meds, chemical imbalance, whatever. But, look, I'm not the guy to ask. I haven't been around in over a month."

"Extended honeymoon?"

Myron shakes his head. "I wish."

He doesn't want me to ask a follow-up, and I don't have time for it.

"So who knows Hank the best?"

Myron gestures at a handsome man with his chin. "David Rainiv."

"For real?"

Myron shrugs and heads onto the court.

I can't imagine two lives on more opposite trajectories than Hank's and David Rainiv's. David was president of our high school class's National Honor Society and is now CEO of one of the country's biggest investment firms. You may have seen him on TV a few years ago when Congress was grilling big-shot bankers. David has a penthouse in Manhattan, but he and his high school sweetheart–cum–wife, Jill, raise their children here in Westbridge. We don't really have socialites in suburbia—more like "keeping up with the Joneses"—but whatever you label it, the Rainivs would be at the top of any heap.

As the next game starts up, David and I find a bench on the other side of the court and sit. David is fit and looks like the love child of a Kennedy and a Ken doll. If you're casting the cleft-chinned senator, you could do worse than David Rainiv.

"I haven't seen Hank in three weeks," David tells me.

"Is that unusual?"

"He pretty much comes every Monday and Thursday."

"And how is he?" I ask.

"He's fine, I guess," David says. "I mean, he's never fine, if you know what I mean. Some of the guys . . ." He looks out at the court. "They don't really want Hank here. He acts out. He doesn't shower enough. On the sidelines when he has to wait a game, he starts pacing and screaming various rants."

"What kind of rants?"

"Nonsensical stuff. He started shouting once about how Himmler hates tuna steaks."

"Himmler like the old Nazi?"

David shrugs. He keeps his eyes on the court, following the game. "He rants, he paces, he scares some of the guys. But on the court"—David smiles now—"it's like he transforms into Hank again. For a little while, the old Hank comes back." He turns to me. "You remember Hank in high school?"

I nod.

"Lovable, right?" David says.

"Yes."

"I mean, a total nerd, but—do you remember that time he pranked the teachers' Christmas party?"

"Something to do with their snacks, right?"

"Right. So the teachers are all getting smashed. Hank sneaks in. He's mixed together bowls of M&M's with bowls of Skittles—"

"Oh gross."

". . . so the teachers, they're wasted, right, and they reach and grab a fistful of candies and . . ." He starts laughing. "Hank filmed it. It was hilarious."

"I remember now."

"He didn't mean any harm. That was Hank. It was more a science experiment to him than a prank." David grows quiet for a moment. I follow his eyes. He's watching Myron take a jump shot. Swish.

"Hank isn't well, Nap. It isn't his fault. That's what I tell the guys who don't want him here. It's like he has cancer. You'd never tell a guy he can't play with us because he has cancer, right?"

"Good point," I say.

David is focused a little too much on the court. "I owe Hank."

"How so?"

"When we graduated, Hank went to MIT. You know that, right?"

"Right," I say.

"I got accepted to Harvard, a mile away. A thrill, right? We were close to each other. So freshman year, Hank and I still hung out. I'd come pick him up and we'd grab a burger somewhere or we'd go to parties, mostly on my campus but sometimes his. Hank could make me laugh like no one else." There is a smile on his face now. "He wasn't one for drinking, but he would stand in the corner and observe. He liked that. And girls liked him too. There was a certain type drawn to him."

The night has a hush to it now. The only sounds are the concentrated cacophony on the court.

The smile slides off David's face like a veil. "But things started to change," he says. "The change was so slow, I barely noticed it at first."

"Change how?"

"Like when I'd come to pick him up, Hank wouldn't be ready. Or as we left, he'd check the door lock two or three times. It got worse. I'd come and he'd still be in a bathrobe. He would shower for hours. He would keep locking and unlocking the door. Not two or three times, but twenty or thirty. I'd try to reason with him: 'Hank, you already checked it, you can stop now, no one wants any of the crap in your room anyway.' He started to worry his dorm would burn down. There was a stove in a public room. We'd have to stop by it and make sure it was off. It would take me an hour to get him outside."

David stops. We watch the game for a few moments. I don't push him. He wants to tell it his own way.

"So one night, we're going out on a double date at this expensive steak house in Cambridge. He says to me, 'Don't pick me up, I'll take the bus.' I say fine. I get the girls. We're there. I'm not telling this right. This girl, Kristen Megargee, I can see Hank is crazy about her. She's gorgeous—and a math geek. He was so excited. Anyway, you can probably guess what happened."

"He didn't show."

"Right. So I make up some excuse and take the girls home. Then I drive over to his dorm. Hank's still locking and unlocking the door. He won't stop. Then he starts blaming me. 'Oh, you said that was next week.'"

I wait. David lowers his head into his hands, takes a deep breath, lifts his head back up.

"I'm in college," David continues. "I'm young, it's exciting, I'm making new friends. I got my studies, I got a life, and Hank, he isn't my job, right? Going over to fetch him is getting to be a real pain in the ass. So after that, I start going less. You know how it is. He texts, I don't answer so fast. We drift apart. Suddenly it's a month. Then a semester. Then . . ."

I stay silent. I can feel the guilt coming off him.

"So these guys"—he gestures to the court—"think Hank is a weirdo. They don't want him here." He sits up. "Well, too bad. Hank is going to play if he wants to play. He's going to play with us, and he's going to feel welcome."

I give it a moment. Then I ask, "Do you have any idea where he might be?"

"No. We still don't . . . we don't really talk, except on the court. Hank and I, I mean. A lot of us go to McMurphy's after we play, you know, for a few pitchers and some pizza. I used to invite Hank, but when I did, he would actually run away. You've seen him walking around town, right?"

"Yes," I say.

"Same route every day, you know. Same time. Creature of habit. I guess that helps. Routine, I mean. We finish here at nine o'clock, give or take. But if we go long, Hank still leaves at exactly nine. No good-bye, no explanation. He has an old Timex with an alarm. It dings at nine, he sprints away, even if it's the middle of a game."

"How about his family? Would he stay with them?"

"His mom passed away last year. She lived in that old condo development in West Orange. Cross Creek Point. His dad might be there now."

"I thought his parents divorced when we were little," I say.

On the court, someone cries out and falls to the ground. He wants a foul, but the other guy is claiming that he's being a drama queen.

"They split up when we were in fifth grade," David says. "His dad moved somewhere out west. Colorado, I think. Anyway, I think they might have reconciled when Mrs. Stroud got sick. I forget who told me that."

The game in front of us ends when Myron hits a fadeaway jumper that kisses the backboard before dropping through the net.

David rises. "I got next," he reminds me.

"Did you ever hear of the Conspiracy Club?" I ask him.

"No, what's that?"

"Some guys in our class back in high school formed it. Hank was a member. So was my brother."

"Leo," he says with a sad shake of his head. "He was a good guy too. Such a loss."

I don't reply to that. "Did Hank ever talk about conspiracies?"

"Yeah, I guess. Nothing specific, though. He never made much sense."

"Did he talk about the Path maybe? Or the woods?"

David stops and looks at me. "The old military base, right?"

I say nothing.

"When we were in high school, Hank was obsessed with that place. He would talk about it all the time."

"What would he say?"

"Nutty stuff, that the government was running LSD testing out of it or mind-reading experiments, stuff like that."

You would sometimes wonder the same kinds of things, wouldn't you, Leo? But I wouldn't call you obsessed. You said it, you had fun with it, but I don't think you ever really bought into it. It seemed to me to be just a game to you, but maybe I misread your interest. Or maybe you were all in it for different reasons. Hank thought about big government plots. Maura liked the edge element, the mystery, the danger. You, Leo, I think you liked the comradery of the friends traipsing through the woods on an adventure like something in an old Stephen King novel.

"Yo, David, we're ready to start!" one guy yells.

Myron says, "Give him a minute. We can wait."

But they are all lined up and ready to play and there is a

protocol here: You don't make the group wait. David looks at me for permission. I nod that we are done and he can go. He starts to step toward the game, but then he turns to me.

"Hank is still obsessed with that old base."

"Why do you say that?"

"The walk Hank takes every morning? He starts by hiking up the Path."

Chapter Eleven

Reynolds calls me in the morning. "I found the divorce attorney who hired Rex."

"Great."

"Not really. His name is Simon Fraser. He's a bigwig partner at bigwig Elbe, Baroche and Fraser."

"You reach out to him?"

"Oh yes."

"I bet he was cooperative."

"I bet you're being sarcastic. Mr. Fraser won't speak with me due to attorney-client privilege and subsequent work product therein."

I frown. "Did he actually say 'therein'?"

"He did."

"We should be able to arrest him for that alone."

"If only we made the laws," Reynolds says. "I was thinking of going back to his clients to see if they would waive privilege."

"You mean the wives he represented?"

"Yes."

"A waste of time," I say. These women won custody cases based in part on Rex's DUI setup. They were not about to admit that. Their exes could use that illegality to reopen custody battles.

"Any ideas?" Reynolds asks.

"Might as well pay Simon Fraser a visit in person."

"I think that too will be a waste of time."

"I can go alone," I say.

"No, I don't think that's a good idea."

"Then we go together. It's your jurisdiction, so you can approach him as a law enforcement officer . . ."

". . . while you play the role of interested civilian?"

"It's the role I was born to play."

"When?"

"I have to make a couple of stops on the way, but I'll be up before lunch."

"Text me when you get close."

I hang up, shower, get dressed. I check my watch. According to David Rainiv, Hank starts his walk up the Path every morning at exactly eight thirty. I park in the teachers' lot, which gives me an unobstructed view of the Path. It's eight fifteen. I flip around the radio and land on Howard Stern for a while. It's eight thirty now. I keep my eyes on the Path. No one approaches.

Where is Hank?

At nine, I give up and head to my second stop.

The shelter Ellie runs caters mostly to battered families. I meet her at one of the transitional residences, an old Victorian located on a quiet street in Morristown. This is a place for the battered women and children to hide from their abusers until we can figure out the next step, which is usually something better but not what anyone would consider desirable.

There are very few big victories here. That's the tragedy. What Ellie does feels like emptying an ocean with a tablespoon. Still, she wades into the ocean tirelessly, time after time, day after day, and while she is no match for the evil in a man's heart, Ellie makes the battle worth it.

"Beth Lashley took her husband's name," Ellie tells me. "She is now Dr. Beth Fletcher, a cardiologist in Ann Arbor."

"How did you find that out?"

"It was harder than it should have been."

"Meaning?"

"I contacted all her closest friends from high school. None keep in touch with Beth, which surprised me. I mean, she was pretty social. I reached out to her parents again. I told them we wanted to get Beth's address for reunions and that kind of thing."

"What did they say?"

"They wouldn't give it to me. They said to mail anything pertinent to them."

I don't know what to make of that. But it's not good. "So how were you able to track her down?"

"Through Ellen Mager. Do you remember her?"

"She was a year behind us," I say, "but I think she was in my math class."

"That's Ellen. Anyway, she went to Rice University down in Houston."

"Okay."

"So did Beth Lashley. So I asked her to call the Rice alumni office and see if as a fellow alum she could get any information on her."

That, I have to admit, is genius.

"Anyway, she got an email address with the Fletcher last name at the University of Michigan Medical Center. I did a little googling to find out the rest. Here's her office number." Ellie hands me a slip of paper.

I look at the slip of paper as though the phone number will give me a clue.

Ellie leans back. "How did it go with tracking down Hank?" she asks.

"Not well."

"The plot thickens."

"It does."

"Oh, before you go, Marsha wanted to see you."

"I'm on my way."

I kiss Ellie on the cheek. Before I head to Ellie's colleague Marsha Stein's office, I veer left and take the stairs to the second level. There is a makeshift day care for the kids. I look inside and see Brenda's youngest working on a coloring book. I continue down the corridor. The door to her bedroom is open. I knock lightly and look inside the small room. Two open suitcases sit on the bed. When Brenda sees me, she rushes over and wraps her arms around me. She has never done that before.

Brenda doesn't say anything. I don't say anything.

When she lets go, she looks up and gives me a small nod. I give her a small nod back.

We still don't say anything.

When I head back into the corridor, Marsha Stein is waiting for me.

"Hey, Nap."

When we were eight and nine years old, Marsha was our teenage babysitter. Do you remember, Leo? She was lithe and gorgeous, a ballerina, a singer, the star of every high school play. We had crushes on her, of course, but so did everyone. Our favorite activity when she babysat was helping her rehearse for her plays. We would read her lines. During her junior year, Dad took us to the high school to see her play Hodel, the beautiful daughter, in *Fiddler on the Roof*. Senior year, Marsha capped off her theater career playing the titular lead in *Mame*. You, my brother, got to play the part of Mame's nephew, listed in the program as "Young Patrick." Dad and I went four times, and Marsha deservedly got a standing ovation at every performance.

Back in those days, Marsha had a ruggedly handsome boyfriend named Dean who drove that black Trans Am and always, no matter how hot or cold the weather, wore his varsity wrestling jacket, the green one with the white sleeves. Marsha and Dean were the "Class Couple" in the Westbridge High School yearbook. They got married a year after graduation. Not long after that, Dean started to beat her. Savagely. Her eye socket is still caved in on the right. Her face looks disjointed now, off-kilter. The nose is too flat from the years of beating.

After ten years, Marsha finally found the courage to run away. As she often tells the abused women here, "You find the courage too late but it's never too late and yes, that's a contra-diction." She joined forces with another "child" she babysat in those days, Ellie, and together they formed these shelters.

Ellie is CEO. Marsha prefers to stay behind the scenes. They now operate one shelter and four transition homes like this. They also have three locations with addresses that are completely unknown to the public, for obvious reasons. They have a pretty good security system, but sometimes I chip in.

I kiss Marsha's cheek. She isn't beautiful anymore. She isn't old, early forties—when life gets beaten out of those who shine brightest, they recover, but sometimes that light never quite comes all the way back. She still likes acting, by the way. The Westbridge Community Players is putting on *Fiddler* in May. Marsha plays Grandma Tzeitel.

She pulls me to the side. "Funny thing."

"Oh?"

"I tell you about what a monster Trey is and suddenly he ends up in the hospital."

I say nothing.

"A few months ago, I told you about how Wanda's boyfriend sexually abused her four-year-old daughter. Suddenly he ends up—"

"I'm kind of in a rush, Marsha," I say to stop her.

She looks at me.

"You can choose not to tell me your problems," I say. "That's up to you."

"I pray first."

"Okay."

"But praying doesn't work. That's when I go to you."

"Maybe you're looking at it wrong," I say.

"How's that?"

I shrug. "Maybe I'm just the answer to those prayers."

I cradle her face in both hands and kiss her cheek again. Then I hurry out before she can say more. You probably wonder how I, as a cop sworn to uphold the law, justify what I did to Trey. I don't. I'm a hypocrite. We all are. I do believe in the rule of law, and I'm not a huge fan of vigilantism. But I don't look at what I sometimes do that way. I look at it like the world is a bar and I see a man across the room beating the crap out of a woman, taunting her, laughing at her, cajoling her to give him one more try like Lucy holding the football for Charlie Brown, and then, after offering her this hope, cruelly smashing her in the face again. I look at it like I just stopped by a friend's house and saw her boyfriend sexually assaulting her four-year-old daughter.

Is your blood boiling?

Should time and distance cool that?

So I pounce. I stop it. I have no illusions. I choose to break the law, and if I'm caught, I'll pay the penalty.

I admit this isn't a great justification, but I don't really care.

I start driving west toward the Pennsylvania border. There is, of course, a great chance Simon Fraser will not be in his office. If so, I will visit his house or wherever he may be. I may miss him. He may refuse to see me. This is how detecting works. You keep going even if what you're doing seems like a momentous waste of time and energy.

I think about you as I drive. Here is my problem: For the first eighteen years of my life, I have zero memories that aren't entangled in you. We shared a womb; then we shared a room. There was, in fact, nothing we did not share. I told you everything. *Everything*. There is nothing I kept from you. There is nothing I was embarrassed or ashamed to tell you because I knew you'd still love me. For everyone else, there is a bit of a facade. There has to be. But with you and me, there was none.

I held nothing—nothing—back. But sometimes I wonder: Did you?

Were you keeping secrets from me, Leo?

An hour later, still driving, I call Dr. Beth Fletcher née Lashley's office. I give my name to the receptionist and ask to speak to Dr. Fletcher. The receptionist tells me the doctor isn't in right now. In that weary, put-out voice only a doctor's receptionist can pull off, she asks what this is regarding.

"I'm an old friend from high school." I give her my name and mobile phone number. Then I add with as much urgency as I can muster: "It's really important I talk to her."

The receptionist is unfazed. "I'll leave a message."

"I'm also a cop."

Nothing.

"Please page Dr. Fletcher and tell her it's important."

The receptionist hangs up without promising that she will.

I place another call to Augie. He answers on the first ring and says, "Yeah."

"I know you want to stay out of this," I say.

No reply.

"But could you tell your patrol guys to keep an eye out for Hank?"

"Won't be hard," Augie says. "He takes the same walk every day."

"Not this morning."

I fill Augie in on my earlier failed stakeout by the Path. I also tell him about my visit to the pickup basketball game last night. Augie is silent for a bit. Then he says, "You know that Hank is not, uh, well, right?"

"Right."

"So what exactly do you think he's going to tell you?"

"Damned if I know," I say.

More silence. I'm tempted to fill it with an apology for abruptly unearthing something he tried hard to keep buried, but I'm not really much in the mood to offer platitudes, and I doubt Augie would want to hear them.

"I'll tell the guys to radio me if they see him."

"Thanks," I say, but he's already hung up.

The law offices of Elbe, Baroche and Fraser are located in a nondescript glass high-rise among a series of nondescript glass high-rises in a development I assume is being satirically labeled "Country Club Campus." I park in a lot slightly larger than a European principality and find Reynolds waiting for me by the door. She's wearing a blazer over a green turtleneck.

"Simon Fraser is here," she says.

"How do you know?"

"I've been staking the place out since I called you. I saw him come in, I haven't seen him leave, his car is still here. From those observations, I deduced that Simon Fraser is here."

"You're good," I say.

"Don't be intimidated by my law enforcement prowess."

The lobby is colorless and cold, like Mr. Freeze's lair. Several law firms and investment entities, and even one of those for-too-much-profit pseudo colleges, are housed in here. We take the elevator up to the sixth floor. The thin kid at reception sports two-day-old stubble, fashionable glasses, and a headset with a microphone. He lifts a finger to indicate we should give him a second.

Then: "May I help you?"

Reynolds takes out her badge. "We're here to see Simon Fraser."

"Do you have an appointment?"

For a moment I think Reynolds is going to spit out, "This badge is my appointment," which would, I confess, disappoint me. Instead she says no but that we would very much appreciate a moment of Mr. Fraser's time. The thin kid hits a button and whispers. Then he asks us to have a seat. We do. There are no magazines, just glossy law firm brochures. I page through one and find a photograph and bio for Simon Fraser. He is a Pennsylvania boy through and through. He attended the local high school, then traveled to the western part of the state to get his BA at the University of Pittsburgh before heading to the far eastern part of the state for his law degree at the University of Pennsylvania in Philadelphia. He is a "nationally recognized family law practitioner." My eyes blur with boredom as I read about how he chaired this and that, authored this and that, served on this and that board, received this and that award for excellence in his chosen field.

A tall woman in a gray pencil skirt saunters toward us. "This way, please."

We follow her down the corridor to a conference room with one glass wall and what I guess is supposed to be a breathtaking view of the parking lot and, if you look farther in the distance, a Wendy's and an Olive Garden. There is a long conference table with one of those speakerphones that looks like a gray tarantula in the center.

Reynolds and I cool our heels for fifteen minutes before the tall woman returns.

"Lieutenant Reynolds?"

"Yes."

"There's a call for you on line three."

The tall woman leaves. Reynolds frowns at me. She puts a finger to her lips indicating that I should keep quiet and hits the speakerphone.

"Reynolds," she says.

A male voice replies, "Stacy?"

"Yes."

"What the hell are you doing at Simon Fraser's office, Stacy?"

"I'm working on a case, Captain."

"What case might that be?"

"The murder of Officer Rex Canton."

"Which our office is not handling because it's been passed on to county."

I had not known that.

"Just following up a lead," Reynolds tells him.

"No, Stacy, you're not following up a lead. You're bothering a prominent citizen who is friends with at least two local judges. Both of the judges called to inform me that one of my lieutenants is harassing a practicing attorney who has already invoked attorney-client privilege."

Reynolds gives me "See what I'm dealing with?" eyes. I nod that I do.

"Do I need to continue, Stacy?"

"No, Captain, I get the message. I'm out of here."

"Oh, and they said you were with someone. Who would—?"

"Bye now."

Reynolds disconnects the call. As though cued, the tall woman opens the conference room door to escort us out. We rise and follow her to the end of the corridor. As we get in the elevator, Reynolds says, "Sorry to make you drive all the way up."

"Yeah," I say to her. "Shame."

When we head outside Reynolds says, "I better get back to the station. Make it okay with my captain."

"Good idea."

We shake hands. She turns and starts to walk away.

"You going to head straight back to Westbridge?" she asks me.

I shrug. "Might have lunch first. How's the Olive Garden?"

"How do you think?"

I don't go to the Olive Garden.

There is an area of the parking lot for reserved parking. I find the sign that reads RESERVED FOR SIMON FRASER, ESQ, which is currently occupied by a shiny red Tesla. I frown but try not to judge. The spot to his left, which is normally reserved for BENJAMIN BAROCHE, ESQ, is open.

Good.

I head back to my car. As I do, I pass a guy in his midforties smoking a cigarette. He's wearing a business suit and a wedding ring, and for some reason, the wedding ring matters to me.

"Please don't smoke," I say to him.

The guy gives me the same look—a hybrid of befuddled and annoyed—I always get when I do this. "Huh?"

"You have people who care about you," I say. "I just don't want you to get sick or die."

"Mind your goddamn business," he snaps, tossing the butt to the ground like it offended him and storming back inside.

But part of me thinks, *Who knows—maybe that'll be his last cigarette ever.*

And they say I'm not an optimist.

I check the entrance. No sign of Simon Fraser. I quickly get in my car and pull it into the BAROCHE spot, hugging the right so that mere inches separate my passenger side from his Tesla's driver's side. There is no way Simon Fraser could squeeze in and reach his door, forget opening it.

I wait. I'm good with waiting. Waiting doesn't bother me. I don't really have to do true surveillance here—he's not going to be able to get into his car in a hurry—so I break out the novel I brought, ease my car seat all the way back, and start to read.

It doesn't take long.

At 12:15 P.M., I spot Simon Fraser exiting the building in my rearview mirror. I stick my bookmark between pages 312 and 313 and place the book on the passenger seat. I wait. Simon is talking animatedly on the phone. He draws closer to the car. With his free hand, he fishes into his pocket and grabs his key fob. I hear the little beep-beep noise of the door unlocking. I wait some more.

When he stops short, I know he's realized the parking situation. I hear his muffled "What the hell?"

I lift my phone and put it to my ear and pretend I'm talking to someone. With my other hand, I take hold of the door handle.

"Hey . . . hey, you!"

I ignore Simon Fraser and keep the phone to my ear. This

angers him. He comes around my side of the car and, using what I assume is his college ring, he raps on the driver's-side window.

"Hey, you can't park here."

I turn toward him and gesture with the phone to indicate I'm kinda busy. His face reddens. Simon Fraser knocks harder with the school ring. I regrip the door handle.

"Listen, assho—"

I open my car door fast, smacking him in the face. Simon Fraser falls back. His phone flies from his hand and crashes against the pavement. I don't know if it's broken or not. I get out of the car before he has time to recover and say, "I've been waiting for you, Simon."

Simon Fraser gently puts his hand to his face as if checking for . . .

"No blood," I say, "yet."

"Is that a threat?"

"Yeah, could be." I put my hand out to help him up. "Here, let me help you up."

He stares at my hand as if I'm holding a turd in it. I smile at him. I give him the crazy "I don't give any Fs" eyes. He scuttles back a bit.

"I'm here to save your career, Simon."

"Who are you?"

"Nap Dumas."

My intent with this whole play is not to hurt him so much as bewilder and disorient. This is a man who is used to being in control, to neat lines and rules, to making his problems go away with phone calls to well-placed sources. He is not accustomed to off-the-beaten-path conflict or lack of control, and if I play it right, I can take advantage of that.

"I'm . . . I'm calling the police."

"No need," I say, spreading my arms. "I'm a cop. What can I do for you?"

"You're a police officer?"

"I am."

His face turns a tad redder. "I'll have your badge."

"For illegal parking?"

"For assault."

"The car door? That was an accident, sorry. But, sure, let's call more cops to the scene. You can see about having my badge for opening a car door. And I"—I point to myself with my thumb—"can see about having you disbarred."

Simon Fraser is still on the ground. I hover over him, not really giving him room to rise without my help. It's not an uncommon power play. I reach out my hand again. If he tries anything—a possibility at this stage—I'm ready. He takes my hand and I pull him up.

Simon Fraser brushes himself off. "I'm leaving," he announces.

He walks over, picks up his phone, brushes that off too like it's a small dog. I can see the cracked screen from here. Now that there is some distance, he glares at me.

"You'll pay for any damage."

I smile back at him. "Nah."

He glances at his car, but mine still blocks the driver's door. I can tell he's now calculating the pros and cons of crawling across the passenger seat and driving away.

"You tell me what I need to know," I say, "we keep this all between us."

"And if I don't tell you?"

I shrug. "I destroy your career."

He snickers. "You think you can?"

"Not sure, to be honest. But I won't rest until I do. I have nothing to lose, Simon. I don't care if you"—I make quote marks with my fingers—"'have my badge.' I'm single. I have no social standing. In sum, to repeat: I have nothing to lose."

I take a step closer.

"But you, on the other hand, well, you have a family, a reputation, what the papers like to call"—again with the finger quotes—"'standing in the community.'"

"You can't threaten me."

"I just did. Oh, and if somehow I can't destroy your reputation, one day I'll come by and kick your ass. Plain and simple. Old-school."

He looks at me in horror.

"My brother is dead, Simon. You may be standing in the way of me finding out who killed him." I take another step toward him. "Do I look like the kind of guy who will just let that slide?"

He clears his throat. "If this has something to do with the work Officer Rex Canton did for our law firm . . ."

"As a matter of fact, it does."

". . . then I can't help you. As I've already explained, the work falls under attorney-client privilege."

"Not when that work you hired him to do is a crime, Simon."

Silence.

"Ever heard of entrapment?"

Another throat clear, less sure this time. "What on earth are you talking about?"

"You hired Officer Rex Canton to get dirt on ex-husbands so as to benefit your clients."

Simon snaps into lawyer mode. "One, I wouldn't character-ize Officer Canton's work in that way. Two, having someone do background checks on the opposition is neither illegal nor unethical."

"He wasn't doing background checks, Simon."

"You have no proof—"

"Sure I do. Pete Corwick, Randy O'Toole, and Nick Weiss. Do those names ring a bell?"

Silence.

"Cat got your tongue, Counselor?"

More silence.

"By startling coincidence, Officer Rex Canton happened to arrest all three of these men for drunk driving. By startling coincidence, your firm represented all three of those men's wives in custody battles at the time of those arrests."

I grin.

He tries: "That isn't proof of a crime."

"Hmm. Think the media will see it that way too?"

"If you breathe a word of these unfounded accusations to the press—"

"You'll have my badge, I get it. Look, I'm going to ask you two questions. If you answer them honestly, that's it. Your short nightmare known as 'me' is over. If you don't answer them, however, I go to the papers and the American Bar Asso-ciation and I tweet out what I know on Facebook or whatever the kids call it nowadays. Fair enough?"

Simon Fraser wouldn't say it, but I could see from the slump in his shoulders that I had him.

"So here is the first question: What do you know about the woman who worked with Rex on the DUI stings?"

"Nothing."

The answer came fast.

"You know he used a woman to seduce the guys into excess drinking, right?"

"Men flirting with women in bars." Simon Fraser shrugs, trying to recover a bit of his normal bluster now. "The law doesn't care why they drink, just how much."

"So who is she?"

"No idea," he says, and his words have the ring of truth. "Do you really think anyone in my firm, especially me, would want to know details like that?"

No. It was a long shot but worth taking. "Second question."

"*Final* question," he counters.

"Who hired your firm to set up the DUI the night Rex Canton was murdered?"

Simon Fraser hesitates. He is thinking it over. I let him. The red is gone from his face now, replaced with something more in the ash family.

"Are you implying that Officer Canton's, uh, work for our firm led to his murder?"

"More than implying."

"You have evidence of that?"

"An assassin flew in for just that purpose. He rented a car and headed to that bar. He pretended to get drunk with Rex's female associate. He waited until Officer Canton pulled him over. Then he shot and killed him."

He seems taken aback by this.

"It was a setup, Simon. Pure and simple."

It shouldn't have come to this—me hanging out in a parking lot making threats. I think Simon Fraser knows that now. He is more dazed now than when the car door knocked him on his ass.

"I'll get you the name."

"Good."

"I can check the billing after lunch," he says, checking his watch. "I'm late to see a client."

"Simon?"

He looks at me.

"Skip the lunch. Get the name now."

I'm blocking on Maura.

I'm doing it for several reasons. The most obvious, of course, is so that I can concentrate on the case at hand. Emotion will not help. I am obviously more driven on this case because of my personal connections here—you, Maura—but I can't let it cloud my brain or allow wants to twist my thinking.

In short: I can't help but hope.

There is a chance, slight as it might be, that there is a reasonable answer to all this and that when Maura and I see each other again . . . when I think of that moment, my mind goes to places it shouldn't. It goes to a future and long walks holding hands and longer nights under the sheets and then it goes to children and repainting the back deck and coaching Westbridge Little League and, yes, of course, I know how silly this all sounds and I would never voice this to anyone and perhaps again you are witnessing what I miss without you in my life.

It's crazy enough I talk to my dead brother, right?

We sit in Simon Fraser's office. The tall woman hands Simon a file. He opens it, and something comes across his face.

"What?" I say.

"I haven't hired Rex Canton in a month." Simon Fraser looks up at me, the relief washing over him. "I don't know who hired him that night, but it wasn't me."

"Maybe someone else in your firm?"

Simon hems a bit here. "I would doubt it."

"Rex worked exclusively for you?"

"I don't know about that, but at this firm, well, I'm a senior partner and the only one who works family law, so . . ."

He doesn't finish the thought, but I get it. Rex was *his* boy here. None of the other lawyers would dare hire him without Simon Fraser's prior consent.

My mobile rings. The caller ID reads WESTBRIDGE PD. I excuse myself and step aside.

"Hello?"

It's Augie's voice on the other end. "I think I know why we can't find Hank."

Chapter Twelve

When I arrive at Westbridge's police station the next morning, Augie is waiting there with a rookie cop named Jill Stevens. I started as a Westbridge patrolman and still work as a sort of hybrid investigator for both the county and this town. Augie brought me in and then pushed me up the ladder. I like this rung—I'm a big-county investigator with a hint of small-town cop. I have zero interest in money or glory. That's not faux modesty. I'm happy being right where I am. I solve the cases and pass on the credit. I want no further advancement or demotion. I am left alone for the most part and free of the political quicksand that sucks down so many.

I'm in my sweet spot.

The Westbridge police station is an old bank on the middle

of Old Westbridge Road. Eight years ago, the new high-tech station opened on North Elm Street and flooded during a storm. With nowhere else to go during repairs, they rented space from the seen-better-days Westbridge Savings Bank, a Greco-Roman-inspired savings and loan built in 1924. It still had the bones—the marble floors and high ceilings and dark oak counters. They turned the old-school vault into a holding cell. The town council still claims that the police will move back into the North Elm Street station, but eight years later, they haven't begun construction.

We all sit in Augie's second-floor office, which used to be the bank manager's. There is nothing on the walls behind him—no artwork, no flags, no awards or degrees or citations like you see in every other police captain's office. There are no photos on his desk. To an outsider, it's like Augie's half packed for retirement already, but this is my mentor. Awards and citations would be boasting. Artwork would be sharing himself in ways he'd rather not. Photos . . . well, even when Augie had family, he didn't want to take them to work.

Augie is behind his desk. Jill sits to my right holding a laptop and a file.

Augie says, "Three weeks ago, Hank came in with a complaint. Jill here took his statement."

We both look at Jill. She clears her throat and opens the file. "The complainant presented himself as very agitated when he entered."

Augie says, "Jill?"

She looks up.

"You can skip the formal talk. We're all friends here."

She nods and closes the file. "I've seen Hank around town.

We all know his reputation. But I just checked the records. Hank has never come to this station before. Well, let me correct that. I mean, he's never *voluntarily* come in. We've picked him up when he acts out, just held him for a few hours until he calms down. Not in a holding cell. Just a chair downstairs. What I mean is, he's never come in to file a complaint."

I try to move this along. "You said he was agitated?"

"I've witnessed his rantings before, so at first I was just sort of humoring him. I figured he needed to vent and that he would calm down. But he didn't. He said people were threatening him, yelling things at him."

"What kind of things?"

"He wasn't clear, but he seemed genuinely scared. He said people were lying about him. Every once in a while, he'd take on a weird studious tone and start talking about defamation and slander. Like he was his own lawyer or something. The whole thing was bizarre. Until he showed us the video."

Jill scooches her chair closer to me and opens the laptop.

"It took a while for Hank to make sense, but eventually he showed me this." She hands me the laptop. There's a still for a video on Facebook. I can't make out what it is yet. A forest maybe. Green leaves from trees. My eyes travel up. The heading of the video shows the name of the page where it'd been posted.

"Shame-A-Perv?" I say out loud.

"The Internet," Augie says, as if that explains everything. He leans back and folds his hands on his paunch.

Jill clicks the play button.

The video starts off shaky. The moving images are narrow with blurry sides, meaning it was shot on a smartphone held vertically. In the distance, I can make out a man standing alone behind the backstop of a baseball diamond.

"That's Sloane Park," Jill says.

I'd already recognized it. It's the field adjacent to Benjamin Franklin Middle School.

The video jerkily zooms in on the man. No surprise—it's Hank. He looks like what you used to call a hobo. He is unshaven. His jeans are loose and faded to the point of near white. He wears a flannel shirt unbuttoned to reveal a once-white, moth-ravaged (one hopes) undershirt.

For a second or two, nothing happens. The camera seems to settle its jitters and come into focus. Then a woman—probably the one doing the filming—whispers, "This dirty pervert exposed himself to my daughter."

I glance at Augie, who remains stoic. Then I turn my attention back to the screen.

Judging by the up-and-down motion and the way the video is closing in on Hank, I assume the woman doing the filming is walking toward him.

"Why are you here?" the woman shouts. "What do you think you're doing?"

Hank Stroud sees her now. His eyes go wide.

"Why are you exposing yourself to children?"

Hank's eyes dart about like scared birds trying to find a place to land.

"Why do our police allow perverts like you to endanger our community?"

For a second Hank puts his hands up to his eyes as though blocking a bright light that doesn't exist.

"Answer me!"

Hank bolts away.

The camera pans to follow him. Hank's pants start to slip. He holds them up with one hand and continues to run toward the woods.

"If you know anything about this pervert," the woman making the video says, "please post it. We need to keep our children safe!"

The video ends on that note.

I look up at Augie. "Did anyone complain about Hank?"

"People always complain about Hank."

"That he exposed himself?"

Augie shakes his head. "Just that they don't like the looks of him, walking around town, disheveled, he smells, he talks to himself. You know the deal."

I do. "But never anything about exposing himself?"

"Never." Augie gestures toward the laptop with his chin. "Take a look at the view count at the bottom of the video."

My jaw drops: 3,789,452 views. "Whoa."

"It went viral," Jill says. "Hank came in here the day after it was uploaded. There were already half a million hits."

"What did he want you to do?" I ask her.

Jill opens her mouth, thinks about it, closes it. "He just said he was scared."

"He wanted you to protect him?"

"Yeah, I guess."

"And what did you do?"

Augie says, "Nap."

Jill shifts in her seat. "What could I do? He was so vague about everything. I told him to come back if there was a specific threat."

"Did you look into who posted the video?"

"Uh, no." Jill looks wide-eyed at Augie. "I put the file on your desk, Captain. Should I have done more?"

"No, you did fine, Jill. I can take it from here. Leave the laptop. Thanks."

Jill looks at me as if I'm supposed to say something to absolve her. I don't blame her for the way she handled it, but I'm not in the mood to let her off the hook, either. I stay quiet as she leaves. When we are alone, Augie frowns at me.

"She's a rookie, for crying out loud."

"Someone on that video is accusing Hank of a pretty serious offense."

"Put it on me, then," Augie says.

I make a face and wave him off.

"I'm the captain. My subordinate left the file on my desk. I should have gone through it better. You want to blame somebody? Blame me."

Right or wrong, this isn't where I want to go with this. "I'm not blaming anybody."

I hit the play button and watch the video again. Then I watch it a third time.

"His pants are loose," I say to him.

"You think maybe they slipped?"

I don't. Neither does he.

"Check out the comments underneath," Augie says.

I move the cursor down. "There are over fifty thousand of them."

"Just click 'Top Comments' and read a few."

I do as he asks. And as always when reading a comments section, my faith in humanity plummets:

*SOMEONE SHOULD CASTRATE THIS GUY
WITH A RUSTY NAIL . . .*

*I WANT TO CHAIN THAT PERV TO THE BACK
OF MY TRUCK AND DRAG HIS ASS . . .*

*THIS IS WHAT'S WRONG WITH AMERICA.
WHY IS THIS PEDO-O-FILE ROAMING
FREE . . .*

*HIS NAME IS HANK STROUD! I SAW HIM
PEEING IN THE PARKING LOT AT THE
WESTBRIDGE STARBUCKS . . .*

*WHY WASTE MY TAX DOLLARS BY PUTTING
THAT DEVIANT IN A PRISON? TAKE THIS
HANK OUT BACK LIKE YOU WOULD A RABID
DOG . . .*

*HOPE THAT FREAK WALKS THROUGH MY
YARD. GOT A NEW RIFLE I'M DYING TO TRY
OUT . . .*

*SOMEONE SHOULD PULL DOWN HIS PANTS,
BEND HIM OVER AND . . .*

You get the idea. Too many posts begin with "Someone should . . ." and then offer up a skew of torture possibilities so creatively sick that Torquemada would have been envious.

"Nice, huh?" Augie says.

"We need to find him."

"I put out a bulletin statewide."

"Maybe we should try his dad."

"Tom?" Augie looks surprised. "Tom Stroud moved away a long time ago."

"Rumor has it he came back," I say.

"For real?"

"Someone told me he's living in his ex's place in Cross Creek Point."

"Huh," Augie says.

"Huh what?"

"We were pretty tight in the day. Tom and I. After the divorce he moved out to Wyoming. Cheyenne. A couple of us went out there, oh, has to be twenty years ago, and took a fly-fishing trip with him."

"When was the last time you saw him?"

"That trip. You know how it is. A guy moves across the country, you lose touch."

"Still," I say. "You just said you two were pretty tight."

I look at him. Augie gets where I'm going with this. He looks down at the main floor of the station. It isn't busy. It rarely is.

"Fine," he says with a sigh, heading for the door. "You drive."

Chapter Thirteen

We drive in silence for a few minutes.

I want to say something to Augie. I want to apologize for unearthing what he'd worked so hard to bury. I want to tell him that I'm going to turn around, that I'm going to drop him back off at the station, that I can handle this entirely on my own. I want to tell him to call Yvonne and maybe give it one more try and forget I said anything about his dead daughter.

But I don't.

Instead I say, "My theory isn't adding up anymore."

"How's that?"

"My theory—if you want to call it that—was that this all has to do with what happened to Leo and Diana."

Out of the corner of my eye, I can see Augie deflate. I push on.

"I figured that it has something to do with that Conspiracy Club. Six possible members that we know of—Leo and Diana—"

"We don't know Diana was a member." There is a snap in his voice, which I completely get. "She wasn't wearing one of those silly pins in the yearbook."

"Right," I say slowly, carefully. "That's why I said *possible* members."

"Fine, whatever."

"If you don't want me to talk about this—"

"Do me a favor, Nap. Just tell me what's now wrong with your theory, okay?"

I nod. As the two of us get older, we get more equal. But Augie is still the mentor, I the mentee. "Six possible members," I say again. "Diana and Leo—"

"—are dead," he says. "So is Rex. That leaves Maura, who was at the scene of Rex's murder, that cardiologist out west—"

"Beth Fletcher née Lashley."

"And Hank," Augie says.

"And he's the problem," I say.

"How so?"

"Three weeks ago, before Rex was murdered, someone posted that viral video of Hank. Then Hank goes missing. Then Rex gets killed. I don't see how there can be a connection. Whoever posted the video—that was a random thing by a school parent. That can't be connected to the old base or the Conspiracy Club, right?"

"Seems unlikely." He rubs his chin with his right hand. "May I make an observation?"

"Shoot."

"You want this too much, Nap."

"And you don't want it enough," I fire back, which is a dumb thing for me to say.

I expect and deserve fireworks. Instead Augie chuckles. "Anyone else, I'd punch them in the mouth for that."

"That was out of line," I say. "I'm sorry."

"I get it, Nap, even if you don't."

"What are you talking about?"

"You aren't just in this because of Leo and Diana," he says. "You're in it for Maura."

I just sit and let the words sting.

"If Maura hadn't run off, you'd have been able to put Leo's death behind you. You'd have questions, of course, like I do. But that's the difference here. Whatever answer we come up with, even if it changes what we know about Leo and Diana, it doesn't really change anything for me. My daughter's dead body will still be rotting in that cemetery. But for you"—there is a deep sadness in Augie's voice, and I think it may be pity for me—"for you, there's Maura."

We pull up to the gate in front of the condo development. I shake it off. Focus. Concentrate.

It is easy to poke fun at these sorts of real estate developments—the placid sameness, the lack of any sense of individuality, the snap-together structuring, the overly orchestrated landscapes—but I've thought of moving into one ever since I reached adulthood. The idea of paying one monthly maintenance fee and doing no exterior work appeals to me. I hate to mow the lawn. I don't like to garden or barbecue or do any of the classic home-ownership rites of passage. I wouldn't care in the slightest if the exterior of my home looked exactly the same as my neighbors'. I don't even feel any special connection to the physical structure where we were raised.

You, Leo, would stay with me wherever I would go.

So why don't I move?

I'm sure a psychiatrist would have a field day with that one, but I don't think the answer is that deep. Maybe it's easier to stay. Moving is an effort. Classic science: A body at rest stays at rest. I don't buy that explanation, but it's the best I've got.

The condo guard is armed with nary a nightstick. I flash my badge at him and say, "We're here to see Tom Stroud."

He studies the badge, hands it back to me. "Is Mr. Stroud expecting you?"

"No."

"Do you mind if I call and let him know you're here? I mean, it's kinda policy."

I look at Augie. Augie nods. I say, "No problem."

The guard places the call. He hangs up, gives us directions to make the second left past the tennis courts, and sticks a parking pass on the windshield. I thank him and drive.

Tom Stroud is standing by an open door as we pull up. It's odd when you see the echo of the son in the father. There is no doubt he's Hank's father, but in a bizarre-world way. Yes, he's obviously older, but he's also better dressed, shaved, groomed. Hank's hair sticks up as though it's a science experiment gone wrong. His father is perfectly coiffed, the gray slicked down and parted by a divine entity.

As we open our car doors, Tom Stroud is wringing his hands. He rocks back and forth. His eyes are a little too open. I glance at Augie. He sees it too. This is a man expecting bad news, the worst sort of news. We have both delivered news of that sort—and, of course, we've both been on the receiving end.

Tom Stroud takes a shaky step forward. "Augie?"

"We don't know where Hank is," Augie says. "That's why we're here."

Relief floods his face. His son is not dead. Tom Stroud ignores me and heads toward Augie. He opens his arms and embraces his old friend. Augie hesitates for a second, almost recoiling in pain, before relaxing and hugging him back.

"It's good to see you, Augie," Tom Stroud says.

"Same, Tom."

When they let go, Augie asks, "Do you know where Hank is?"

Tom Stroud shakes his head and says, "Why don't you come inside?"

Tom Stroud makes us coffee with a French press.

"Doris liked to use one of those K-Cup machines, but I think the coffee ends up tasting like plastic." He hands me a cup, then Augie. I take a sip. It's excellent, by the way—or maybe it's my Francophile bias popping up again. Augie and I sit on stools in the small kitchen. Tom Stroud stays standing. He looks out a window that faces a building that looks exactly like this one.

"Doris and I got divorced when Hank was ten. The two of us, Doris and me, we started dating when we were fifteen. That's too young. We got married when we were still in college. I ended up working for my dad. He manufactured pallet nails and staples. I was third generation. The factory was in

Newark when I was a kid, until the riots. Then we moved it overseas. My job, it was the most boring job in the world. At least that's what I thought at the time."

I look at Augie. I expect an eye roll, but Augie is either faking paying attention to keep the guy talking or he's genuinely moved by his old friend's story.

"Anyway, I'm in my thirties, I hate my job, we're not doing well financially, I'm getting old before my time and I'm miserable and . . . it's all my fault. The divorce, I mean. You reach an edge and then you step off and you just keep tumbling down. Doris and I fought. We started to hate each other. Hank, my 'ungrateful' son, started to hate me too. So you know, the hell with them, right? I moved far away. Started a fish-and-tackle business with a gun range in the back. I tried to come back a few times, visit Hank. But he was just sullen when I came around. A pain in the ass. So why bother, you know? I got married again, but it didn't last. She left me, no kids this time, no big deal, neither of us ever really thought it was forever. . . ."

His voice drifts off.

"Tom?"

"Yeah, Augie."

"Why did you come back?"

"I'm out there in Cheyenne. I'm living my life, doing my thing. Then Doris calls and tells me she has cancer."

There are tears in his eyes now. I look at Augie. He's close to welling up too.

"I catch the next flight back here. Doris and me, we don't fight when I get back. We don't talk about the past. We don't rehash what happened or even ask why I'm back. I just move back in. I know that makes no sense."

"It makes sense," Augie says.

Tom shakes his head. "So much waste. A lifetime of it."

No one says anything for a moment. I want to move on, but this is Augie's play now.

"We had six healthy months and then six not-so-healthy months. I don't call them 'good' or 'bad' months. They're all good if you're doing the right thing. Do you know what I mean?"

"Yeah," Augie says. "I know what you mean."

"I made sure Hank was here when Doris died. We were both with her."

Augie adjusts himself on the stool. I stay very still. Tom Stroud finally turns away from the window.

"I should have called you, Augie."

Augie shakes it off.

"I wanted to. I really did. I was going to call, but . . ."

"No need to explain, Tom." Augie clears his throat. "Does Hank ever come by?"

"Yeah, sometimes. I've been thinking about selling this place. Putting the money in a trust for him. But I think the condo gives Hank some semblance of stability. I try to get him help. Sometimes . . . sometimes he's fine. Which makes it almost worse. Like he gets a glimpse of what his life could be and then it's snatched away."

Tom Stroud looks toward me for the first time. "You went to school with Hank?"

"I did, yes."

"Then maybe you know this already. Hank is ill."

I give him a small nod.

"People don't get it's an illness. They expect Hank to behave a certain way—to get over it or snap out of it or something—but it's like asking a man with two broken legs to sprint across a field. He can't."

"When was the last time you saw Hank?" I ask.

"It's been a few weeks, but it's not like his visits are consistent."

"So you weren't worried?"

Tom Stroud hems on that one. "I was, and I wasn't."

"Meaning?"

"Meaning even if I was, I didn't really know what I could do about it. Hank's an adult. He's not committed. If I had called you guys, what would you have done?"

There is no need to answer. It's obvious.

"Did Hank show you the video someone took of him in the park?" I ask.

"What video?"

I take out my mobile phone and play it for him.

When it is over, Tom puts his hand to his face. "My God . . . who posted that?"

"We don't know."

"Can I . . . I don't know . . . can I issue a missing person's report for Hank or something?"

"You can," I say.

"Then let's do that. Augie?"

Augie looks up at him.

"Find my boy, okay?"

Augie gives a slow nod. "We'll do our best."

Before we leave, Tom Stroud leads us to a room his ex-wife set aside for Hank.

"He never stays here. I don't think Hank's been inside this room since I've been back."

When he opens the door, you can smell the stale. We step in and see the far wall, and I just turn to look for Augie's reaction.

The wall is blanketed with black-and-white photos, newspaper clippings, and aerial shots of the Nike missile base in its prime. The material is mostly old, the photos rolling in on the corners, the clippings yellowing like tobacco-stained teeth. I scan for something recent or maybe something that I couldn't just find routinely online, but I don't see anything special.

Tom notices us staring. "Yeah, I guess Hank was pretty obsessed with that old base."

Again I glance at Augie. Again Augie is having none of it.

"Did Hank ever say anything about it to you?" I ask.

"Like what?"

I shrug. "Like anything?"

"Nothing that made sense."

"How about stuff that didn't make sense?"

Tom Stroud looks over at Augie. "You think this base has something—?"

"No," Augie says.

Tom turns back to me. "Hank just ranted about it. You know the kind of crazy stuff—they were keeping secrets, they were evil men, they were doing mind experiments." A sad smile comes to his face. "Funny."

"What?" I say.

"Well, not funny, but ironic. Like I said, Hank was really obsessed with the place. Even as a kid."

He hesitates here. Augie and I say nothing.

"Anyway, Doris used to joke that maybe Hank was right— maybe some secret lab did do weird experiments at the base. Maybe one night, when Hank was a little kid, he walked up that path and the bad guys grabbed him and did something to his brain and that's why he's like he is now."

The room is silent. Tom tries to laugh it off.

"Doris was only joking," Tom says. "Gallows humor. Something like this happens to your kid, you grasp at any straw, you know?"

Chapter Fourteen

Principal Deborah Keren is pregnant.

I know it may not be good form to notice a pregnancy, but she is a tiny woman everywhere except the belly, and she's dressed in orange, which is a curious choice unless she is intentionally embracing the pumpkin look. She steadies herself on the sides of the chair. It takes a bit of effort for her to rise. I tell her there is no need, but she is already past the halfway point, and it looks like it might take a crane and crew to stop her momentum and safely lower her back into the chair.

"I'm in the eighth month," Keren says. "I tell you that because everyone is suddenly afraid if you ask, 'Are you pregnant,' they'll be wrong and get in trouble or something."

"Wait," I say, "you're pregnant?"

Keren gives a side smile. "No, I swallowed a bowling ball."

"I was going to say beach ball."

"You're an amusing guy, Nap."

"This your first kid?"

"It is."

"That's wonderful. Congrats."

"Thanks." She moves toward me. "You done charming me with small talk?"

"How did I do?"

"So charming that if I wasn't already pregnant, I would be now. So what can I do for you, Nap?"

We don't know each other super-well, but we both live in Westbridge and when you're a local principal and a local cop, you bump into each other at the too-many town gatherings. She starts waddling down the corridor. I walk with her, trying not to subconsciously copy her. The corridors are an empty only a school corridor during classes can be. The place hasn't changed much since we were here, Leo—hard tile floors, lockers lining both sides, the wall above them painted a Ticonderoga-pencil yellow. The biggest change, which isn't a change, is perspective. They say that schools seem smaller as you age. That's true. I think maybe it's that perspective that keeps the old ghosts at bay.

"It's about Hank Stroud," I say to her.

"Interesting."

"Why do you say that?"

"As I'm sure you're aware, the parents complain about him all the time."

I nod.

"But I haven't seen him in weeks. I think that viral video scared him off."

"You know about the video?"

"I try to know what's going on in my school"—she peeks through a small rectangular window into a classroom, moves to the next door, peeks in again—"but I mean, come on, half the country knows about that."

"Have you ever seen Hank expose himself?"

"If I had, don't you think I would have called you guys?"

"So that's a no."

"That's a no."

"Do you think he did it?" I ask.

"Exposed himself?"

"Yes."

We keep walking. She checks out another classroom. Someone in the room must catch her eye, because she waves. "I'm of two minds on Hank." A student turns the corner, sees us, stops in her tracks. Principal Keren says, "Where are you going, Cathy?"

Cathy looks everywhere but at us. "To see you."

"Okay. Wait in my office. I'll be there in a few minutes."

Cathy does that scared-servant shuffle past us. I look at Keren, but it's not my business. She's already back on the move.

"You are of two minds on Hank," I say to prompt us back on subject.

"Those are public grounds out there," she says. "Open to the public. That's the law. Hank's got as much right to be on them as anyone. We have joggers run past there every day too. Kimmy Konisberg jogs by. You've noticed her, right?"

Kimmy Konisberg is, for lack of more adequate terminology, the town MILF. She has it, and boy does she flaunt it. "Who?"

"Right. So every morning, Kimmy jogs by in the tightest and

yet least supportive Lycra imaginable. If I was a certain type of person, I would say she wants these adolescent boys to stare."

"Would that type of person be truthful?"

"Touché. And this town is such a hypocritical protective bubble as it is. And I get that. I get that's why people move out here to raise their families. To keep them safe. Heck"—she rests her hand on her belly—"I want my kids safe too. But it can become too sheltered. That's not healthy. I grew up in Brooklyn. I'm not going to tell you how rough I had it. We walked past six Hanks every day. So maybe our kids can learn compassion. Hank is a human being, not something to be scorned. A few months back, the kids found out Hank went to school here. So one of the kids—do you know Cory Mistysyn?"

"I know the family. Good people."

"Right, been in town a long time. Anyway, Cory dug up an old middle-school yearbook from Hank's last year." She stops and turns to me. "You and Hank were here at the same time, right?"

"Right."

"So you know. The kids were shocked. Hank used to be just like them—in chorus, won the science fair, was even treasurer of the class. It got the kids thinking."

"There but for the grace of God."

"Exactly." She takes two more steps. "God, I'm hungry all the time, and then when I eat, I feel sick. This eighth month just sucks. I'm hating all men right now, by the way."

"I'll keep that in mind." Then I say, "You said two minds."

"Pardon?"

"With Hank. You said you're of two minds. So what's Mind Two?"

"Oh." She starts up again, her belly leading the way. "Look, I hate the stigma attached to mental illness—that goes without saying—but I don't like Hank hanging around here either. I don't *think* he's a danger, but I don't *know* that he's not, either. I worry I'll be so politically correct about it that I'm not protecting my students. Do you know what I mean?"

I let her know that I do.

"So I don't like Hank standing out there. But so what? I don't like that Mike Inga's mom always illegally drops him off in the no-drop-off zone. I don't like that Lisa Vance's dad clearly helps her with her art projects. I don't like that Andrew McDade's parents storm in whenever the report cards arrive to grade-grub for their kid. I don't like a lot of things." She stops and puts a hand on my arm. "But do you know what I don't like most?"

I look at her.

"Online shaming. It's the worst sort of vigilante justice. Hank is just the most recent example.

"Last year, someone tweets a picture of a kid with a caption saying, 'This punk stole my iPhone but forgot all the pics he takes are on my cloud, please retweet to find him.' The purported 'punk' was Evan Ober, a student here. You know him?"

"Name doesn't ring a bell."

"No reason it should. Evan's a good kid."

"Did he steal the iPhone?"

"No, of course not. That's my point. He started dating Carrie Mills. Carrie's ex Danny Turner was furious about it."

"So Turner posted that pic."

"Yep, but I can't prove it. That's the shit-bird anonymity of online shaming. Did you see that girl who just walked past us?"

"The one you sent to your office?"

138

"Yeah, that's Cathy Garrett. She's a sixth-grade girl. Sixth grade, Nap. So a few weeks ago, Cathy accidentally left her phone in the bathroom. Another girl found it. So this other girl takes the phone, snaps a close-up of her, uh, privates, and then sends the pic to Cathy's entire contact list, including her parents, her grandparents, everyone."

I make a face. "That's sick."

"I know, right?" She grimaces and puts both hands on her lower back.

"You okay?"

"I'm eight months pregnant, remember?"

"Right."

"I feel like I got a school bus parked on my bladder."

"Did you ever catch the girl who took the pics?"

"Nope. We have five or six suspects, all twelve-year-old girls, but the only way to know for certain . . ."

I hold up my hand. "Say no more."

"Cathy's been so traumatized by the whole thing, she pretty much visits my office every day. We talk, she calms down, she heads back to class."

Keren stops and looks back over her shoulder. "I should get to Cathy now."

We start walking back.

"Your talk about the anonymity of online shaming," I say. "Is this your way of telling me you don't believe Hank exposed himself?"

"No, but you're making my point for me."

"What's that?"

"I *don't* know because I *can't* know. That's always the problem with this sort of innuendo. You want to just dismiss it. But sometimes you can't. Maybe Hank did, maybe he didn't. I can't unring that bell, and, sorry, that's wrong."

"You've watched the video of Hank, right?"

"Right."

"Any idea who filmed it?"

"Again, I have no proof."

"I don't need proof."

"I wouldn't want to cast aspersions without evidence, Nap. That's what the online shaming does."

We reach her office. She looks at me. I look at her. Then she lets loose a long sigh.

"But I can tell you that there is an eighth-grade girl named Maria Hanson. My secretary can give you her address. Her mother, Suzanne, has come to see me frequently to complain about Hank. When I tell her that there is nothing that legally can be done, she becomes particularly agitated."

Principal Keren looks through the glass at Cathy. Her eyes start to water.

"I better get to her," she says.

"Okay."

"Damn." She wipes the tears from her eyes with her fingers and looks at me. "All dry?"

"Yeah."

"Eighth month," she says. "My hormones are on crack."

I nod. "You having a girl?"

She smiles at me. "How did you guess?"

She waddles away. I watch her through the glass as she takes Cathy in her arms and lets the young girl sob on her shoulder.

Then I leave to find Suzanne Hanson.

Chapter Fifteen

Westbridge doesn't have a poor side of town. It has a poor acre, maybe.

There's a grouping of aging three-family houses located between a Ford dealership and a Dick's Sporting Goods near the town center. Maura and her mom moved in here the summer before our senior year. They sublet two rooms from a Vietnamese family after Maura's father cleaned them out and ran off. Maura's mom worked a few part-time jobs and drank too much.

The Hanson family lives on the first floor of a rust-brick edifice. The wood stoop groans as I step up. When I ring the bell, a big man in mechanic's coveralls comes to the door. The name "Joe" is stenciled on the right chest pocket. Joe does not look happy to see me.

"Who are you?" Joe asks.

I show him my badge. A woman I assume is Suzanne Hanson comes into view from behind him. When she sees my badge too, her eyes widen, probably in parental worry. I reassure them right away.

"Everything is fine," I say.

Joe remains suspicious. He steps in front of his wife and gives me narrow eyes. "What do you want?"

I pocket my badge. "Several concerned citizens have filed complaints against a man named Hank Stroud. I'm looking into them."

"See, Joe?" the woman I assume is Suzanne says. She slides in front of her husband and pushes open the door. "Come in, Officer."

We move though the front room into the kitchen. She offers me a seat at the table. I take it. The floor is Formica. The table is round and faux wood. The chair is chipped-white Windsor. There is a clock above the door that uses red dice for numbers. The inscription on top reads FABULOUS LAS VEGAS. Toast crumbs litter the table. Suzanne sweeps them with one hand over the table's side and into her free palm. Then she dumps the crumbs into the sink and runs the water.

I take out a pad and pen for show. "Do you know who Hank Stroud is?"

Suzanne sits across from me. Joe stands over her, his hand on her shoulder, still eyeing me like I'm here to either shoplift or bed his wife. "He's that horrible pervert who hangs around the school," she says.

"I assume you've seen him more than once," I say.

"Almost every day. He ogles all the girls, including my daughter, Maria. She's only fourteen!"

I nod, trying on a friendly smile. "You've seen this personally?"

"Oh, sure. It's terrible. And by the way, it's about time the police got on this. You work hard, you scrape together enough money to move to a beautiful town like Westbridge; I mean, you expect your kids to be safe, right?"

"Definitely," I say.

"And what do you have? Some hobo— Do people still say 'hobo'?"

I smile and spread my hands. "Why not?"

"Right. Hobo. He hangs around our children. You move to a town like this and every day you have to see this bum—that's what he is, I know you shouldn't use the word—this bum every day lurking around your children. It's like this giant, awful weed in a beautiful flower garden, you know?"

I nod. "We need to pull the weed out."

"Exactly!"

I take some pretend notes. "Have you ever seen Mr. Stroud do more than ogle?"

She's about to blurt something out, but now I notice the hand on her shoulder gently squeeze to silence her. I look up at Joe. He looks back at me. He gets why I'm here. I get that he gets it, and he gets that I get that.

Shorter: The game is over. Or is just beginning.

"You posted a video of Hank Stroud, didn't you, Mrs. Hanson?"

Her eyes are aflame. She shakes Joe's hand off her shoulder. "You don't know that."

143

"Oh, I know it," I say. "We already ran a voice analysis. We also traced down the Internet IP address from which the video originated." I give what I said a second to land. "They both confirm that you, Mrs. Hanson, filmed and posted that video."

This is a lie, of course. I ran no voice analysis or Internet trace.

"And what if she did?" Joe asks. "Not saying she did or she didn't, but if she did, there's no law against it, is there?"

"I don't care," I say. "I'm here to find out what happened, that's all." I look her straight in the eyes. She looks down a second, then back up at me. "You filmed Hank. If you keep denying it, you're just going to piss me off. So tell me what you saw."

"He . . . he pulled down his pants," she says.

"When?"

"You mean like the date?"

"For starters, sure."

"It was maybe a month ago."

"Before school, after school, when?"

"Before school. That's when I see him. I drop my daughter off at seven forty-five A.M. Then I stay and watch her walk all the way in every day because, well, wouldn't you? You drop your fourteen-year-old daughter off at this beautiful school, and there is a creepy pervert right across the way. I don't understand why the police don't do something."

"Tell me exactly what happened."

"I told you. He pulled down his pants."

"Your daughter was walking. And he pulled down his pants."

"Yes."

"On your video, his pants are up."

"He pulled them back up."

"I see. So he pulled his pants down and then he pulled them back up."

"Yes." She is looking up to the left. I forget if that means a lie is coming or a memory. Doesn't matter. I don't believe much in that stuff. "He saw me fiddling with my phone and he panicked and so he pulled them back up."

"How long would you say his pants were down?"

"I don't know. How could I know?"

Joe adds, "You think she was carrying a stopwatch or something?"

"It was long enough, that I can tell you."

I bite back the obvious joke and say, "Go on."

Suzanne looks confused. "What do you mean, go on?"

"He pulled his pants down, he pulled his pants up." I look very unimpressed. "That's it?"

Joe doesn't like that. "What, that's not enough for you?"

"How do you know his pants didn't just fall down?" I ask.

Once again Suzanne's eyes drop to the table before lifting toward me. I know a lie is coming. I am not disappointed. "He pulls his pants down," she says again. "Then he yells at my daughter to look at his . . . I mean, he starts stroking it and everything."

Ah, human nature. So predictable sometimes. I see this a lot, Leo. You hear a witness tell you something that they hope will shock your senses. Then I, as an investigator, act blasé. The truthful person lets it go. But the liar starts embellishing, trying to up the story so I share their outrage. I use the word "embellishing" here, but really it's straight-up lying. They can't help themselves.

I know now and don't want to waste much more time here. Time to cut to it.

Watch and learn, Leo.

"You're lying," I say.

Suzanne's mouth turns into a shocked perfect O.

Joe's face reddens. "Are you calling my wife a liar?"

"What part of 'you're lying' left that in doubt, Joe?"

If Suzanne had been wearing pearls, she'd have clutched them. "How dare you!"

I smile now. "I know it's a lie," I say, "because I just talked to Maria."

The anger rises.

"You did what?" Suzanne shouts.

"It took a while for your daughter to cave," I say, "but eventually Maria admitted to me it never happened."

They are both apoplectic. I try not to enjoy this.

"You aren't allowed to do that!"

"Do what?"

"You can't talk to our daughter without our permission," she says. "I'll have your badge."

I frown. "Why does everyone say that?"

"What?"

"That threat. 'I'll have your badge.' You saw it on TV, right?"

Joe takes a step toward me. "I don't like the way you're talking to my wife."

"And I don't care. Sit down, Joe."

He sneers at me. "Tough guy. Because you have a badge."

"Again with the badge." I sigh, take out the badge, slide it across the table. "Here, you want it? Take it." I stand and get right in Joe's face. "You ready to go now?"

Joe takes a step back. I step closer to him. He tries to look me in the eyes, but he can't hold it.

"Not worth it," he mutters.

"What did you say?"

Joe doesn't reply. He circles the table and sits in the chair next to his wife.

I glare down at Suzanne Hanson. "If you don't tell me the truth, I'm going to launch a full investigation and charge you with two counts of violating federal Internet Act Section 418, which upon conviction could lead to a penalty of one hundred thousand dollars and up to four years in prison."

I'm making this up. I don't think there is any federal Internet act. The specific section number is a nice touch, don't you think?

"That bum shouldn't be there!" she insists. "You people wouldn't do anything about it!"

"So you did," I say.

"He shouldn't be allowed to be that close to a school!"

"He has a name. It's Hank Stroud. And he's missing."

"What?"

"Since you posted your video, no one has seen him."

"Good," she says.

"How's that?"

"Maybe the video scared him."

"And you feel good about that, do you?"

Suzanne opens her mouth, then closes it again. "I was just

trying to protect my child. To protect all the children at the school, really."

"You better tell me everything."

She did.

Suzanne admitted that she "exaggerated" to the point of making it all up. Hank never exposed himself. Tired and frustrated by what she perceived as the lack of action by school administrators and law enforcement, Suzanne Hanson did what she thought best.

"It's only a question of time before he did something awful. I was just trying to prevent that."

"Noble," I reply with as much disdain as I can muster.

Suzanne was "cleaning up the filth" by trying to twist the reality of her town into the idyllic haven she believed it should be. Hank was mere refuse. Best to dump him curbside where he could be trucked out of sight and smell. I would lecture Suzanne Hanson on her lack of empathy, but what's the point? I remember once when we were maybe ten, driving through a rough neighborhood in Newark. Parents always tell their kids to look out the windows and be grateful for what they've got. But our dad handled it differently. He just said one line that has always stuck with me:

"Every person has hopes and dreams."

It is something I try to remember every time I cross a fellow human being. Does that include low-life turds like Trey? Of course. He has hopes and dreams too. That's fine. But when your hopes and dreams crush the hopes and dreams of others . . .

I'm rationalizing again. I don't care about the Treys of the world. Simple as that. Maybe I should. But I don't. Or maybe I doth protest too much.

What do you think, Leo?

When I finally leave their stuffy house—when Joe slams the door behind me to make some kind of stand, to himself at least—I take a deep breath. I glance over to where Maura used to live. She never brought me here, and I was inside only once. This was about two weeks after you and Diana were killed. I turn now and look at the tree across the street. That was where I waited, hidden. First I saw the Vietnamese family exit. Fifteen minutes later, Maura's mom stumbled out in an ill-fitted summer dress. She managed to weave her way down the street toward the bus stop.

When she was out of sight, I broke into the house.

The answer to why is probably obvious. I was looking for clues to where Maura might have gone. When I had cornered her mother earlier, she said something about her transferring to a private school. I asked where. She wouldn't tell me.

"It's over, Nap," Mrs. Wells told me, her breath stinking of booze. "Maura has moved on. So should you."

But I didn't believe her. So I broke in. I rummaged through all the drawers and cabinets. I went into Maura's room. Her clothes and backpack were still there. Did she pack anything? It didn't look like it.

I also searched for my varsity jacket.

For all Maura's eye rolling about my being a jock and the stupid intensity of sports in this town and the anti-hip, quasi-sexist idea of it all, Maura got a kick out of wearing my varsity jacket. Retro maybe. Ironic, I don't know. Or maybe it wasn't a contradiction at all. Maura was an old soul.

So I searched for my varsity jacket, the green one with the white sleeves and the crossed hockey sticks on the back and my name and "Captain" stenciled on the front.

But I couldn't find it.

Did Maura take the jacket with her? I always wondered. Why wasn't the jacket in her room?

I turn away from the house now and look out into the distance. I have a few minutes. I know where I want to go. I cross the road and find the railroad tracks. I know you are not supposed to walk beside them, but I'm living on the edge today. I follow the tracks out of the town center, up past Downing Road and Coddington Terrace, past the storage facility and the old industrial plant that's been converted into a party space and circuit-training studio.

I am away from civilization now, high up on that hill between the station for Westbridge and the one for Kasselton. I skirt past broken beer bottles and reach the edge. I look down and see the steeple from Westbridge Presbyterian. It lights up at 7:00 P.M., so I assume you saw it that night. Or were you too stoned or high to take notice? I knew that you were starting to get a little too fond of recreational drugs and drinking. In hindsight, I guess I should have stopped it, but at the time it didn't hit me as a big deal. Everyone was doing it—you, Maura, most of our friends. The only reason I didn't partake was because of my training.

I take another deep breath.

So how did it all go down, Leo? Why were you here, on the other side of Westbridge, and not hanging out in the woods near the old Nike base? Did you and Diana want to be alone? Were you trying to avoid your Conspiracy Club friends? Were you intentionally staying away from the old base?

Why were you here? Why were you on these train tracks?

I wait for you to say something. You don't.

I wait a little more because I know it won't be long now. The Main Line runs every hour this time of day. I wait until I hear the whistle as it pulls out of the Westbridge station. Not far away now. Part of me wants to stand on the tracks. No, I don't want to end it. I'm not suicidal. But I want to know what it was like for you. I want to reconstruct that night so I know exactly what you experienced. I watch now as the train hurtles over the horizon. The tracks vibrate to the point where I can't believe they don't come apart. Did you feel that vibration under your feet? Did Diana? Or were you standing off to the side, just as I am? Did you both look down at the steeple, turn, and then decide to jump across at the last possible second?

I can see the train now. I watch it come closer. Did you see it that night? Hear it? Feel it? You must have. It bears down on these tracks with unfathomable power. I take another step back. When it rushes by, I am a full ten yards away from the train and yet I'm forced to close my eyes and raise my hand to protect my face. The swoosh of air nearly knocks me off my feet. The pure might of the locomotive, the sheer mass times velocity, is awesome, devastating, unstoppable.

A mind, like a heart, goes where it wants, and so I imagine that hard-steel front grille crushing human flesh. I imagine those churning wheels grinding bone into dust.

I pry my eyes open and squint at the train speeding by. It seems to take forever, that the train is endless, crushing and churning and grinding. I stare straight at it, letting it blur without trying to focus. My eyes water.

I've seen the horrific, splatter-filled crime scene photos from that night, but they oddly don't move me. The destruction was so great, the disfigurement so immense, that either I can't link the misshapen waxy chunks to you and Diana or, more likely, my mind won't let me.

When the train finally passes, when the quiet slowly returns, my eyes start to take in the scene. Even now, all these years later, I am searching for clues, evidence, something that may have been missed. Being up here is strange. The horror is obvious, but it also feels somehow holy, somehow right, to be in the place where you drew your final breath.

As I start back down the hill, I check my phone for messages. Nothing from our old classmate Beth Fletcher née Lashley, MD. I call her office in Ann Arbor again. The receptionist gives me a bit of the runaround, so I get more pointed. Soon a woman who introduces herself as Cassie and calls herself the "office manager" gets on the line.

"Dr. Fletcher is unavailable at this time."

"Cassie, I'm getting tired of being jerked around. I'm a cop. I need to speak to her."

"I can only pass that message on to her."

"Where is she?"

"I wouldn't know."

"Wait, you don't know where she is?"

"It is not my concern. I have your name and number. Is there any other message you'd like me to give her?"

In for a penny, in for a pound. "Do you have a pen, Cassie?"

"I do."

"Tell Dr. Fletcher that our friend Rex Canton has been murdered. Tell her Hank Stroud is missing. Tell her Maura Wells briefly resurfaced and then went missing again. Tell the good doctor that it all goes back to the Conspiracy Club. Tell her to call me."

Silence. Then: "Is that Laura with an *L* or Maura with an *M*?"

Completely unflustered.

"Maura with an *M*."

"I'll give Dr. Fletcher the message."

She hangs up.

I don't like this. Maybe I'll call the Ann Arbor Police Department, ask them to send one of their people over to Beth's home and office. I keep walking. I think again about all the strands—your and Diana's "accident," Rex's murder and Maura being at the scene, Hank and that viral video, the Conspiracy Club. I try to find connections, draw lines, work Venn diagrams of these events in my head. But I see no overlap or link.

Perhaps there is none. That's what Augie would tell me. He's probably right, but of course, accepting that possible reality gets me nowhere.

I see the Westbridge Memorial Library up ahead now, and that sparks an idea. The front facade is that kind of red school brick that dates back a hundred years. The rest of the building is modern and sleek. I still love libraries. I love the hybrid quality, the new computer sections and the books yellowing with age. Libraries for me have always had a cathedral-like ambiance, a hushed sanctuary where learning is revered, where we the people elevate books and education to the level of the religious. When we were kids, Dad would take us here on Saturday mornings. He would leave us in the children/young adult section with strict instructions not to misbehave. I would browse through dozens of books. You would grab one—usually one meant for an older reader—sit in a beanbag chair in the corner, and read the entire book.

I head down two levels to the dingy basement area. It is old-school down here—rows and rows of books upon books, most no longer of interest to the casual library visitor, sit on aluminum shelves. There are a few cubby desks for true homework grinders. In the corner, I find the old room. The plaque next to it reads TOWN HISTORY. I lean my head in and rap on the wood.

As Dr. Jeff Kaufman looks up at me, his reading glasses drop off his nose. The glasses are on a chain, so they bounce against his chest. He's wearing a thick knit cardigan sweater buttoned up to the sternum. He's bald on top with shocks of gray hair on the sides that look as if they are trying to flee from his scalp.

"Hey, Nap."

"Hey, Dr. Kaufman."

He frowns. Dr. Kaufman was a librarian and town historian long before we moved to Westbridge, and when you call someone of authority "doctor" or even "mister" as a kid, it is hard to convert to a casual use of their first name as an adult. I move into the cluttered room and ask Dr. Kaufman what he can tell me about the old Nike missile base located by the middle school.

Kaufman's eyes light up. He takes a moment or two to gather his thoughts; then he invites me to have a seat across the table from him. The table is a mess of black-and-white photographs from days of yore. I scan them hoping to see one of the old base. I don't.

He clears his throat and dives in: "The Nike missile bases were constructed in the midfifties throughout northern New Jersey. This was during the height of the Cold War. Back then, we would run school drills where kids would duck under their desks in case of nuclear attack, if you can believe it. Like that would help. The base here in Westbridge was constructed in 1954."

"The army just stuck these bases right in the middle of suburban towns?"

"Sure, why not? Farmland too. New Jersey used to have a lot of farms back then."

"And what were the Nike missiles used for exactly?" I ask.

"They were surface-to-air. Put simply, the missiles were an air defense designed to shoot down attacking Soviet aircrafts, most notably their Tu-95, which could fly six thousand miles without needing to refuel. The missile batteries were in approximately a dozen sites in northern New Jersey. Sandy Hook still has remnants if you want to visit. The one in Livingston is now an art colony, of all things. There were missile batteries in Franklin Lakes, East Hanover, Morristown."

It is hard to believe. "Nike missiles in all these towns?"

"Sure. They started with the smaller Nike Ajax missiles, but those were still thirty feet long. They kept them in underground launch sites and would bring them to the surface the same way a body shop would lift a car up in a garage."

"I don't get it," I say. "How could the government keep something like this a secret?"

"They didn't," Kaufman says. "At least not at first."

He stops now, leans back, and folds his hands over his belly.

"In fact, the bases were celebrated. When I was seven—that would have been in 1960—my Cub Scout pack got a tour of the facility, if you can believe it. The idea that your friendly local missile site was keeping you safe from the long-range aircraft of the Soviet Union was supposed to make you sleep better."

"But that changed?" I ask.

"Yes."

"When?"

"Early sixties." Jeff Kaufman sighs and rises to his feet. He opens a tall file cabinet behind him. "See, they replaced the Nike Ajax missiles with the larger Nike Hercules." He plucked out two photographs of a scary-ass-looking white missile marked US ARMY on the side. "Forty-one feet tall. Traveled at Mach 3—that's about twenty-three hundred miles per hour. Range of seventy-five miles."

He moved back to the seat, sat, and put his hands on the table in front of him. "But the big change with the Nike Hercules—the reason they clammed up about the program—had to do with the payload."

"Meaning?"

"The missiles were armed with W31 nuclear warheads."

It is hard to fathom. "There were nuclear weapons . . . ?"

"Right here, yes. Armed warheads. There were even reports of a few near misses. One slid off a dolly when they were moving it higher up a hill. Landed on the concrete and the warhead cracked. Smoke started pouring out. No one knew about it at the time, of course. Everything was kept hush-hush. Anyway, the Nike program ran until the early 1970s. The control center in Westbridge was one of the last to close. That would have been 1974."

"And then what?" I ask. "I mean, what happened to the land after they closed?"

"There wasn't much interest in anything military in the seventies. Vietnam was ending. So they just sat there. Most fell into disrepair. Eventually most were sold off. A condo development was built over a missile battery in East Hanover, for example. One of the roads is called Nike Drive."

"What about the base in Westbridge?"

Jeff Kaufman smiles at me. "What happened to our base," he says, "is a tad murkier."

I wait.

He leans toward me and asks what I'm surprised he hadn't asked earlier. "Do you mind me asking why you're suddenly interested in all of this?"

I was going to make something up or tell him that I'd rather not, but then I figure what's the harm. "It involves a case I'm working on."

"What kind of case, if you don't mind me asking?"

"A long shot," I say. "Something from years ago."

Jeff Kaufman meets my eyes. "Are you talking about your brother's death?"

Ka-pow.

I don't say anything—in part because I've learned to stay silent and let others jump in to break it, in part because I don't think I can.

"Your father and I were friends," he says. "You knew that, right?"

I manage to nod.

"And Leo . . ." Kaufman shakes his head and sits back. His face has lost a bit of color. "He wanted to know about the history of the base too."

"Leo came to you?" I ask.

"Yes."

"When?"

"I can't say exactly. A few times, probably within a year of his death. Leo was fascinated by the base. Some of his friends came with him too."

"Do you remember their names?"

"No, sorry."

"What did you tell them?"

He shrugs. "The same things I'm telling you now."

My mind is whirring. I feel lost yet again.

"At Leo's memorial service, I shook your hand. I doubt you'd remember. So many people were there and you looked so shell-shocked. I told your dad."

That startles me back. "Told my dad what?"

"That Leo used to come here and ask about the base."

"You told my dad?"

"Sure."

"What did he say?"

"He seemed grateful. Leo was so bright and inquisitive. I thought that your father would want to hear that, that's all. I never thought his death could be connected . . . I mean, I still don't. Except now you're here too, Nap. And you're no fool either." He looks up. "So tell me. Is there a connection?"

Rather than answer him I say, "I need to know the rest of the story."

"Okay."

"What happened to the Westbridge base after the Nike program closed down?"

"Officially? It was taken over by the Department of Agriculture."

"And unofficially?"

"When you were a kid, did you ever go up there?"

"Yes."

"We did in my day too. We used to sneak in through a hole in the fence. I remember one time we got so trashed one of the soldiers took us home in an army jeep. My dad grounded me for three weeks." The memory brings a small smile to his face. "How close did you get to the base?"

"Not very."

"Exactly."

"I'm not following."

"Security was tighter for the Department of Agriculture than a nuclear missile control center." Kaufman tilted his head. "Why do you think that was?"

I don't answer.

"Think about it. You have these empty military bases. The security apparatus is already in place. If you were a government agency that wanted to fly under the radar, do something clandestine . . . Look, think of some three-letter government agencies that might like to hide in plain sight like that. It wouldn't be the first time. The old Montauk Air Force Station had dozens of rumors swirling around it."

"What kind of rumors?"

"Nazi scientists, mind control, LSD experiments, UFOs, all kinds of crazy nonsense."

"And you believe those? You believe the United States government hid Nazis and aliens in Westbridge?"

"For crying out loud, Nap, they hid nuclear weapons here!" There was a glint in Kaufman's eyes now. "Is it really such a stretch to think they hid something else?"

I say nothing.

"It doesn't have to be Nazis and aliens. They could have been testing some advanced technology—DARPA, lasers, drones, weather modification, Internet hacking. Does that really seem so far-fetched with all the security around the place?"

No, it doesn't.

Jeff Kaufman stands now, starts pacing. "I'm a damn good researcher," he says. "Back in the day, I dug into this pretty deeply. I even took a trip down to Washington, DC, to check records and archives. All I found going on there were innocuous corn and livestock studies."

"You told all this to my brother?"

"Him and his friends, yeah."

"How many of them?"

"What?"

"How many kids came with Leo?"

"Five, maybe six, I don't remember."

"Boys, girls?"

He thought about it. "I think there were two girls, but I can't swear to it. Might have been just one."

"You know that Leo didn't die alone."

He nods. "Of course. Diana Styles was with him. The captain's daughter."

"Was Diana one of those girls who visited you with my brother?"

"No."

I am not sure what to make of that, if anything. "Is there anything else you can think of that could help me?"

"Help you what, Nap?"

"Let's say you're right. Let's say the base was doing something top secret. And let's say somehow these kids found out about it. What would happen to them?"

Now it was his turn to not reply. His mouth just drops open.

"What else did you learn, Dr. Kaufman?"

"Just two more things." He clears his throat and sits back down. "I found the name of one of the commanders. Andy Reeves. He was supposedly an agriculture expert out of Michigan State, but when I looked into his background, let's just say it was muddled."

"CIA?"

"He fits the pattern. And he still lives in the area."

"Did you ever talk to him about it?"

"I tried."

"And?"

"He just said the base did boring agriculture stuff. Counting cows and crops, that's how he put it."

"What's the second thing?"

"The closing of the base."

"Right, when was that?"

"Fifteen years ago," Kaufman says. "Three months after your brother and Augie's daughter were found dead."

As I head back toward my car, I call Augie.

"I just talked to Jeff Kaufman."

I think I hear a sigh. "Oh, great."

"He had some interesting stuff to say about the old base."

"I bet he did."

"Do you know Andy Reeves?"

"I did."

I'm cutting across town now. "How?"

"I've been head of this police department for almost thirty years, remember? He was running the base when it was doing agriculture studies."

I pass a new place that only sells various chicken wings. The smell is enough to harden my arteries.

"Did you buy that?" I ask.

"Buy what?"

"That they were doing agricultural studies."

"I buy that," Augie says, "a lot more than I buy those mind-control rumors. As police chief, I knew all the commanders at the base. My predecessor knew all the ones from before that."

"Kaufman says back in the day the base used to control nuclear missiles."

"That's what I heard too."

"And then he said when it changed hands, the base became even more guarded and more secretive."

"No offense to Kaufman, but he's being overly dramatic."

"How so?"

"The Nike bases were out in the open at first. Kaufman told you that, right?"

"Right."

"So when they went nuclear, it would have been suspicious to all of a sudden be hunkering down and acting too secretive. There was a ton of added security when they went nuclear, but it was more subtle."

"And when the Nike bases closed down?"

"There may have been tighter security, but that was just normal updating and technology. A new team comes in, they put up a better fence."

I cross Oak Street, Westbridge's own Restaurant Row. I walk past—in order—Japanese, Thai, French, Italian, dim sum, and something called "California fusion" restaurants. After that, you hit a slew of bank branches. I don't see the point. I never see any customers in bank branches, other than to use the ATMs.

"I'd like to talk to this Andy Reeves," I say to Augie. "Can you arrange it?"

I expect pushback. I don't get it. "Okay, I'll set it up for you."

"You're not going to try to stop me?"

"No," Augie says. "You seem to need this."

He hangs up then. As I reach my car, my phone rings. The caller ID tells me it's Ellie.

"Hey," I say.

"We need you at the shelter."

I don't like the tone. "What's wrong?"

"Nothing. Just get here as soon as you can, okay?"

"Okay."

She hangs up. I slip into the car and grab the portable police siren light. I almost never use it, but this seems like a good time. I slap it on the roof and drive fast.

I arrive at the shelter in twelve minutes. I hurry-walk inside, turn left, and half rush down the hall. Ellie is waiting outside her office door. The expression on her face tells me that this is something big.

"What?" I ask.

Ellie doesn't speak, instead choosing to gesture toward the inside of her office. I turn the knob, push the door open, and look inside.

There are two women in the room.

The one on the left I don't recognize. The other . . . It takes me a second to process. She has aged well, better than I would have expected. The fifteen years have been a friend to her. I wonder now if those years had been about sobriety and yoga or at least something along those lines. Anyway, it looks like it.

Our eyes meet. I say nothing for a moment. I just stand there.

"I knew it would come back to you," she says.

I flash back to standing across the street from the row houses, the ill-fitted summer dress, the walk-weave as she headed down the street. It's Lynn Wells.

Maura's mother.

Chapter Sixteen

I don't waste time. "Where's Maura?"

"Close the door," the other woman says. Her hair is the color of carrots, with lipstick to match. She's wearing a tailored gray suit with a frilly shirt. I'm not a fashionista, but it looks expensive.

"And you are?"

I turn back and reach for the door. Ellie gives me a quick nod as I close it.

"My name is Bernadette Hamilton. I'm Lynn's friend."

I get a sense that they are more than friends, though I don't care in the slightest. My heart is thumping so hard I'm sure they can see it through my shirt. I turn back to Mrs. Wells, all ready to repeat my question more forcefully, when something makes me pull up.

Slow down, I tell myself.

I have a million questions to ask her, of course, but I also understand that the best interrogations require almost supernatural patience. Mrs. Wells has come to me, not vice versa. She has sought me out. She has even used Ellie as a go-between, so that she didn't have to show up at my home or office or leave a phone trail. That all took effort.

The obvious conclusion?

She wants something from me.

So I should let her talk. I should let her give up something without being asked. Stay quiet. That is my normal modus operandi. No reason to change that because it's personal. So I stay calm. Don't ask her questions. Don't prompt her or make demands.

Not yet. Take your time. Plan.

But one thing, Leo: There is no way Mrs. Wells is leaving this room without telling me where Maura is.

I stay standing and wait for her to make the first move.

Finally, Mrs. Wells speaks. "The police came to see me."

I say nothing.

"They said Maura might be involved in a murder of a police officer." When I still don't reply, she says, "Is that true?"

I nod. I see her friend Bernadette reach over and put her hand on Mrs. Wells's.

"Do you really think Maura could be involved in a murder?" Lynn Wells asks.

"Probably, yeah," I say.

Her eyes widen a bit. I see the hand tighten over hers.

"Maura wouldn't kill anyone. You know that."

166

I bite back a sarcastic rejoinder and stay silent.

"The police officer who visited me. Her name was Reynolds. From somewhere in Pennsylvania. She said you were helping in the investigation?"

Mrs. Wells says it like a question. Again I don't take the bait.

"I don't understand, Nap. Why would you be investigating a murder in another state?"

"Did Lieutenant Reynolds tell you the name of the victim?"

"I don't think so. She just said he was a police officer."

"His name is Rex Canton." I keep an eye on her face. Nothing. "Does the name ring a bell?"

She considers it. "No, I don't think so."

"Rex was in our high school class."

"At Westbridge High?"

"Yes."

The color starts to ebb from her face.

The heck with patience. Sometimes you startle them with the surprise question: "Where's Maura?"

"I don't know," Lynn Wells says.

I lift my right eyebrow, offering up my most incredulous expression.

"I don't. That's why I came to you." She looks up at me. "I hoped you could help me."

"Help you find Maura?"

"Yes."

My voice is thick. "I haven't seen Maura since I was eighteen years old."

The phone on the desk starts to ring. We all ignore it. I look toward Bernadette, but she only has eyes for Lynn Wells.

"If you want me to help find Maura," I say, trying to keep

my tone calm, professional, matter-of-fact, all while my heart rate is spiking, "you need to tell me what you know."

Silence.

Lynn Wells looks at Bernadette, who shakes her head. "He can't help us," Bernadette says.

Lynn Wells nods. "This was a mistake." Both women rise. "We shouldn't have come."

They both start for the office door.

"Where are you going?" I ask.

Lynn Wells's voice is firm. "We're leaving now."

"No," I say.

Bernadette ignores me and circles toward the door. I shift my body to block her.

"Move," she says.

I look at Lynn Wells. "Maura is in over her head."

"You don't know anything."

When Bernadette goes for the knob, I'm still in the way.

"Are you going to hold us here by force?"

"Yes."

I'm not bluffing. I have spent my entire adult life waiting for answers, and now that those answers are standing in front of me, I will not let them walk out the door. No way, no how. I will keep Lynn Wells here until I know what she knows. I don't care what that takes. I don't care about the ethics or legalities.

Lynn Wells will not leave this room without telling me all she knows.

I don't move.

I try the crazy eyes, but they won't come. There is a quake inside of me, an internal shake, and I think they can see it.

"You can't trust him," Bernadette says.

I ignore her and focus on Mrs. Wells. "Fifteen years ago," I begin, "I came home from a hockey game. I was eighteen years old. A senior in high school. I had a great best friend in my twin brother. And I had a girlfriend I thought was my soul mate. I sat at my kitchen table and waited for my brother to come home . . ."

Lynn Wells studies my face. I see something I can't quite comprehend. Her eyes start to water. "I know. Both our lives changed forever that night."

"Lynn—"

She waves Bernadette to silence.

"What happened?" I ask. "Why did Maura run away?"

Bernadette snaps, "Why don't you tell us?"

That reply puzzles me, but Lynn puts a hand on Bernadette's shoulder. "Wait outside."

"I'm not leaving you."

"I need to talk to Nap alone."

Bernadette protests, but she isn't going to win this one. I move away from the door just a bit. I'm still not taking chances. I open the door just enough so that Bernadette can slip through. I'm actually crazy enough to keep an eye on Maura's mom as though she might try to bolt through it too. She doesn't. Bernadette eventually slides through the opening, throwing a baleful glare in my direction as she does.

Maura's mom and I are alone now.

"Let's sit down," she says.

"You know how it was between Maura and me back then."

Lynn Wells and I have turned the two chairs in front of Ellie's desk so that they are facing each other. I notice now that
there is a wedding band on her left hand. She keeps turning
and twisting it as she speaks.

She waits for me to reply, so I say, "I do."

"It was rough. That was my fault. At least, most of it. I
drank too much. I resented how being a single mother held me
back from . . . I don't even know what. More drinking, I guess.
And the timing didn't help, what with Maura being a teenager
and all that goes along with that. Plus she was naturally rebellious. Of course, you knew that. It was part of what drew you
to her, don't you think? So you mix all that together and . . ."

She makes two fists and then spreads her fingers, indicating
an explosion.

"We were struggling. I was working two jobs. One at a Kohl's.
Another waitressing at a Bennigan's. Maura worked part-time at
Jenson Pet Store for a while. You remember that, right?"

"Yes."

"Do you know why she quit?"

"She said something about allergies to the dogs."

There is a smile on her face, but there is no joy there. "Mike
Jenson kept putting his hand on her ass."

Even now, even all these years later, I feel the heat rush
through me. "Are you serious?"

But of course she is. "Maura said you were hotheaded. She
was afraid if she told you . . . Anyway, it doesn't matter. We lived
in Irvington at the time, but when she worked at the pet store,
we got a little taste of Westbridge. This woman I worked with at
Kohl's gave me an idea. She said I should move into the cheapest
housing in a town with good schools. 'Your daughter will get the

best education that way,' she said. That made sense to me. Whatever else you can say about Maura, she was whip smart. Anyway, that's what we did. You two met a short time later . . ."

Lynn Wells fades away.

"I'm stalling," she says.

"So skip ahead to that night," I tell her.

She nods. "Maura didn't come home."

I keep still.

"I didn't realize this right away. I was working a late shift
and then I went out with some friends. Drinking, of course. I
didn't get home until four in the morning. Maybe four, I don't
even know. I don't remember. I don't think I checked her bedroom. Great mom, right? I also don't know if that would have
made a difference. If I saw Maura wasn't there, what would I
have done differently? Probably nothing. I would have figured
that she stayed at your place. Or went to the city. She visited
friends in Manhattan a lot, though not as much once you two
started dating. And when I finally woke up and Maura wasn't
there, well, it was close to noon. I figured she'd gone out already. That made the most sense, right? So I didn't think much
of it. Then I went to work. I had a double shift at Bennigan's. It
was near closing time when the bartender said there was a call
for me. That was odd. I got scolded by the manager for that.
Anyway, it was Maura."

In my pocket, I feel my phone vibrate. I ignore it.

"What did she say?"

"I was worried, you know. Because like I said, she never
called me at work. So I hurried over and said, 'You okay, hon?'
and she just said, 'Mom, I'm going away for a little while. If
anyone asks, I'm too upset by what happened and I'm changing

171

schools.' Then she tells me, 'Don't talk to the police.'" She takes a deep breath. "You know what I say back?"

"What?"

The sad smile is back. "I ask her if she's high. That's the first thing I ask my daughter who is calling me for help. I say, 'Are you high or something?'"

"What did she say?"

"Nothing. She hung up. I'm not even sure she heard me. And I didn't even know what Maura meant by being upset by what happened. See, I was that out of it, Nap. I didn't even know about your brother and that Styles girl yet. So I just went back to work, you know, waitressing. I got two tables complaining by now. And I was taking an order at a table across from the bar, you know they got all those TVs on?"

I nod.

"Well, usually it's on sports, but someone flipped it over to the news station. That's when I saw . . ." She shakes her head. "God, how awful. They didn't say any names. So I didn't even know it was your brother or anything. Just two Westbridge students got run over by a train. So maybe now Maura's call made a little bit of sense to me. I figured she was upset by this, wanted a few days away to deal with it. I didn't know what to do, but I've learned a few things in my life. One was not to react too quickly. I'm not the smartest woman. Sometimes if you have a choice of taking Road A or Road B you should just stay where you are until you know the lay of the land. So I calmly finished my shift. Like I said, it all made sense. Except, well, what about the part about not talking to cops? That part bothered me, but I was too busy working to think about it much. So anyway, when my shift was over, I went out to my car. I was supposed to meet up with a guy I'd started seeing, but I didn't want to anymore. I just wanted to get home and hunker down. So I walked out to the lot. It was pretty empty by then. And there were these men there waiting for me."

She turns away and blinks.

"Men?" I repeat.

"Four of them."

"You mean like cops?"

"That's what they said. They flashed badges at me."

"What did they want?"

"They wanted to know where Maura was."

I'm picturing this. Bennigan's had closed down years ago, replaced by another chain restaurant called the Macaroni Grill, but I know the parking lot.

"What did you tell them?"

"I said I didn't know."

"Okay."

"They were very polite. The lead guy, the one who did all the talking, he had this pale skin and whispery voice. Gave me the chills. His fingernails were too long. I don't like that on a man. He said that Maura wasn't in trouble. He said that if she just came forward now it would all be okay. He was very persistent."

"But you didn't know."

"Right."

"So then what?"

"So then . . ." I see her eyes fill with tears. She reaches her hand up and puts it on her own throat. "I don't even know how to tell this part."

I reach out now and put my hand on hers. "It's okay."

Something has changed in the room. You can feel it like an electric surge.

"What happened next, Mrs. Wells?"

"What happened next . . ." She stops, shrugs. "It's a week later."

I pause. Then I say, "I don't understand."

"Neither do I. Next thing I remember I hear pounding on my back door. I open my eyes, and I'm in my own bed. I peek through the shade to see who was there."

She looks at me.

"It was you, Nap."

I remember this, of course. I remember going to their house and pounding on that back door, searching for Maura, who had not contacted me since my brother's death other than to say that the news about my brother was too awful, that she was going away.

That we were over.

"I didn't answer the door," she says.

"I know."

"I'm sorry about that."

I wave it off. "You said something about it being a week later."

"That's just it. See, I thought it was the next morning, but a full week had passed. I didn't know what to do. I tried to re-create what had happened. The most likely thing was that I drank myself into an extended blackout, right? I figured the pale man with the whispery voice thanked me for my time, told me to get in touch if I heard from Maura, and left me. Then I got in my car and went on a bender." She tilted her head. "Doesn't that sound like the most likely explanation, Nap?"

The room feels ten degrees cooler.

"But I don't think that's what happened."

"What do you think happened?" I ask.

"I think the pale man with the whispery voice did something to me."

I can hear my breathing like seashells pressed against my ears. "Like what?"

"I think they took me someplace and asked me about Maura again. I had these memories when I first woke up. Bad memories. But they disappeared, like after a dream. You ever have that? You wake up and you remember the nightmare and you think you'll never forget it and then the images just slip away?"

I hear myself say, "Yes."

"That's what it was like. I know it was bad. Like the worst dream possible. I reach out and try to remember, but it's like grabbing smoke."

I nod more just to have something to do, some way to handle the blows. "So what did you do?"

"I just . . ." Lynn Wells shrugs. "I went to work at Kohl's. I thought I'd get in huge trouble for missing shifts, but they said I called in sick."

"And you don't remember doing that."

"No. The same thing when I went to Bennigan's. They said I called in sick too."

I lean back now, try to take it in.

"I . . . I got paranoid too. I kept thinking I was being followed. I would see a man reading a newspaper and I'd be sure he was watching me. You started coming around the house too, Nap. I remember snapping at you to go away, but I couldn't keep that up. I knew I had to do something until Maura told me what was going on. So I did what she said. I told you that lie about her transferring schools. I contacted Westbridge High too. I told them we were moving and would let them know where to forward Maura's records. The school didn't really ask too many questions. I think a lot of your classmates were devastated and taking time off."

Lynn Wells puts her hand to her throat again. "I need some water."

I get up and circle behind the desk. Ellie keeps a small fridge under the windowsill. I wonder why Mrs. Wells came to me via Ellie, but there are more pressing matters. I open the fridge, see the anally laid-out water bottles, and grab one for her.

"Thank you," she says.

She twists open the top and takes a deep pull like, well, an alcoholic. "You quit drinking," I say.

"You're always an alcoholic," she says. "But, yes, it's been thirteen years since my last drink."

I nod my approval, not that she needs it.

"I owe Bernadette for that. She's my rock. Just when I was at my lowest, I found her. We got legally married two years ago."

I don't know what to say to that—I want to get back on topic—so I just say, "Okay." Then I add, "When did you next hear from Maura?"

She takes another swig and twists the top back on the bottle.

"Days passed. Then weeks. I jumped every time the phone rang. I thought about telling someone, but who? Maura had said not to go to the police, and after what I experienced with that pale guy, well, like I said, if you aren't sure about Road A or B, just stay where you are. But I was scared. I had terrible dreams. I could hear that whispery voice asking me over and over about where Maura was. I didn't know what to do. The whole town was grieving over your brother and Diana. Diana's father, the police chief, he came by one day. He wanted to know about Maura too."

"What did you tell him?"

"The same thing I told everyone else. Maura was freaked out by what happened. I said she was staying with my cousin in Milwaukee for a while and then transferring schools."

"Was there a cousin in Milwaukee?"

She nods. "He said he would cover for me."

"So when did you hear from Maura again?"

She stares at the water bottle, one hand on the white top, the other cupping the bottom. "Three months later."

I stand there, trying not to look stunned. "So for three months . . . ?"

"I had no idea where she was. I had no contact. Nothing."

I don't know what to say. My phone vibrates again.

"I worried a million times over. Maura was a smart girl, resourceful, but you know what I figured?"

I shake my head.

"I figured she was dead. I figured the pale man with the whispery voice found her and killed her. I was trying to stay calm, but really, what could I do? If I went to the police, what would I say? Who would believe me about that missing week or any of it, really? Whoever those guys were, they either killed her—or if I made too much noise, I was going to help them kill her. Do you see my choices? Going to the police wasn't going to help her. Maura either was making it on her own or . . ."

"Or she was dead," I say.

Lynn Wells nods.

"So where did you finally see her?"

"At a Starbucks in Ramsey. I went to the bathroom in the back and suddenly she came in behind me."

"Wait, she didn't call you first?"

"No."

"She just showed up?"

"Yes."

I try to comprehend this.

"So what happened?"

"She said she was in danger, but that she'd be okay."

"What else?"

"Nothing."

"That was all she said?"

"Yes."

"And you didn't ask—?"

"Of course I asked." For the first time, Lynn Wells has raised her voice. "I grabbed her arm and desperately hung on. I begged her to tell me more. I apologized for everything I did wrong. She hugged me, and then she pushed me away. She got out the door and headed out the back. I followed her, but . . . you don't get it."

"So explain it to me."

"When I came out of the bathroom . . . there were men there again."

I give it a second to make sure I'm hearing right. "The same men?"

"Not literally the same, but . . . one headed out the back door too. I got to my car and then . . ."

"Then what?"

When Lynn Wells looks up—when I see the tears come to her eyes and her hand go to her throat again—I feel my heart plummet down a mine shaft. "Some might say that the pressure of seeing my daughter again sent me on another bender."

I reach out again and take her hand. "How many days this time?"

"Three. But you see it now, don't you?"

I nod. "Maura knew."

"Yes."

"She knew that they would interrogate you. Maybe with drugs. Maybe harshly. And if you didn't know anything—"

"I couldn't help them."

"More than that," I say.

"What do you mean?"

"Maura was keeping you safe," I tell her. "Whatever made her run, if you knew about it, you'd be in danger too."

"Oh my God . . ."

I try to focus.

"So what then?" I ask.

"I don't know."

"Are you saying you haven't seen Maura since that day in Starbucks?"

"No. I've seen her six times."

"In the past fifteen years?"

Lynn Wells nods. "Always by surprise. Always a quick visit to let me know she's okay. For a while she set up an email account for us. We never sent anything. We would both just leave it in our draft files. We both had the password. She used a VPN to keep it anonymous. But then she started to think that was too risky. And in a way, oddly, she had nothing to say to me. I

told her about my life. About my quitting drinking and Bernadette. But she never said anything about her own life. It was
torture for me." She holds the water bottle a little too tightly. "I
have no idea where she's been or what she's been doing."

My mobile phone vibrates again.

This time I glance at it. It's Augie. I put the phone to my ear.
"Hello?"

"We found Hank."

Chapter Seventeen

D o you remember Hank's tenth birthday party, Leo?

It was a big year for laser tag and Nerf wars and sports-themed parties. Eric Kuby had that soccer party in an indoor bubble. Alex Cohen had her birthday at that mall with mini-golf and a Rainforest Cafe. Michael Stotter's had video games and virtual-reality rides. They strapped us in and shook the seats and we stared at the screen. It really felt like we were on a roller coaster. You got sick on that one.

Hank's party, like Hank, was different. His was held in a science laboratory at Reston University. Some guy with thick glasses and a white lab coat led us through a series of experiments. We made slime using borax powder and Elmer's Glue. We made high-bouncing polymer balls and giant ice marbles. We did lab stuff involving chemical reactions and fire and static electricity. The party was better than I thought it would be—a geek heaven even the jocks would love—but the part I remember best is the expression on Hank's face sitting right up front, his eyes wide and dreamy, that dorky smile plastered to his face. Even then, even as a ten-year-old, I got how happy Hank was, how much in his element (ha-ha), how rare it was for any of us to reach this particular high. Even then—and I doubt I could have articulated this—part of me wanted to stop time for him, just let him stay in this moment, this room, his friends and his passions locked together for longer than the forty-five minutes of entertainment followed by fifteen minutes of cake. I think back now about that party, about the purity of that moment for Hank, about the directions our lives take, and what the timeline was between that moment and now, the link between that happy boy with the dorky smile and the naked and mutilated dead man hanged by his neck from a tree.

I can still look on the face—bloated, grotesque, decaying, even—and see that little boy at the party. It's weird how you can do that with people you grew up with. The stench knocks everyone else back a step, but for some reason it doesn't bother me. I have seen my share of dead bodies. Hank's naked corpse looks like someone ripped out his bones, a marionette held up by one string. Cut marks, probably made by a sharp blade, cover his torso, but the thing that keeps drawing your attention is the most obvious one.

Hank was castrated.

I'm surrounded by my two superiors. On one side of me is

Essex County Prosecutor Loren Muse. On the other side is Augie. We are all staring up in silence.

Muse turns to me. "I thought you asked for a few personal days."

"Not anymore. I want this case."

"You knew the victim, right?"

"Years ago."

"Still. No way." Muse is one of those tiny women who seem to emanate great strength. She gestures to a man heading down the hill. "Manning will take it."

Augie still hasn't spoken. He too has seen his share of dead bodies, but his face is ashen. County has jurisdiction in homicides. The town of Westbridge—Augie's department—offers only support. My job will be to liaise between the two.

Muse looks back over the hill. "Did you see all those media trucks?"

"Yes."

"You know why so many showed up?"

I do. "That viral video."

Muse nods. "A man is outed as a sexual predator via online vigilantism. The video has, what, three or four million hits. Now that man is found in the woods, hung from a tree. When it gets out that he was castrated . . ."

She doesn't have to finish. We all get it. A total shit show. I'm almost glad now I'm not the lead on this one.

Alan Manning walks past us like we aren't there. He stands by Hank's slightly swaying remains and makes a show of inspecting him. I know Manning. He's not a bad detective. But he's not a good one either.

Muse takes a step back. Augie and I follow her.

"Augie tells me you spoke to the mom who posted the video," she says to me.

"Suzanne Hanson."

"What did she say?"

"That she lied. That Hank didn't really expose himself."

Muse slowly turns toward me. "Come again?"

"Mrs. Hanson just didn't like an undesirable hanging around the school."

"And now he's dead," Muse says with a shake of her head.

I don't reply.

"Ignorant, stupid . . ." She shakes her head again. "I'm going to see if we can charge her with something."

I have no issue with that.

"Do you think maybe Mrs. Hanson is involved in this?" Muse asks.

No, I think to myself. And I want to be honest. I don't want to lead Manning off the scent, but I also want what's best for the case, which may involve slight misdirection. So I say, "I think the Hansons might be a good place for Manning to start."

We stare up at the body again. Manning is circling underneath it, his face scrunched up. His manner is too showy, like something he saw on TV, and I half expect him to whip out a giant magnifying glass à la Sherlock Holmes.

Augie still has his eyes on the corpse. "I know Hank's father."

"Then maybe you should be the one to notify him," Muse says. "And with the press already buzzing around, the sooner, the better."

"Do you mind if I go with him?" I ask.

She shrugs a "suit yourself."

Augie and I start walking away. Franco Cadeddu, the county medical examiner and a good guy, has just arrived. He passes us with a stern nod. Franco is always all business on the scene. I return the stern nod. Augie does not. We keep walking. The crime scene guys, dressed in full body suits and surgical masks and gloves, hurry past us. Augie doesn't so much as glance at them. His face is set, trudging toward a dreaded task.

"Doesn't make sense," I say.

It takes a moment or two for Augie to reply. "How's that?"

"Hank's face."

"What about it?"

"It isn't purple or even a different hue than the rest of his body."

Augie says nothing.

"So he didn't die from strangulation or a broken neck," I say.

"Franco will figure that out."

"Another thing: The smell—it's beyond rancid. You can see the start of decay."

Augie keeps walking.

"Hank disappeared three weeks ago," I say. "My guess is, he's been dead that long."

"Again, let's wait for Franco."

"Who found the body?"

"David Elefant," Augie says. "He was walking his dog off leash. The dog ran this way and started howling."

"How often does Elefant do that?"

"Do what?"

"Walk his dog here. This ravine is somewhat out of the way, but it isn't that remote."

"I don't know. Why?"

"Let's say I'm right. Let's say Hank has been dead for three weeks."

"Okay."

"If Hank's body had been hung up on that tree all that time, don't you think someone would have spotted it by now? Or noticed that smell? We aren't that far away from civilization, right?"

Augie doesn't reply.

"Augie?"

"I hear you."

"Something isn't right."

He finally stops and turns back toward the crime scene in the distance. "A man was castrated and hung from a tree," he says. "Of course something isn't right."

"I don't think this is about that viral video," I say.

Augie doesn't reply.

"I think it's about the Conspiracy Club and that old military base. I think it's about Rex and Leo and Diana."

I see him flinch when I say his daughter's name.

"Augie?"

He turns and starts walking again. "Later," he says.

"What?"

"We'll talk about it later," Augie says. "Right now I just need to tell Tom that his boy is dead."

Tom Stroud stares down at his hands. His lower lip trembles. He has not spoken, not one word, since he opened the door. He knew. Right away. He looked at our faces and

knew. They often do. Some claim that the first step in the grieving process is denial. Having delivered my share of life-
shattering news, I have found the opposite to be true: The first
step is complete and immediate comprehension. You hear the
news and immediately you realize how absolutely devastating it
is, how there will be no reprieve, how death is final, how your
world is shattered and that you will never, ever be the same.
You realize all that in seconds, no more. The realization floods
into your veins and overwhelms you. Your heart breaks. Your
knees buckle. Every part of you wants to give way and collapse
and surrender. You want to curl up into a ball. You want to
plummet down that mine shaft and never stop.

That's when the denial kicks in.

Denial saves you. Denial throws up a protective fence. Denial grabs hold of you before you leap off that ledge. Your hand
rests on a hot stove. Denial pulls your hand back.

The memories of that night rush in as we enter Tom Stroud's
home, and part of me longs for that protective fence. I had
thought that it was a good idea to come, but seeing Augie deliver
bad news—the worst news, just as he did that night you died—is
hitting me harder than I had anticipated. I blink and somehow
Tom Stroud becomes Dad. Like Dad, he stares down at the table. He, too, winces as though absorbing punches. Augie's
voice—a blend of tough, tender, compassionate, detached—
brings me back more than any sight or smell, the nightmarish
déjà vu, as he tells yet another father about the death of his child.

The two older men sit in the kitchen. I stand behind Augie,
maybe ten feet back, ready to come off the bench but hoping
the coach doesn't call my number. My legs feel wobbly. I am
trying to put it together, but it is making less and less sense.

The official investigation, the one undertaken by Manning and the county office, will, I'm certain, concentrate on the viral video. It will seem simple to them: The viral video goes public, the public is outraged, someone takes matters into their own hands.

It is neat. It makes sense. It may even be correct.

The other theory, of course, is the one I will follow. Someone is killing off the old Conspiracy Club members. Of the six possible members, four have been killed before their thirty-fifth birthday. What are the odds that there is no connection? First Leo and Diana. Then Rex. Now Hank. I don't know where Beth is. And of course, there's Maura, who saw something that night that caused her to run away forever.

Except.

Why now? Let's say somehow they all saw something they shouldn't have that night. Again, this may sound like paranoid thinking, even if the group was called the Conspiracy Club, but I need to play it out.

Suppose they all saw something that night.

Maybe they ran—and the bad guys only, what, caught Leo and Diana? Okay, stay with that. So then—again, what?—they dragged Leo and Diana to the railroad tracks on the other side of town and made it look like they were killed by a train. Okay, fine. Let's assume the others ran. Maura they couldn't find. That all works.

But what about Rex and Hank and Beth?

Those three never hid. They stayed in high school and graduated with us.

Why didn't the bad guys from the base kill them?

Why would they wait fifteen years?

And talk about coincidental timing—why would the bad guys finally kill Hank around the same time that viral video came out? Did that make sense?

No.

So how is the viral video tied into this?

I'm missing something.

Tom Stroud finally starts to cry. His chin goes down to his chest. His shoulders start to spasm. Augie reaches across and puts a hand on Tom's upper arm. It's not enough. Augie moves closer. Tom leans forward and starts sobbing onto Augie's shoulder. I see Augie in profile now. He closes his eyes, and I see the pain on his face. Tom's sobs grow louder. Time passes. No one moves. The sobs start to subside. Eventually they fade away. Tom Stroud pulls back and looks at Augie.

"Thank you for telling me yourself," Tom Stroud says.

Augie manages a nod.

Tom Stroud wipes his face with his sleeve and forces up a smile of some sort. "We have something in common now."

Augie looks a question at him.

"Well, something horrible," Tom continues. "We've both lost children. I know your pain now. It's like . . . it's like being members of the worst club imaginable."

Now it is Augie who winces as though absorbing blows.

"Do you think that awful video had something to do with it?" Tom asks.

I wait for Augie to answer, but he seems lost now. I take the question for him.

"They'll certainly be looking into that," I say.

"Hank didn't deserve that. Even if he did expose himself—"

"He didn't."

Tom Stroud looks at me.

"It was a lie. A mother didn't like Hank hanging around the school."

Tom Stroud's eyes grow big. I think about those grieving steps again. Denial may be quickly giving way to anger. "She made it up?"

"Yes."

Nothing in his expression changes, but you can feel his temperature rising. "What's her name?"

"We can't tell you that."

"Do you think she did it?"

"Do I think she killed Hank?"

"Yes."

I answer honestly. "No."

"Then who?"

I explain how the investigation has just started and offer the expected "doing all we can" platitudes. I ask him if he has someone he can call to be with him. He does—a brother. Augie barely says a word, hanging by the door, rocking back and forth on his heels. I settle Tom in as best I can, but I'm not a babysitter. Augie and I have been here long enough.

"Thanks again," Tom Stroud says to us at the door.

Just in case I haven't uttered enough banalities, I say, "Sorry for your loss."

Augie heads out first, starting up the walk. I have to hurry to catch up with him.

"What's up?"

"Nothing."

"You got awfully quiet in there. I thought maybe you got an update on your phone or something."

"Nope."

Augie reaches the car and opens the door. We both get in.

"So what gives?" I ask.

Augie glares through the front windshield at Tom Stroud's house. "Did you hear what he said to me?"

"You mean Tom Stroud?"

He keeps glaring at that door. "He and I have something in common now." I see a tremor hit his face. "He knows my pain."

His voice is thick with disdain. I can hear his breathing thicken and grow labored. I don't know what to do here, how to play it, so I just wait.

"I lost a beautiful, vibrant seventeen-year-old daughter, a girl with all the promise in the world. She was my everything, Nap. You get that? She was my life."

He looks at me now, the same glare. I meet his eyes and don't move.

"I woke Diana up for school in the morning. I made her chocolate-chip pancakes every Wednesday. When she was a little girl, I took her every Saturday morning to the Armstrong Diner, just the two of us, and then we'd go to Silverman's and buy ponytail holders or neon scrunchies or those tortoiseshell clips for her hair. She collected hair stuff. I was just the clueless dad, what do I know? All of that stuff was still there when I cleaned out her room. Threw them all away. When she had rheumatic fever in seventh grade, I slept in a chair at Saint Barnabas for eight straight nights. I sat in that hospital and watched her and begged God to never hurt her. I went to every field hockey game, every holiday concert, every dance recital, every graduation, every parents' day. When she went on her first date, I secretly followed them to the movies because I was so nervous. I stayed up every night she went out because I couldn't fall asleep until I knew she was home safe. I helped her work on college essays no one ended up having to read because she died before she could apply. I loved that girl with all my might every single day of her life, and he"—Augie practically spits the word out toward Tom Stroud's house—"he thinks now we have something in common? He thinks, what, that he, a man who abandoned his son when things got tough, knows my pain?"

He hits his own chest when he says the word "my." Then he stops, grows quiet. His eyes close.

A small part of me wants to say something comforting, something along the line that Tom Stroud just lost his son and so we need to cut him a little slack. But most of me gets exactly what Augie means and doesn't feel the need to be that generous.

When Augie opens his eyes, he stares at the house again. "Maybe we need to look at this in a new way," he says.

"How's that?"

"Where was Tom Stroud all those years?"

I stay quiet.

"He claims he was out west," Augie continues, "opening a fish-and-tackle business."

"With a gun range in the back," I add.

Now we both stare at the house.

"He also claims he came back every once in a while. Tried to bond with his kid, who rejected him."

"So?"

Augie doesn't answer for a moment. Then he lets loose a

long breath and says, "So maybe he came back fifteen years ago."

"Seems a stretch," I say.

"It does," Augie agrees. "But it might be a good idea to check on his whereabouts."

Chapter Eighteen

When I arrive back home, the Walshes are outside. I give them the big Mr. Friendly smile. Look how harmless the single guy is. They wave back.

They all know your tragic story, of course. It's legend in these parts, as they say. I'm surprised none of Westbridge's wannabe Springsteens has written the "Ode to Leo and Diana." Still, they all think that it can't happen to them. That's how people are. They all hunger for the details not solely because they are ghoulish—that's part of it, no question—but more because they need to know that it can't possibly happen to them. Those teens drank too much. They took drugs. They took foolish chances. Their parents didn't raise them right. They didn't watch close enough. Whatever. Can't happen to us.

Denial isn't just for the grieving.

I still haven't heard back from Beth Lashley. That troubles me. I call the Ann Arbor Police Department and locate a detective named Carl Legg. I explain to him that I'm looking for a cardiologist named Beth Fletcher née Lashley and am getting the runaround from her office staff.

"Is she wanted in connection to a crime?" Legg asks me.

"No. I just need to talk to her."

"I'll head over to her office myself."

"Thanks."

"No worries. I'll call you when I know more."

The house is quiet, the ghosts all sleeping. I head up to the second floor and pull the handle. The ladder to the attic comes down. I climb up and try to remember the last time I was up here. I guess I helped bring your stuff to the attic, but if I did, that memory is gone. Maybe Dad spared me and did it himself. Your death was sudden. Dad's was not. He and I had time. He accepted his fate, even as I denied it. By the time his body gave out, Dad had already unburdened himself and thus me of most of his worldly possessions. He gave away his own clothes. He packed up his room.

He tidied up before the Reaper arrived, so I wouldn't have to.

The attic, no surprise, is musty and hot. It's hard to breathe. I expect there to be a ton of boxes and old trunks, all the stuff you see in movies, but there is very little. Dad put down a few planks of wood, that's it, so that most of the floor is pink insulation. That's what I remember most. You and I would come up here as kids and we'd play a game of having to stay on the boards because if we stepped on the pink, we would fall right straight through the ceiling and land on the floor below. I don't know if that's true, but that's what Dad always told us. I remember as a kid being scared of that, like the insulation was quicksand, and I would step on it and sink in and be gone forever.

You never run into quicksand in real life, do you? For something so huge in movies and TV, you never actually hear about anyone getting trapped or dying in quicksand.

This is how my mind is roaming as I spot the box in the corner. That's it. One box, Leo. You know Dad wasn't big on material goods. Your clothes are gone. Your toys are gone. Purging was part of his grieving process—not sure what stage that would be. Acceptance maybe, though acceptance is supposed to be the last step and Dad had a bunch more to go through after the purge. We know Dad was an emotional man, but his full-body sobs—the way his chest heaved and his shoulders trembled, his wails of thunderous agony—frightened me. There were times I thought he would physically break in half, that his ceaseless anguish would cleave his torso or something.

And, no, we never heard from Mom.

Did Dad reach out and tell her? I don't know. I never asked. He never told me.

I open the box to see what Dad saved. Here is a thought I haven't had until right this second: Dad obviously knew that you would never be able to open this box. He also knew that he himself would never open it either. That means whatever is in here, whatever he chose to save, would hold value only to me. Whatever Dad saved, he saved thinking that I might one day want it.

The box is sealed with tape. It's hard to peel off. I take a key out of my pocket and use it to slice down the seam. Then I pull back the cardboard and peer inside. I don't know what I expect to see. I know you. I know your life. We shared a room for your entire life. It isn't like anything huge is unaccounted for.

But as I see the photograph on the top, I feel newly lost. It's a snapshot of the four of us—you and Diana, Maura and me. I remember it, of course. The photo was taken in Diana's back-yard. Her seventeenth—and last—birthday. It was a warm October night. We'd spent the day down at Six Flags Great Adventure. Augie had a friend, a retired cop who now worked for a major park sponsor, and he was able to get us wristbands that gave us limitless access to the fast-pass lane. No lines for the coasters, Leo. Do you remember? I don't have a lot of memories of you or Diana on that day. We broke off, you and Diana staying mostly in the arcade area—I remember you won her a stuffed Pikachu—and Maura and I went on the hard-core coasters. Maura wore a crop top that made my mouth dry. You and Diana took a goofy picture with one of the Looney Tunes characters. Which one? I bet it's . . . yes, the second photo. I pull it into view. You and Diana standing on either side of Tweety Bird, the Six Flags fountain spouting water behind you.

Two weeks later you'd both be dead.

I study the photograph of the four of us some more. In the picture, night has fallen. Other partygoers are mingling behind us. We are all tired, I guess, a long day. Maura sits on my lap, our bodies entwined in a way only dating teenagers can achieve. You sit next to Diana. She isn't smiling. You look stoned. Your eyes are glassy and hazy. You also look . . . troubled maybe. I didn't notice then. I was into my own stuff, wasn't I? Maura and hockey and making a first-tier college. Fate, I was certain, would secure my future happiness, though I had no real plan, no clue what I wanted to be. I only knew that I would be a huge success.

The doorbell rings.

I put the photo back and start to stand, but the ceiling is too low. With my back bent, I head toward the opening. As I climb down the ladder, the doorbell sounds again. Then again. Impatient.

"Coming!" I shout.

I trot down the stairs and see out the window that it's my old classmate David Rainiv. His high-end business suit seems tailored by a higher entity. I open the door. His face is ashen and crumpled, even as his Hermès tie stays perfectly Windsored.

"I heard about Hank."

I don't bother to ask him how. The old saw about bad news traveling fast has never been truer than in the age of the Internet.

"Is it true?"

"I can't really talk about it."

"They say he was found hung from a tree."

The sadness is etched all over his face. I remember him wanting to help when I asked about Hank at the basketball courts. There is no point in being a hard-ass here. "I'm sorry for your loss."

"Did Hank hang himself," David asked, "or was he murdered?"

I'm about to tell him again that I can't talk about it, but there is an odd desperation on his face. I wonder now whether he came to me for confirmation or something more.

"Murdered," I say.

His eyes close.

"Do you know something about this?" I ask.

His eyes stay closed.

"David?"

"I'm not sure," he says at last. "But I think I might."

Chapter Nineteen

The Rainivs live at the far end of a tony new cul-de-sac in one of those McMansions with an indoor pool, a formal ballroom, eight hundred bathrooms, and a million square feet of mostly useless space. Everything about the house screams nouveau riche. The driveway gate is an overly ornate metal sculpture of children flying a kite. It is all wanting to look too old by looking too new. It's labored, trying too hard, tacky. But that's my take. I've known David a long time. He's always been a good guy. He's generous to charities. He gives his time and energy to the town. I've seen him with his kids. He's not one of those poseur fathers—you know, the ones who make a big production out of watching their kids at the mall or park so you think, *Wow, what a caring father,* but you can see it's just an act for public consumption. That's not David. Most of all, I see his devastated face now and I remember how he went through the timeline of his friendship with Hank. That kind of loyalty is the mark of a man. So I don't like his or maybe his wife's taste in houses. Who the hell cares? Get over ourselves. Stop judging.

We pull into a garage the approximate dimensions of a college gymnasium—is that judging?—and park. He leads me through a side door and down into what some homes call a basement, but this one has a theater room and wine cellar, so we need to find a new term. Lower level, maybe? He heads into a small room and flicks on a switch. In the back right corner, there is a four-foot-high old-fashioned safe with a big dial.

"You're not the cop on the case, right?"

This is the third time David has asked me that. "No. Why is that a big deal?"

He bends down and starts fiddling with the dial. "Hank asked me to hold something for him."

"Recently?"

"No. Eight, nine years ago. He said if he was ever murdered, I should find a way to give it to someone I trust. He warned me not to give it to anyone in law enforcement or anyone involved in the investigation." David looks back at me. "You see my dilemma?"

I nod. "I'm in law enforcement."

"Right. But like I said, this was eight, nine years ago. Hank was already pretty out of it by then. I figured it was nothing, just the ramblings of a diseased mind. But he was pretty adamant about it. So I made a promise to him—that if he was ever murdered, I would do the right thing by him. I never really thought of what that meant because, I mean, it was just incoherent rambling, right? Except now . . ."

He makes one last turn of the dial. I hear a click. He reaches for the handle, and as he does, he turns back and looks up at me. "I trust you, Nap. You're in law enforcement, but I somehow think Hank would be okay with my giving this to you."

He opens up the safe, reaches into the back, digs through whatever else is there—I don't pry by looking—and pulls out a videocassette tape that smacks me in the face with déjà vu and sends me—pardon the pun—reeling. I remember Dad buying you a Canon PV1 digital video camcorder sophomore year. You freaked out with joy. For a while, you filmed everything. You wanted to be a director, Leo. You talked about making a documentary. The pain hits me anew at the thought.

The cassette David hands me is in a red plastic case that reads MAXELL, 60 MINUTES—the exact same kind you used. Of course you weren't the only one who used Maxell tapes back in the day. They were pretty common. But seeing one again, after all these years . . .

"Did you watch it?" I ask.

"He told me not to."

"Any idea what's on it?"

"None. Hank asked me to keep it safe for him."

I just stare at the cassette another moment.

"This probably has nothing to do with it," David says. "I mean, I heard about that viral video of him exposing himself."

"That was a lie."

"A lie? Why the hell would someone do that?"

He's Hank's friend. I owe him something. I give him the quick rundown on Suzanne Hanson's moronic motives. David nods, closes the safe, spins the dial.

"I assume you don't have anything that plays this kind of tape," I say.

"I don't think so, no."

"Then let's find someplace that does."

On the phone, Ellie says, "Bob found an old Canon in the basement. He thinks it still works, but it may need a charge."

I am not surprised. Ellie and Bob throw out nothing. Even more disturbing, they keep everything organized so even something like an old video camera that hasn't seen the light of day in a decade will be neatly labeled and kept complete with its charging cord.

"I can be over in ten minutes."

"You'll stay for dinner?"

"Depends on what's on the tape," I say.

"Right, yeah, that makes sense." Ellie hears something in my voice and knows me too well. "Everything else okay?"

"We'll talk."

I hang up first.

David Rainiv is driving, both hands on the wheel at ten and two. "I don't want to make a big thing of it," he says, "but if there is no next of kin, could you send the body to Feeney's Funeral Home when you're done and tell them to send me the bill?"

"His father is back in town," I remind him.

"Oh right," David says with a frown, "forgot about that."

"You don't think he'll step up?"

He shrugs. "The guy let Hank down his whole life. I don't know why we'd assume he'll come through now."

Good point. "I'll check and see."

"I'd take care of it anonymously, if that's okay. Get the guys from basketball there. Pay their respects. Hank deserves that."

I don't know what people deserve or don't deserve, but I'm okay with whatever.

"It would mean something to him," David continues. "Hank was big on honoring the dead: his mom"—his voice grows soft now—"your brother, Diana."

I don't say anything. We drive a bit more. I have the tape in my hand. Then I think hard about what he just said and ask, "What did you mean?"

"About?"

"About Hank honoring the dead. About my brother and Diana."

"You serious?"

I look at him.

"Hank was crushed by what happened to Leo and Diana."

"That's not the same thing as 'honoring.'"

"You really don't know?"

I assume the question is rhetorical.

"Hank took the same walk pretty much every day. You know that, right?"

"Right," I say. "He started at the Path, by the middle school."

"And do you know where he ended up?"

It suddenly feels like a cold finger is traveling down the back of my neck.

"The railroad tracks," David says. "Hank ended his walk on the exact spot where . . . well, you know."

There is a buzzing in my ears. My words seem to be coming from very far away now. "So every day, Hank started his walk by the old military base"—I'm trying not to sputter—"and ended it where Leo and Diana died?"

"I thought you knew."

I shake my head.

"Some days he would time the walk," David continues. "A couple of times . . . well, this was strange."

"What?"

"He'd ask me to drive him so he could time how long a car ride would take."

"A car ride between the military base and the tracks on the other side of town?"

"Yes."

"Why?"

"He never said. He was jotting down calculations and muttering to himself."

"Calculating what?"

"I don't know."

"But he was focused on how long it would take to get from one place to another?"

"Focused?" David is quiet for a moment. Then he says, "I'd say he was more like obsessed. I only saw him at the tracks, I don't know, three or four times. It would be when I took the train into the city and we'd drive by him. He was always crying. He cared, Nap. He wanted to honor the dead."

I try to absorb all this. I ask David for more details, but there is nothing. I ask him about anything else he might know connecting Hank to Leo, connecting Hank to the Conspiracy Club, connecting Hank to Rex, Maura, and Beth, connecting Hank to anything else about the past. But again I come up empty.

David Rainiv pulls up to the front of Ellie and Bob's house. I thank him. We shake hands. He reminds me again that if anything is needed to give Hank a proper funeral, he's ready to step up. I nod. I see he wants to ask something more but he shakes it off.

"I don't have to know what's on the tape," he says.

I get out and watch him drive off.

Ellie and Bob's lawn is manicured as though they are preparing for a PGA Tour event. Their flower boxes are coordinated and symmetrical to the point that the right half of the house looks like a precise mirror image of the left. Bob opens the door and greets me with the big smile and the firm handshake.

Bob works in commercial real estate, though I don't quite get exactly what he does with it. He's a terrific guy, and I would take a bullet for him. We tried going out a few times on our own to Yag's Sports Bar to watch some NCAA March Madness or the NHL playoffs—Bro Time—but the truth is, our relationship fizzles without Ellie. We are both okay with this. I have heard that men and women can't be friends without there being some kind of sexual component, but at the risk of sounding horribly PC, that's horseshit.

Ellie comes over more warily than usual and kisses me on the cheek. I think we both know after the whole meeting with Lynn Wells that there is unfinished business between us, but right now I have bigger concerns.

"I have the video camera out in the workshop," Bob says.

"It doesn't have a charge yet, but as long as you keep it plugged in, it works."

"Thanks."

"Uncle Nap!"

Their two girls, Leah, age nine, and Kelsi, age seven, come ripping around the corner as only two young girls can. They both wrap their arms around me as only two young girls can, nearly tackling me with their loving onslaught. I would do a lot more than take a bullet for Leah and Kelsi—I would shoot plenty in return.

As godfather to both—and a man with virtually no other family—I dote on Leah and Kelsi and spoil them right up to the line where Ellie and Bob have to admonish me. I quickly ask them now about school, and they enthusiastically tell me. I'm no fool. They are getting older and soon they won't tear around the corner so fast, but I'm okay with that. Some might wonder whether I feel a pang, not having a family of my own yet or missing being an uncle for your kids.

We would have made great uncles for each other's kids, Leo.

Ellie starts to shoo them off me. "Okay, girls, that's enough. Uncle Nap has to do something in the workshop with Daddy."

"What does he have to do?" Kelsi asks.

"Some work stuff," Bob says to her.

Leah: "What kind of work stuff?"

Kelsi: "Is it police work stuff, Uncle Nap?"

Leah: "Are you catching bad guys?"

"Nothing that dramatic," I say, and then I wonder whether they know the word "dramatic" and then I don't like saying that since "nothing dramatic" may be a lie so I add, "I just need to watch this tape."

"Ooo, can we watch?" Leah asks.

Ellie rescues me from that. "You certainly cannot. Go set the table."

They do very little moaning before heading off to do their chore. Bob and I head toward the workshop in the garage. A sign above the door reads BOB'S WORKSHOP. The sign is carved in wood, and every letter is a different color. As you might expect, you could film handyman how-to videos in Bob's workshop. The tools are hung in size order, equidistant from one another. Lumber and piping are stored in perfect pyramids against the back wall. Fluorescent fixtures hang from the ceiling. Plastic bins, all properly labeled, hold nails, screws, fasteners, connectors. The floor is snap-together rubber modules. All the colors in the room are neutral and soothing. There is no dirt, no sawdust, nothing to dispel the relative calm of the place.

I can't hammer a nail, but I see why Bob loves being in here.

The camera sitting on the workbench is an exact match—a Canon PV1—and I wonder whether it is indeed your old one. Like I said, Dad gave away most of your stuff. Maybe somehow that camera ended up with Ellie and Bob, who knows? The Canon PV1 stands upright with the viewing lens on the top. Bob turns it over and presses the eject button. He reaches back for me to hand him the cassette. I do. He sticks it in and pushes it into the designated slot.

"It's ready," Bob tells me. "You just hit the play button here"—he points to it—"and you can watch it here." Bob pulls on something, and a little screen hinges out from the side.

Everything about this is reminding me of you. Not in a pleasant way.

"I'll be in the kitchen if you need any help," Bob says.

"Thanks."

Bob heads back into the house, closing the door behind him. No reason for me to drag this out. I hit the play button. It starts with static, which then gives way to darkness. The only thing I can see is the date stamp.

One week before you and Diana were killed.

The picture is shaky, like whoever is holding the camera is walking. It gets shakier, so that maybe whoever was walking is now running. I can't make out anything yet. Just black. I think I hear something, but it's faint.

I find the volume knob and turn it all the way up.

The shaking stops, but the picture is still too dark to make anything out. Playing with the brightness knob doesn't help, so I turn out the lights for better contrast. The garage turns spooky now, the tools more menacing in the shadows. I stare hard at the small screen.

Then I hear a voice from the past say, "Is it on, Hank?"

My heart stops.

The voice on the tape is yours.

Hank says, "Yeah, it's on."

Then another voice: "Point it up at the sky, Hank."

It's Maura. My stopped heart explodes in my chest.

I put my hands on the workbench to steady myself. Maura sounds animated. I remember that tone so well. I watch now as the camera pans up. Hank had been pointing the lens at the ground. As he raises it, I can see the lights from the military base.

You again, Leo: "Do you guys still hear it?"

"I do. It's faint, though."

That sounds like Rex.

You: "Okay, let's stay quiet."

Then I hear Maura say, "Holy shit, look! Just like last week."

"My God." You again. "You were right, Maura."

There are lots of overlapping gasps and excited voices now. I try to make them out—you for sure, Maura, Rex, Hank . . . another female voice. Diana? Beth? I'll have to back it up later and listen closer. I'm squinting at the screen, hoping to see what is taking them all by surprise.

Then I see it too, coming out of the sky, seemingly floating into view. I gasp along with them.

It's a helicopter.

I try to up the volume so I can hear the rotors, but it's already turned up all the way. As though reading my thoughts, Hank fills me in.

"Sikorsky Black Hawk," Hank says. "Stealth copter. Barely makes a sound."

"I can't believe it." That sounds like Beth.

The screen is tiny and even with the lights off in Bob's workshop, it is hard to see exactly what is going on. But there is no question about it now. A helicopter is hovering above the old military base.

As the copter starts to descend, Maura whispers, "Let's get closer."

Rex: "They'll spot us."

Maura: "So?"

Beth: "I don't know . . ."

Maura: "Come on, Hank."

The camera grows shaky again as Hank moves, it seems,

closer to the base. At one point he stumbles. The camera points to the ground. I see a hand reach out to help him up, and now . . . now I can see the white sleeve of my varsity jacket. As the camera comes back up, Hank lands the focus right on Maura's face. My whole body jolts. Her dark hair is a perfectly tangled mess, her eyes lit with excitement, her killer smile just south of sane.

"Maura . . ."

I actually say this out loud.

From the tinny speaker, I hear you say, "Shh, stop."

The copter lands. It is hard to see much, but the rotors are still spinning. I can't believe how quiet they are. I'm still not sure what I'm seeing—it may be a door sliding open. There is a flash of bright orange. Could be a person. Not sure. Probably has to be.

The bright orange reminds me of prisoner garb.

There is a noise like someone stepping on a branch. Hank jerks the camera to the right. Rex shouts, "Let's get the hell out of here!"

And the picture goes black.

I hit the fast-forward button. But that's it. There is nothing else on the tape. I rewind and watch the scene with the helicopter again. Then a third time. It never gets easier to hear your voice or see Maura's face.

During the fourth viewing something new occurs to me. I start putting myself into this timeline. Where was I that night? I wasn't part of the Conspiracy Club. I didn't really think much of it at the time—this "clandestine group" was somewhere between cute and childish, in my view, between harmless and (when I was unkind) pathetic. You had your games and secrets. I get that.

But how could you guys keep something like this secret from me?

You used to tell me everything.

I try to travel back in time. Where was I that night? It was, like the night you died, a Friday. Friday was hockey night. Who did we play that night? I don't remember. Did we win? Did I see you when I got home? I don't remember. I know I got together with Maura. We headed into the clearing in those woods. I can still see the tangled hair, the killer smile, the eyes lit with excitement, but something was different that night, something even more electrifying when we made love. I don't think I wondered why back then—Maura liked the edge—but I probably selfishly chalked it up to my own wonderfulness. That's how wrapped up I, the big jock senior, was in my own stuff.

And my twin brother?

I think back to that photograph in the attic. The four of us. The stoned, lost look on your face. Something was going on with you, Leo. Something big and probably obvious, and because I was a self-involved prick, I missed it and you died.

I unplug the camera. I'm sure that Bob won't mind if I take it with me. But I need to think on it. I don't want to act in haste. Hank hid this video because whatever issues he had, he knew this was big. He was paranoid and probably mentally unwell, and come hell or high water, I still want to honor his wishes.

So where do I go with this?

Do I take it to the authorities? Do I tell Muse or Manning? Do I tell Augie?

First things first. Make copies. Put the original in a safe place.

I run it through my head, try to see how this all fits together. The old Nike base stayed under government control. It pretended to be some kind of harmless agriculture center so as to hide its real purpose. Okay, I get all that. I even get that you guys saw something that night that could open the place up to public scrutiny.

I might even be able to take it a step further. I might even get why they—and by "they" I just mean the "bad guys" working at the base—would want to silence you and Diana, even though I didn't hear Diana on the tape. Was she there? I don't know. But either way, the two of you ended up dead.

Question: Why would the others still be alive?

Possible answer: "They" didn't know about Rex, Hank, and Beth. "They" only knew about you and Diana. Okay, that makes a modicum of sense. Not much. But I'll take a modicum. And I can add Maura into this equation. Somehow "they" knew about Maura too. That's why she ran and hid. On the tape, you and Maura are clearly the leaders. So maybe you two went back and did something careless. You got caught. She ran.

That all makes some sense.

But again: What about the others? Rex and Hank and Beth continued their lives. None of them hid. Maybe after fifteen years they started looking again. Maybe something happened after fifteen years so that suddenly they did know.

Like what?

No idea. But maybe Augie was onto something when he wondered about Tom Stroud. Maybe I need to figure out when exactly Tom Stroud came back to Westbridge.

Enough speculating. I'm still missing something. And there is something else I need to do right now.

Confront Ellie.

It can't be a coincidence that Maura's mother came to me via Ellie. Ellie knows something. This realization is one I half want to ignore. I've taken enough blows today, thank you very much, but if I can't trust Ellie—if Ellie lied to me and doesn't have my back—then where am I?

I take a deep breath and open the workshop door. The first sounds I hear are Leah's and Kelsi's laughter. I realize I'm making this family seem somewhat unreal, a little too perfect, but this is what I see. I once asked Ellie how she and Bob did it, and she said, "We've both been through some wars, so now we fight to preserve this." Maybe I understand, but I'm not sure. Ellie's parents' late-in-life divorce was hard on her. Maybe that's part of it, I don't know. Or maybe we don't know anybody that well.

I look for the seams in Ellie and Bob's life. Just because I can't see them doesn't mean they aren't there. And just because Ellie and Bob may hide them doesn't make them any less wonderful or human.

Dad's quote: Every person has hopes and dreams.

I head into the kitchen, but Ellie isn't there. There is an open seat. Bob turns to me and says, "Ellie had to run out. She left you a plate."

Out the window, I see Ellie heading to her car. I make a quick excuse and sprint after her. She's opening her car door and readying to slide in when I shout, "Do you know where Maura is?"

That stops her. Ellie turns toward me. "No."

I meet her eyes. "To reach me, her mother came through you."

"Yes."

"Why you, Ellie?"

"I promised her I wouldn't say anything."

"Who?"

"Maura."

I know that name is coming, and it still punches me in the teeth. "You"—it takes me a second—"you promised Maura?"

My mobile rings. It's Augie. I don't answer. Whatever happens now—whatever Ellie tells me—I know nothing will be the same between us anymore. There is very little in my world that keeps me grounded. I have no family. I let very few people into my world.

The person who is dearest to me just pulled the life rug, if you will, out from under me.

"I have to go," Ellie says. "There's an emergency at the center."

"All these years," I say. "You lied to me."

"No."

"But you never told me."

"I made a promise."

I try to keep the hurt out of my voice. "I thought you were my best friend."

"I am. But being your friend doesn't mean I betray everyone else."

My mobile keeps buzzing. "How could you keep something like this from me?"

"We don't tell each other everything," she says.

"What are you talking about? I trust you with my life."

"But you don't tell me everything, do you, Nap?"

"Of course I do."

"Bullshit." Ellie's voice comes out as a surprise whisper-scream, one of those things adults do when they're angry but don't want to wake the kids. "You keep plenty from me."

"What are you talking about?"

Something flashes in her eyes. "You want to tell me about Trey?"

I am about to say *Who?* That's how focused I am on this investigation, into the possibility of discovering the truth about that night and feeling betrayed by, of all people, the woman who is closest to me. But then, of course, I remember the baseball bat and the beating.

Ellie stares hard at me.

"I didn't lie to you," I say.

"You just didn't tell me."

I say nothing.

"You don't think I know it was you who put Trey in the hospital?"

"It has nothing to do with you," I say.

"I'm complicit."

"No, you're not. It's on me."

"Are you really that dense? There's a line between wrong and right, Nap. You drag me across it. You break the law."

"To punish slime," I say. "To help a victim. Isn't that what we're supposed to be doing?"

Ellie shakes her head, her anger flushing her cheeks. "You don't get it, do you? When the police come around because they figure there might be a connection between an injured man and a battered woman, I have to lie to them. You know that, right? So like it or not, I'm complicit. You involve me, and you don't have the decency to face me with the truth."

"I don't say anything to keep you safe."

Ellie shakes her head. "Are you sure that's it, Nap?"

"What are you talking about?"

"Maybe you don't tell me because I'd stop you. Maybe you don't tell me because what you do is wrong. I set up that shelter to help the abused, not to go vigilante on the abusers."

"It's not on you," I say again. "I'm the one who makes that call."

"We all make calls." Her voice is quieter now. "You made the call that Trey deserved a beating. I made the call to keep my word to Maura."

I shake my head as my phone starts up. It's Augie again.

"You can't keep this from me, Ellie."

"Let it go," she says.

"What?"

"You didn't tell me about Trey to protect me."

"So?"

"So maybe I'm doing the same for you."

The phone still rings. I have to take it. As I put it to my ear, Ellie jumps into the car. I'm about to stop her, but then I notice that Bob is standing by the door, watching with a funny look on his face.

It'll have to wait.

"What?" I shout into the phone.

"I finally got hold of Andy Reeves," Augie tells me.

The "agriculture" commander at the military base. "And?"

"You know the Rusty Nail Tavern?"

"That's a dive bar in Hackensack, right?"

"Used to be. Meet him there in an hour."

Chapter Twenty

copy the old videotape in the least-tech but fastest way possible. I simply play it on the little camera screen while recording it with my smartphone. The quality is not as terrible as I thought it would be, but I won't be winning any cinematography awards either. I upload a copy of the video to my cloud, and then, to be on the safe side, I email it out to another one of my email addresses.

Should I send a copy to someone else for safekeeping?

Yes. The question is, who? I consider David Rainiv, but if it ever got traced back—and, yes, I'm being paranoid—I don't want to put him in danger. I think about sending it to Ellie, but same issue. Plus I need to think it through. I need to really consider my next move with her.

The obvious answer is Augie, but again, do I want to just send this out to his computer without any kind of warning?

I call Augie on the phone.

"You at the Rusty Nail yet?" Augie asks.

"On my way. I'm emailing you a video."

I fill him in on David Rainiv's visit and the rest of it. He stays quiet. When I finish, I ask if he's still on the line.

"Don't send it to my work," he says.

"Okay."

"You got my personal email address?"

"Yes."

"Okay, send it there." There is a longer pause. Then Augie clears his throat and says, "Diana . . . you said she wasn't on the tape?"

I can always hear it when he says Diana's name. I lost you. A brother. A twin. Devastating, sure. But Augie lost his only child. Whenever he says Diana's name, it comes out hoarse, pained, like someone is pummeling him as he speaks. Each syllable rains down new hurt.

"I didn't see or hear Diana," I tell him, "but the tape isn't great quality. You might pick up something I didn't."

"I still think you're heading down the wrong path."

I think about that. "I do too."

"So?"

"So it's the only path I have right now. I might as well stay on it and see where it leads."

"Sounds like a plan."

"Though not a good one."

"No, not a good one," Augie agrees.

"What did you tell Andy Reeves?" I ask.

219

"About you?"

"About my reason for visiting, yeah."

"Not a damn thing. What could I tell him? I don't even know."

"Part of my plan," I say. "The not-good one."

"Better than none at all, I guess. I'm going to watch the tape. I'll call you if I see anything."

The Rusty Nail is a converted house with cedar-shake vinyl siding and a red door. I park between a yellow Ford Mustang with the license plate EBNY-IVRY and a bus-van hybrid with the words "Bergen County Senior Center" painted on the side. I don't know what Augie meant by saying it used to be a dive bar. From the outside it still looks like one to me. The only change I notice is the extensive wheelchair ramp. That didn't used to be there. I head up the steps and open the heavy red door.

Initial observation: The crowd is old.

Very old. I'm guessing the median age is close to eighty. Probably came in from the senior center. Interesting. Seniors take field trips to supermarkets and racetracks and casinos.

Why not taverns?

The second thing I notice: There is an ostentatious white piano with silver trim, like something Liberace would have considered too garish, in the middle of the room, complete with a tip jar. Straight out of Billy Joel. I almost expect a real estate novelist and Davy from the navy to be nursing drinks. But I don't see anyone fitting that description. I see a variety of walkers and canes and wheelchairs.

The piano player is pounding out "Sweet Caroline." "Sweet Caroline" has become one of those songs, played at every wedding and sporting event, beloved by children and seniors alike. The old patrons sing along enthusiastically. They are off-key and have no pitch and don't care. It's a nice scene.

I'm not sure which one is Andy Reeves. In my head, I'm expecting someone in his midsixties with a crew cut and military bearing. A few of the older men fit the bill, I guess. I step into the room. I spot several strong young guys now, their eyes moving around like wary security guards, and I'm tagging them as bartenders or maybe orderlies for the seniors.

The piano player looks up and nods at me. He does not have a crew cut or military bearing. He has feathered blond hair and that kind of waxy complexion I associate with chemical peels. He beckons with a head gesture for me to take a seat at the piano as the older crowd builds to a giant "Bah-bah-bah, good times never seemed so good."

"So good, so good, so good . . ."

I sit. One of the old guys throws his arm around me, nudging me to sing along. I join in for a very unenthusiastic "I've been inclined" and wait for someone else—preferably Andy Reeves—to approach me. No one does. I glance around the room. There is a poster featuring four of the happiest, healthiest seniors this side of a Viagra ad with the words "Tuesday Afternoon Bingo—$3 Drinks" emblazoned across their chests. At the bar, a few of the guys I figure are orderlies-bartenders pour a red beverage into laid-out plastic cups.

When "Sweet Caroline" finishes up, the old folks hoot and holler their approval. I'm almost looking forward to the next song, enjoying this quasi normalcy, but the feathered-hair piano man stands up and announces a "quick break."

The old-timers register their disappointment with gusto.

"Five minutes," the piano man says. "Your drinks are at the bar. Think up a few requests, okay?"

That placates them a bit. The piano man scoops the money out of what looks like an oversized brandy snifter, heads toward me, and says, "Officer Dumas?"

I nod.

"I'm Andy Reeves."

First thing I notice: His speaking voice is a little breathy. Or whispery.

He takes the seat next to me. I try to guess the age. Even with whatever weird cosmetic work has made his face shiny, he can't be more than midfifties, but then again, the military base closed down only fifteen years ago. Why does he have to be older than that?

I glance around. "This place," I say.

"What about it?"

"It seems a far distance from the Department of Agriculture."

"I know, right?" He spreads his hands. "What can I say? I needed a change."

"So you no longer work for the government?"

"I retired, what, seven years ago. Worked for the USDA for twenty-five years. Got a nice pension and now I'm pursuing my passion."

"Piano."

"Yes. I mean, not here. This is, well, you have to start somewhere, right?"

I study his face. The tan is from a bottle or bed, not the sun. I can see some very pale skin near the hairline. "Right," I say.

"We had a piano at that old Westbridge office. I used to play there all the time. Helped us relax when the job got too stress-ful." Reeves shifts in his seat and flashes teeth so big and daz-zlingly white that they could double as piano keys. "So what can I do for you, Detective?"

I jump right in. "What kind of work were you guys doing at the military base?"

"Military base?"

"That's what it used to be," I say. "A control center for Nike missiles."

"Oh, I know." He shakes his head in awe. "What a history that place has, am I right?"

I say nothing.

"But all of that, well, it was years before we moved in. We were just an office complex, not a military base."

"An office complex for the USDA," I say.

"That's right. Our mission was to provide leadership on food, agriculture, natural resources, rural development, nutri-tion, and related issues based on sound public policy, the best available science, and efficient management."

It sounds rehearsed, probably because it is.

"Why there?" I ask.

"Pardon?"

"The USDA has an office on Independence Avenue in Wash-ington, DC."

"Headquarters, sure. We were a satellite."

"But why there, in the woods like that?"

"Why not?" he says, lifting his palms to the ceiling. "It was a great space. Some of the work we did, well, I don't want to boast or make it sound more glamorous than it was, but many of our studies were absolutely top secret." He leans forward. "Did you ever see the movie *Trading Places*?"

"Eddie Murphy, Dan Aykroyd, Jamie Lee Curtis," I say.

He's very pleased that I know it. "That's the one. If you remember, the Duke brothers were trying to corner the orange juice market, right?"

"Right."

"Do you remember how?" Reeves smiles as he sees on my face that I do. "The Dukes were bribing a government official to obtain an advance copy of the USDA's monthly crop report. The USDA, Detective Dumas. That was us. Many of our studies were that important. We needed privacy and tight security."

I nod. "So that's why you had the fence and all the No Trespassing signs."

"Exactly." Reeves spreads his hands again. "Where better for us to conduct our testing than a former military base?"

"Anybody ever defy those signs?"

For the first time I think I see the smile flicker. "What do you mean?"

"Did you ever have trespassers?"

"Sometimes," Reeves says as casually as he can muster. "Kids would sneak into the woods to drink or smoke pot."

"And then what?"

"What do you mean?"

"Would the kids ignore the warning signs?"

"Something like that."

"What would they do then?"

"Nothing. They'd just walk past the signs."

"And what would you do about that?"

"Nothing."

"Nothing?"

"We might tell them that this was private property."

"Might?" I ask. "Or did?"

"Sometimes we did, I guess."

"How would you do that exactly?"

"Pardon?"

"Walk me through it. A kid goes past your sign. What would you do?"

"Why are you asking?"

I put a little snap in my voice. "Just answer the question, please."

"We'd tell him to go back. We'd remind him that he was trespassing."

"Who would remind him?" I ask.

"I don't understand."

"Would you be the one to remind him?"

"No, of course not."

"Then who?"

"One of our security guards."

"Were they guarding the woods?"

"What?"

"The signs started probably fifty yards away from your fence."

Andy Reeves considers this. "No, the guards wouldn't be that far out. They would be more interested in controlling the perimeter."

"So you probably wouldn't see a trespasser until he reached your fence, is that correct?"

"I don't see the relevance—"

"How would you spot this trespassing kid?" I ask, changing gears. "Would you rely on the guard's vision, or did you have cameras?"

"I think we may have had a few . . ."

"*Think* you had cameras? You don't remember?"

I'm testing his patience. That's not unintentional. Reeves starts tapping the top of the table with a fingernail. A long fingernail, I notice. Then he gives me a toothy grin and whispers again: "I'm really not going to take much more badgering, Detective."

"Yeah, okay, sorry," I say. I tilt my head. "So let me ask you this: Why would stealth Black Hawks be landing at a 'USDA'"—I do finger quotes—"'office complex' at night?"

Drop the mic, as one of my goddaughters might say.

Andy Reeves hadn't been expecting that one. His mouth drops open, though not for long. His eyes harden. The big wide smile has been replaced with something closemouthed and far more reptilian.

"I have no idea what you're talking about," he whispers.

I try to stare him down, but he has no problem with too much eye contact. I don't like that. We all think eye contact is great or a sign of honesty, but like most things, too much indicates an issue.

"It's been fifteen years, Reeves."

He doesn't stop staring.

"I don't care what you guys were doing." I try to keep the pleading out of my voice. "I just need to know what happened to my brother."

Exact same volume, exact same cadence, exact same words: "I have no idea what you're talking about."

"My brother's name was Leo Dumas."

He pretends to be thinking about it, trying to dredge up the name from his memory bank.

"He was hit by a train with a girl named Diana Styles."

"Oh, Augie's daughter." Andy Reeves shakes his head the way people do when they speak of someone else's tragedy. "Your brother was the young man killed with her?"

He knows this. I know this. He knows I know.

"I'm sorry for your loss."

The condescension drips off his voice like maple syrup off a stack of pancakes. Intentionally, of course. Striking back at me.

"I already told you I don't care what you were doing at the base," I try. "So if you want me to stop digging into this, all you have to do is tell me the truth. Unless."

"Unless what?"

"Unless you killed my brother," I say.

Reeves doesn't take the bait. Instead he makes a scene out of checking his watch. He looks over at the old folks starting to meander back toward the piano. "My break is over."

He stands.

"Before you go," I say.

I take out my phone. The video is already up. It's cued to the first time the helicopter appears. I click the play button and hold it up for him. Even the fake tan is leaving his face now.

"I don't know what that's supposed to be," he says, but his voice just isn't making it.

"Sure you do. It's a Sikorsky Black Hawk stealth helicopter flying over what you claim is a Department of Agriculture office complex. If you watch a few more moments, that helicopter will land. And after that, you'll be able to see a man in a prisoner-issue orange jumpsuit get out of that copter."

That's a touch of an exaggeration—you really just see an orange dot—but a touch is all you need.

"You can't verify—"

"Sure I can. There is a date stamp. The buildings and landscape are unique enough. I have the volume turned down, but the whole thing is narrated." Another exaggeration. "The teenagers who made the tape spell out exactly where they are and what they are witnessing."

His glare is back.

"One more thing," I say.

"What?"

"You can hear three teenage boys on the tape. All three have died under mysterious circumstances."

One of the old men shouts out, "Hey, Andy, can I request 'Livin' on a Prayer'?"

"I hate Madonna," another says.

"That's 'Like a Prayer,' you moron. 'Livin' on a Prayer' is Bon Jovi."

"Who you calling a moron?"

Andy Reeves ignores them. He turns to me. The facade is gone now. The whisper is harsher. "Is that the only copy of the tape?"

"Yes," I say, giving him flat eyes. "I was dumb enough to come here without making copies."

He speaks through gritted teeth. "If that tape is what you claim—and I stress the word '*if*'—revealing it would be a federal offense punishable by a prison sentence."

"Andy?"

"What?"

"Do I look scared?"

"It would be treason to reveal that."

I point to my calm face, indicating again that I do not in any way, shape, or form appear frightened by this threat.

"If you dare show it to anyone—"

"Let me stop you there, Andy. I don't want you to worry your pretty head about it. If you don't tell me what I want to know, I'll definitely show it. I'll post it all over Twitter and Facebook with your name on it." I pretend to have a pen and paper and prepare to mime writing. "Is Reeves spelled with two *e*'s or *ea*?"

"I had nothing to do with your brother."

"How about my girlfriend, then? Her name is Maura Wells. You want to tell me you had nothing to do with her either?"

"My God." Andy Reeves slowly shakes his head. "You have no clue, do you?"

I don't like the way he says it, with sudden confidence. I don't know how to reply, so I go with a simple "So tell me."

Another patron shouts, "Play 'Don't Stop Believin',' Andy. We love that one."

"Sinatra!"

"Journey!"

Murmurs of agreement. One guy starts singing, "'Just a small town girl.'" The others answer, "'Livin' in a lonely world.'"

"One second, fellas." Reeves waves and smiles, just a good ol' guy enjoying the attention. "Save your energy."

Andy Reeves turns back to me, lowers his mouth until it's close to my ear, and whispers, "If you release that tape, Detective Dumas, I'll kill you and everyone you love. Do I make myself clear?"

"Crystal." I nod. Then I reach out, grab him by the balls, and squeeze.

His scream shatters the night air.

A few of the old folks jump up, startled. When I let go, Reeves flops to the floor like a fish hitting a dock.

The younger guys, the orderlies, react. They rush toward me. I back up, take out my shield.

"Stay where you are," I warn. "Police business."

The old folks don't like this. Neither do three of the order-lies. They come closer, circling me. I take out my phone and snap a quick pic. The old-timers yell at me.

"What do you think you're doing? . . . If I was ten years younger . . . You can't just do that . . . 'Livin' on a Prayer'!"

One drops to his knee to tend to the wounded Reeves as the orderlies move closer.

I need to close this down now.

I show the approaching orderlies the gun in my hip holster. I don't pull it out, but the sight is enough to slow them down.

An old man shakes his fist at me. "We're going to report you!"

"Do what you must," I say.

"You better get out of here now."

I agree. Five seconds later, I'm out the door.

Chapter Twenty-one

'm not worried about my behavior being called in to law enforcement. Andy Reeves will recover, and when he does, he won't want anyone reporting the incident.

I am more worried, however, about Reeves's threat. Four people—you, Diana, Rex, and Hank—have been murdered. Yes, I'm going to use that term now. Forget the claims of accident and suicide. You were murdered, Leo. And I'll be damned if I'm going to let that go.

I call Ellie. She doesn't answer, which pisses me off. I look on my phone and check the photo I took of Reeves. He's on the floor, his face scrunched up in pain, but it's clear enough. I attach it to a text and send it to Ellie. The text reads:

See if Maura's mom recognizes him.

I start to drive home, but I realize that I haven't eaten anything. I veer to the right and make my way to the Armstrong Diner. It's open twenty-four hours. Through the window I see that Bunny is on duty. As I get out of the car, my phone rings. It's Ellie.

"Hey," she says.

"Hey."

That's our way of realizing we went too far, I guess.

"Where are you?" she asks.

"The Armstrong."

"I'll be there in half an hour."

The phone goes dead. I get out and start toward the diner. Two girls, probably late teens, maybe early twenties, stand outside, smoking and jabbering away. One is blond, one brunette, both resembling "Internet models" or wannabe reality stars. That's the look, I guess. I walk past them as they take deep drags. Then I stop and turn back toward them. I stare at them until they feel my eyes. They keep talking for a second or two, glancing toward me. I don't move. Eventually their voices fade away.

The blonde makes a face at me. "What's your problem?"

"I should just go inside," I say. "I should just mind my own business. But I want to say one thing first."

They both look at me the way you do at a crazy person.

"Please don't smoke," I say.

The brunette puts her hands on her hips. "Do we know you?"

"No," I say.

"You a cop or something?"

"I am, but that has nothing to do with it. My father died of lung cancer because he smoked. So I can just walk right past you—or I can try to save your life. Chances are, you won't listen to me, but maybe if I do this enough, maybe just one time, someone will stop and think and maybe even quit. So I'm asking you—I'm sort of begging you—please don't smoke."

That's it.

I head inside. Stavros is behind the cash register. He gives me a high five and nods toward a table in the corner. I'm a single guy who doesn't like to cook, so I'm here a lot for dinner. Like the menus at most New Jersey diners, the Armstrong's menu is Bible-length. Bunny just gives me the specials menu. She points to the salmon with couscous and gives me a wink.

I look out the window. The two smoking girls are still outside. The brunette has her back to me, the cigarette between her fingers. The blonde gives me a baleful look, but there is no cigarette in her hand. I give her a thumbs-up. She turns away. She probably finished it already, but I take the victories where I can.

I'm just about finished with my meal when Ellie comes through the door. Stavros's face lights up when he sees her. It's a cliché to say that someone lights up a room when she enters it, but at the very least, Ellie raises the average level of goodness, of decency, of virtue in it.

This is the first time I just don't take all that for granted.

She slides in across the booth, tucking one foot under her.

"Did you get that photograph to Maura's mom?" I ask.

Ellie nods. "She hasn't replied yet."

I see her blink away tears.

"Ellie?"

"Something else I never told you."

"What?"

"Two years ago, when I spent that month in Washington."

I nod. "For that conference on the homeless."

She makes a "yeah right" noise. "A conference"—she picks up the napkin and starts dabbing at her eyes—"that lasts a month?"

I don't know what to make of that, so I stay silent.

"This has nothing to do with Maura, by the way. I just . . ."

I reach out and put my hand on her arm. "What is it?"

"You're the best person I know, Nap. I trust you with my life. But I didn't tell you."

"Didn't tell me what?"

"Bob . . ."

I stay perfectly still.

"There was this woman at work. Bob started staying late. So one night I surprised him. The two of them . . ."

I feel my heart bottom out. I don't know what to say and I don't think she wants me to say anything, so I tighten the grip on her arm a little. I want to offer some kind of comfort. But I blew that chance.

A monthlong conference. Man.

My best friend was in horrible pain. And I never saw it.

Some great detective, right?

Ellie wipes her eyes and forces up a smile. "It's better now. Bob and I cleared the air."

"You want to talk about it?"

"Not right now, no. I came to talk to you about Maura. About my promise to her."

Bunny comes over, drops a menu in front of Ellie, gives her a wink. When she leaves, I don't know how to continue. Neither does Ellie. So finally I say, "You made a promise to Maura."

"Yes."

"When?"

"The night Leo and Diana died."

Another punch in the teeth.

Bunny comes back over and asks Ellie if she wants to order anything. Ellie says a decaf. I manage to order a mint tea. Bunny asks whether either of us wants to try the banana pudding, it's to die for. We both decline.

"That night," I say. "Did you see Maura before or after Leo and Diana died?"

Her answer sends me into another tailspin: "Both."

I don't know what to say, or maybe I'm afraid of what I might say. She looks out the window, into the parking lot.

"Ellie?"

"I'll break my promise to Maura," she says. "But, Nap?"

"What?"

"You're not going to like it."

"Let me start with the after," Ellie says.

The diner is emptying out, but we don't care. Bunny and Stavros have been steering newcomers to the opposite end of the diner, giving us privacy.

"Maura came to my house," she says.

I wait for Ellie to say more. She doesn't.

"That night?"

"Yes."

"What time?"

"About three in the morning. My parents had broken up, and Dad . . . he wanted me happy, so he converted the garage into a bedroom for me, which was pretty awesome for a teenager. My friends could come at all hours because you could reach my room without waking anybody."

I'd heard rumors about Ellie's back door always being open, but this was before Ellie and I became tight, before my brother and Ellie's best friend, Diana, were found on those railroad tracks. I wonder about that now. The two sturdiest relationships in my adult life are with Ellie and Augie, both born from that tragic night.

"So anyway, when I first heard the knock, I didn't think much of it. People knew that if they couldn't go home yet—if they were too drunk or whatever—they could crash at my place."

"Had Maura ever come by before?" I ask.

"No, never. I know I've told you this, but I was always a little in awe of Maura. She just seemed, I don't know, cooler than the rest of us. More mature and worldly. You know what I mean?"

I nod. "So why did she come to you?"

"I asked her that, but at first, Maura was just a wreck, crying and hysterical. Which, like I said, was weird to me because she always seemed above it all. It took me like five minutes to calm her down. She was covered in dirt. I thought she'd been attacked or something. I actually started checking her clothes to see if anything had been ripped. I read about that in some rape-trauma class. Anyway, when she started to calm down, it almost happened too quickly. I don't know how else to put it.

Like someone had slapped her in the face and shouted, 'Snap out of it!'"

"What did you do?"

"I broke out a bottle of Fireball whisky I had hidden under my bed."

"You?"

She shakes her head. "You really think you know everything about me, don't you?"

Evidently not, I think.

"Anyway, Maura shook me off, said she needed to keep a clear head. She asked if she could stay with me for a while. I said of course. Truthfully, I was kinda flattered that she chose me."

"This is three in the morning?"

"Around three, yeah."

"So you didn't know about Leo and Diana yet," I say.

"Right."

"Did Maura tell you?"

"No. She just said she needed a place to hide." Ellie leaned forward. "Then she looked me dead in the eyes and made me promise. You know how intense she could be, right? She made me promise not to tell anyone she was there, not ever, not even you."

"She specifically said me?"

Ellie nods. "I actually thought at first maybe you two had a big fight, but she was too scared. She came to me, I think, because, well, I'm Reliable Ellie, right? There were people closer to her. That's what I kept wondering about. Why me? Now I know."

"Know what?"

"Why she came to me. You heard her mom. People were looking for her. I didn't know that back then. But Maura must have figured anyone close to her would be watched or questioned."

I nod. "So she couldn't go home."

"Right. And she probably thought that they'd spy on you or question your dad. If they wanted to find her, they'd search the people close to her."

I see it now. "And you really weren't a friend."

"Exactly. She figured that they wouldn't go to me."

"So what were they after? Why were these people looking for her?"

"I don't know."

"You didn't ask?"

"I asked. She didn't tell me."

"And you let that go?"

Ellie almost smiles. "You don't remember how persuasive Maura could be?"

Oh, I do. I get it.

"I learned later that Maura told me nothing for the same reason she told her mother nothing."

"To protect you."

"Yes."

"If you didn't know anything," I continue, "you couldn't tell them anything."

"She also made me promise, Nap. She made me swear that until she came back on her own, I couldn't tell anyone. I tried to keep that promise, Nap. I know you're angry about it. But something about the way Maura said it . . . I wanted to keep my word. And I was really afraid that breaking my word would lead to disaster. To tell you the truth, even now, even as we sit here, I think it's the wrong thing. I didn't want to tell you."

"So what changed your mind?"

"Too many people are dying, Nap. And I wonder whether Maura is one of them."

"You think she's dead?"

"Her mom and I . . . we naturally bonded after this. That first call at the Bennigan's? I helped set that up. Lynn left that part out when she talked to you, to protect me."

I don't know what to say to all this. "You lied to me all these years."

"You were obsessed."

Again that word. Ellie says I am obsessed. David Rainiv says Hank was obsessed.

"If I told you about this promise," Ellie says, "well, I had no idea how you'd react."

"Wasn't your place to worry about my reaction."

"Maybe not. But it wasn't my place to break a promise either."

"I still don't get it. How long did Maura stay with you?"

"Two nights."

"And then?"

Ellie shrugs. "I came home and she was gone."

"No note, no nothing?"

"Nothing."

"And since then?"

"More nothing. I haven't seen her or heard from her since."

Something isn't adding up. "Wait, when did you learn about Leo's and Diana's deaths?"

"I heard about it the day after they were found. I called Diana's house and asked for her and"—I see her eyes water up again—"her mom . . . God, her voice."

"Audrey Styles told you over the phone?"

"No. She asked me to come over. But I could hear it. I ran the whole way. She sat me down. In the kitchen. When she finished, I went home to ask Maura. But she was gone."

Still not adding up. "But . . . I mean, you had to figure it was connected, right?"

She didn't reply.

"Maura comes to you the night Leo and Diana die," I say. "You had to think there was some link."

Ellie nods slowly. "I figured it couldn't be a coincidence, that's right."

"And yet you didn't tell anyone?"

"I made a promise, Nap."

"Your best friend had just been killed," I say. "How could you not tell anyone?"

Ellie lowers her head. I stop for a second.

"You were the most responsible girl in the school," I say. "I could see you keeping a promise. That makes sense. But once you found out Diana was dead—"

"We all thought it was an accident, remember? Or maybe a weird double suicide, though I never believed that. But I didn't think Maura had anything to do with it."

"Come on, Ellie, you can't be that naïve. How could you not tell someone?"

She lowers her head again. I know it now. She's hiding something.

"Ellie?"

"I did tell someone."

"Who?"

240

"But that was part of Maura's genius, when I look back at it. What could I tell anyone? I had no idea where she was."

"Who did you tell?"

"Diana's parents."

I freeze. "You told Augie and Audrey?"

"Yes."

"Augie . . ." I think I can't be stunned anew, yet here I am. "He knew that Maura had stayed at your house?"

She nods, and I'm reeling again. Can you trust anyone in this world, Leo? Ellie lied to me. Augie lied to me. Who else? Mom, of course. When she said she was coming right back.

Did Dad lie too?

Did you?

"What did Augie say to you?" I ask.

"He thanked me. Then he told me to keep my promise."

I need to see Augie. I need to go over to his house and figure out what the hell is going on here. But then I remember something else Ellie told me.

"You said before and after."

"What?"

"I asked you if you saw Maura before or after Leo and Diana died. You said both."

Ellie nods.

"You told me about the after. What about the before?"

She looks off.

"What is it?" I ask.

"This is the part," Ellie says, "you're not going to like."

Chapter Twenty-two

She stands across the street from the Armstrong Diner and watches them through a window.

Fifteen years ago, after the gunfire shattered the still night, she ran and hid for two hours. When she ventured out and saw the parked cars with the men in them, she knew for sure. She made her way toward the bus stop. It didn't matter which bus she got on. She just wanted distance. All the buses leaving Westbridge ended up in either Newark or New York City. From there, she could find friends and support. But it was late. Very few buses were still operating at that hour. Even worse, when she started up near the station by Karim Square, she again noticed men nearby in parked cars. For the next two nights, she stayed with Ellie. The three days after that, she hid in the Livingston basement / art studio of Hugh Warner, her art teacher.

Mr. Warner was single, wore a ponytail, and always smelled like a bong. Then she started moving. Mr. Warner had a friend in Alphabet City. She stayed there for two days. She cut her hair and dyed it blond. For a few weeks, she followed groups of foreign tourists in Central Park and stole cash, but when she nearly got caught by an off-duty cop from Connecticut, she knew that had to end. A panhandler told her about a guy in Brooklyn who did fake IDs. She bought four new names. The IDs weren't perfect, but they were good enough to get her temporary employment. For the next three years, she moved around. A lot. In Cincinnati, she waitressed at a luncheonette. In Birmingham, she worked the cash register at Piggly Wiggly. In Daytona Beach, she donned a bikini and sold time-shares, which felt grimier than robbing the tourists. She slept on streets, in public parks, in chain motels (they were always clean), in the homes of strange men. She knew that if she just kept moving, she would be safe. They couldn't put out an APB on her. There were no Wanted posters. They were looking, but they were limited. The public couldn't help them. She joined various religious groups, feigning a reverence for whatever egomaniac served as minister, and used that to find housing, nourishment, protection. She danced at remote "gentlemen's clubs"—the strangest of euphemisms because they are neither—where the money was good but the attention too great. She was robbed twice, beaten, and one night she got in way over her head. She blocked on that and moved on. She started carrying a knife. In a parking lot outside of Denver, two men attacked her. She stabbed one deep in the gut. Blood poured from his mouth. She ran. He may have died. She never knew. She sometimes hung around community colleges, where the security wasn't too tight, and even attended classes. Near Milwaukee, she tried to settle down for a bit, even getting her real estate license, but an attorney noticed something wrong with her ID during a closing.

In Dallas, she prepared taxes at a storefront accounting chain—they pretended to hire real accountants, but her training was a three-week seminar at a Courtyard Marriott—and for the first time, perhaps because the loneliness was getting overwhelming, she made a real friend in a coworker named Ann Hannon. Ann was great fun and warm, and they became roommates. They double-dated and went to movies and even took a vacation together to San Antonio. Ann Hannon was the first person she trusted enough to tell the truth, but of course, for both their protection, she never did. One day as she approached the storefront, she noticed two men in suits sitting in the waiting area reading newspapers. There were often people in the waiting area. But these guys looked wrong. She could see Ann through the window. Her always-smiling friend was not smiling. So she ran again. Just like that. Never called Ann to say good-bye. That summer she worked in a cannery in Alaska. She then did a three-month stint selling excursions on a cruise ship running from Skagway to Seattle. There were a few kind men along the way. But most were not kind. Most were anything but kind. As the years passed, she twice ran into people who recognized her as Maura Wells—one in Los Angeles, one in Indianapolis. That was bound to happen when she looked back on it now. You spend your life on streets or in public places, someone is going to see you. It was no big deal. She didn't pretend that they were mistaken or claim that she was someone else. She had stories ready, usually involving doing a graduate program. As soon as the person was out of sight, she would be gone. She always had a backup plan, always knew where the nearest truck stop was, because that was the easiest way to get a ride when you looked like she did. A guy was bound to give her a lift. Sometimes, if she got to the stop early enough, she would watch them eat and converse and interact, trying to decide which driver looked the least predatory. You could tell. Or you could be wrong. She didn't ask the women drivers for lifts, even the seemingly friendly ones, because women on the road had learned to be suspicious, and she was afraid that they might call her in. She had a series of wigs now and various glasses with no prescription. That was enough of a disguise in the event that anyone said anything.

There are various theories about why the years seem to pass faster as you get older. The most popular is also the most obvious. As you get older, each year is a smaller percentage of your life. If you are ten years old, a year is ten percent. If you are fifty years old, a year is two percent. But she had read a theory that spurned that explanation. The theory states that time passes faster when we are in a set routine, when we aren't learning anything new, when we stay stuck in a life pattern. The key to making time slow down is to have new experiences. You may joke that the week you went on vacation flew by far too quickly, but if you stop and think about it, that week actually seemed to last much longer than one involving the drudgery of your day job. You are complaining about it going away so fast because you loved it, not because it felt as though time was passing faster. If you want to slow down time, this theory holds: If you want to make the days last, do something different. Travel to exotic locales. Take a class.

In a sense, this was her life.

Until Rex. Until more gunfire. Until Hank.

Through the window, she can see the devastation on Nap's face. It is the first time she has seen him in fifteen years. Her life's greatest what-if. The road not taken. She lets the emotions ricochet through her. She doesn't fight them.

At one point, she even steps out from the shadows.

She stands under a light in the parking lot, in plain view now, not moving, letting fate take the chance that Nap might turn and look out the diner window and see her and then . . .

She gives him ten seconds to look. Nothing. She gives him another ten.

But Nap never looks out the window.

Maura turns and disappears back into the night.

Chapter Twenty-three

Diana and I had plans," Ellie begins.

There are only two other tables of patrons left, and they are way on the other side of the counter. I am trying hard to not get ahead of myself, to listen before jumping to conclusions, to absorb first and process later.

"We probably seemed like silly clichés, looking back on it. I was president of the student council. Diana was vice president. We were cocaptains of the soccer team. Our parents were close friends. They'd go out to dinner as a foursome." She looks up at me. "Does Augie date much?"

"Not really."

"You said he went down south with a girlfriend recently."

"Yvonne. Hilton Head."

"Is that in Georgia?"

"It's an island off South Carolina."

"How did it go?" Ellie asks.

How did Augie put it? "I don't think it's going to work out."

"I'm sorry to hear that."

I say nothing.

"He should be with someone. Diana wouldn't want her father alone like that."

I catch Bunny's eyes, but she looks away, giving us privacy. Someone has hit one of the old jukeboxes. Tears for Fears remind us in song that "Everybody Wants to Rule the World."

"You said you saw Maura before Leo and Diana died," I say, trying to get us back on course.

"I'm getting to that."

I wait.

"So Diana and I are in the school library. You probably don't remember this—no reason you would—but we had our big fall dance coming up the week after. Diana was head of the planning committee. I was her second."

She's right. I don't remember. The annual fall dance. Maura wouldn't have wanted to go. I wouldn't have cared.

"I'm not telling this right," Ellie says.

"It's okay."

"Anyway, the dance was a big deal to Diana. She'd been working on it for over a month. She couldn't decide between two themes. One was Vintage Boardwalk, the other was called Once Upon a Storybook, and so Diana suggested that we do both." Ellie looks off now, a small smile toying with her lips. "I was adamantly against this idea. I told Diana we have to, *have to,* pick only one, because otherwise it would be anarchy, and because I was a stupid, pathetic little perfectionist, this—what theme to choose—is what my best friend and I argued about the last time we ever spoke."

Ellie stops. I give her the time to put herself back together.

"So we're arguing about this and it's getting kinda heated— and then Maura walks in and starts talking to Diana. I was in a snit about the idea of two themes, and so I didn't listen to the first part too closely. But Maura wanted Diana to come with her somewhere that night. Diana said no, that she had kinda had it."

"Had it with what?" I ask.

"She didn't say. But then Diana told us both something . . ."

Ellie stops again and looks at me.

"What?" I say.

"She said that she'd had it with the whole group of them."

"And by 'group,' she meant . . . ?"

"Look, I didn't really care. I was focused on how someone could possibly think you could have two themes for one dance and how would you possibly mesh Vintage Boardwalk, which I liked, with carnival games and peanuts and popcorn, with Once Upon a Storybook, which I didn't even get. I mean, what the hell does that even mean? But now? After what we saw in the yearbook? I guess maybe Diana was talking about the Conspiracy Club. I don't know. That's not the part you won't like."

"What is the part I won't like?"

"What Diana said next."

"Which was?"

"Diana wanted to wait another couple of weeks—until after the fall dance because, well, she was the planning chair. But Diana said she was tired of your brother and his friends. She swore us both to secrecy, but she said she was going to break up with Leo."

I just react: "That's crap."

Now it's Ellie's turn to stay quiet.

"Diana and Leo were solid," I say. "I mean, yeah, it was high school, but . . ."

"He changed, Nap."

I shake my head.

"Leo was moodier. That's what Diana said. He would snap at her. Look, a lot of kids were experimenting senior year, partying or whatever—"

"That's all he was doing too. Leo was fine."

"No, Nap, he wasn't fine."

"We lived in the same room. I knew everything about him."

"And yet you didn't know what was going on with the Conspiracy Club. You didn't know he and Diana were having a rough time of it. That's not your fault. You had Maura and your hockey. You were just a kid . . ."

Her voice trails off when she sees my face.

"Whatever happened that night—" Ellie begins.

I interrupt her. "What do you mean, 'whatever happened'? That military base was guarding a secret. Leo and Maura and, I don't know, the rest of them found out what it is. I don't care if Leo was stoned or that maybe, *maybe* Diana considered breaking up with him a week later. They all saw something. I have the proof now."

"I know," Ellie says gently. "I'm on your side."

"You don't sound like it."

"Nap?"

I look at her.

"Maybe you should let this go," she finally says.

"Yeah, that's not going to happen."

"Maybe Maura doesn't want to be found."

"I'm not doing this for Maura," I say. "I'm doing this for Leo."

But once we are out in the parking lot, once I kiss Ellie's cheek and make sure she's in her car, a thought rises from the ashes and won't so easily be put down: Maybe Ellie is right. Maybe I should let this go.

I watch Ellie pull out. She doesn't turn around and wave good-bye. She's always waved good-bye in the past. Dumb thing to notice, but there you go. I wonder about this. It may have been a promise, but she has been keeping a secret from me for fifteen years. You would think unburdening herself might lead us to a higher level of trust.

That doesn't seem to be the case.

I glance around the parking lot for the smoking girls, but they are long gone. Still I feel eyes on me. I don't know whose. I don't really care. Ellie's words rip through my head like talons.

"Maybe you should let this go. Maybe Maura doesn't want to be found."

What exactly am I trying to do here?

Proclaiming that I'll do anything in my quest for justice sounds honorable and brave. But that doesn't make it right. How many more have to die before I step back? By flushing out Maura, am I putting her and others in danger?

I'm stubborn. I'm determined. But I'm not reckless or suicidal.

Should I let this go?

I still feel like I'm being watched, so I turn. Someone is standing behind a tree at the Jersey Mike's Subs shop down the street. Doesn't seem like a big deal, but I'm full of paranoia right now. I put my hand to the gun in my hip holster. I don't pull it. I just want to know it's there.

As I step toward the tree, my phone buzzes. The number is blocked. I step toward my car. "Hello?"

"Detective Dumas?"

"Yep."

"This is Carl Legg with the Ann Arbor Police Department. You asked me to look into finding a cardiologist named Dr. Fletcher."

"Any luck?"

"No," Legg says. "But there are a few things you should know. Hello, you there?"

I slide into my car. "I'm listening."

"Sorry, sounded like you cut out for a second. So I visited Dr. Fletcher's office and spoke to the office manager."

"Cassie."

"Yep," Legg says. "You know her?"

"She wasn't cooperative on the phone."

"She wasn't Miss Congeniality in person either, but we pushed a bit."

"I appreciate that, Carl."

"Brothers of the badge and all that. Anyway, Dr. Fletcher called out of the blue last week and said she was taking a sabbatical. She canceled all her appointments and transferred as many as she could to a Dr. Paul Simpson. That's her partner."

I look over at the tree. No movement. "Has she done this kind of thing before?"

"No. According to Cassie, Dr. Fletcher is a very private person but completely dedicated to her patients. Canceling suddenly like this was out of character. I then spoke to her husband."

"What did he say?"

"He said they're separated and he has no idea where she is. He said she called him and said the same thing about a sabbatical. He agreed it was out of character, but he also said that since the separation, she's been—and I quote—'discovering herself.'"

I start my car and pull out of the lot. "Okay, Carl, thanks."

"You could take it to the next level, of course. Get her phone records, her credit card statements, that kind of thing."

"Yeah, I might do that."

Except that means legalities like getting warrants, and I'm not sure I want to go that route. I thank Carl Legg again and hang up. I start driving toward Augie's apartment on Oak Street. I go slow because I need to clear my head and think this through.

Augie was told Maura had gone to Ellie's that night to hide.

What did that mean, exactly? I'm really not sure. Did Augie follow up? Did he do anything with that information?

Most of all, why didn't Augie tell me?

My mobile rings again, and this time it's my boss, Loren Muse.

"Tomorrow morning," Muse says. "Nine A.M. My office."

"What's this about?"

"Nine A.M."

She hangs up.

Great. I wonder now if maybe one of the old-timers at the Rusty Nail did report the testicular assault on Andy Reeves. Nothing to be gained by worrying about that now. I hit Augie's number on my speed dial. No answer. I'm surprised that he hasn't called me back since I sent him a copy of Hank's videotape.

The turn for Oak Street is already upon me. So much for head clearing. I pull into the lot behind the brick apartments and turn off my car. I sit and stare out the window at nothing. That doesn't help. I get out and circle toward the front of the building. The streetlights are a dull amber. A hundred yards ahead of me I see an older woman walking an enormous dog. A Great Dane maybe. Something like that. I can only really see her in silhouette. When I make out what looks like a cigarette in her hand, I sigh and debate calling her out.

Nah. I'm a nosy pain in the ass, but I'm not a crusader.

Still, as I watch her stoop down with a plastic bag in her hand to clean up, something catches my eye.

A yellow car.

Or at least it looks yellow. I've seen those amber streetlights play havoc with the colors of white and cream, and even certain light metallic colors. I get to the sidewalk and hurry toward it. As I rush past the older woman, I figure it won't cost me anything not to be a total hypocrite.

"Please don't smoke," I say.

The woman just watches me rush by, which is fine by me. I've had every kind of response. One smoker was a vegan who lectured me on how my eating habits were far worse than anything tobacco and nicotine could do to me. Maybe he had a point.

The car is yellow. It's also a Ford Mustang.

Just like the car parked in front of the Rusty Nail.

I get right up next to it and see the license plate: EBNY-IVRY.

I didn't think about it before, but I get it now.

EBONY and IVORY. Piano terminology.

This yellow Ford Mustang belongs to Andy Reeves.

Again I reach and touch my gun. Not sure why. I do that sometimes. I wonder where Andy Reeves is right now, but I think the answer is obvious:

Augie's.

I start back toward Augie's apartment. As I pass by the old woman, she says, "Thank you."

Her voice is thick with phlegm. I stop.

"Too late to do me any good," she says, and I see something heavy in her eyes. "But I appreciate the kindness. Keep it up."

I think of several things to say, none of them in the slightest way profound, all of them ruining this moment, so I just nod and head off.

This apartment development is old-school and utilitarian, so there are no fancy names for the buildings. Buildings A, B, and C line the road from left to right. Buildings D, E, and F are in the row behind them. Buildings G, H, I, you get the drift. Each building houses four apartments, two on the first floor (Apartments 1 and 2) and two on the second floor (Apartments 3 and 4). Augie is in Building G, Apartment 2. I sprint up the path and turn left.

I almost run right into him.

Andy Reeves is leaving Augie's apartment, his back to me,

closing the door behind him. I move back down the path. Out of sight. Then I realize that chances are, he'll take this path and see me.

I move off the pavement and duck behind a bush. When I glance at the window behind me—Building E, Apartment 1—I see a black woman with big hair staring out at me.

Great.

I try to smile at her reassuringly. She doesn't look reassured.

I hop away and move down toward Building D. I'm not overly concerned about someone dialing 911 on me. By the time anyone responds, this will have been played out. I'm also a cop, and Augie is our captain.

Andy Reeves does indeed saunter down the path where I had recently been standing. If he looks to his right, there is a slight chance he'll see me, but I'm mostly blocked by a non-functioning lamppost. I pick up my phone and hit Augie's number again. It goes right into voice mail.

I don't like that.

Suppose Andy Reeves has done something to Augie. Am I just going to let him go?

My mind whirs. Two choices here—check on Augie or stop Andy Reeves. Decision made, I spin around Building D and head for Augie's apartment. Here is the way I look at it: If I rush in now and find Augie . . . whatever . . . either there will still be time to run back and catch the sauntering Andy Reeves before he gets to his car—or if not, if I get there a little late, the guy is making his escape in a neon-yellow Ford Mustang. Need I say more?

The windows at Augie's apartment are dark, meaning the

lights are out. I don't like that either. I rush to the door and pound on it hard.

"Wow, relax. It's open."

Relief courses through me. The voice belongs to Augie.

I turn the knob and push the door open. No lights are on. Augie sits in the dark with his back to me. Without turning around, he says, "What were you thinking?"

"About?"

"Did you really assault Reeves?"

"I might have squeezed his balls."

"Jesus, are you out of your mind?"

"He threatened me. He threatened you too, actually."

"What did he say?"

"That he'd kill me and everyone I loved."

Augie sighs. He still hasn't turned around. "Sit down, Nap."

"Can we turn a light on? This is kind of spooky."

Augie reaches his hand out and flicks on a table lamp. It's not a lot of illumination, but it's enough. I move to my familiar seat and take it. Augie stays in his.

"How did you know about the ball grab?" I ask.

"Reeves was just here. He's really upset."

"I bet he is."

I notice now that there is a glass in Augie's hand. Augie notices me noticing. "Pour yourself one," he says.

"I'm good."

"That tape you sent me," he says. "The ones the kids took of the copter."

"What about it?"

"You can't show it to anybody."

No need to ask why, so I take another approach. "You watched it?"

"Yes."

"I'd love to hear your thoughts."

Augie gives a heavy sigh. "A bunch of teenagers defied government no-trespassing warnings and filmed a helicopter landing at a government site."

"That's it?"

"Did I miss something?"

"Could you make out who was talking on the tape?" I asked.

He considered that. "The only voice I recognized for sure was your brother's."

"How about Diana?"

Augie shakes his head. "Diana wasn't on the tape."

"You seem pretty certain."

Augie raises the glass to his lips, stops, thinks better of it, places it back down. He stares off now, beyond me and into the past. "The weekend before she died, Diana was in Philadelphia doing college tours. All three of us—Diana, Audrey, and me—were there. We visited Villanova, Swarthmore, and Haverford. We liked them all, though Diana thought Haverford might be too small and Villanova might be too big. When we got home on Sunday, she was deciding between two colleges for early decision—Swarthmore and Amherst, which we'd visited over the summer." He still looks off, his voice devoid of any emotion. "If Diana made that decision, she never got the chance to tell me. Both applications were on her desk on the night she died."

Now he takes a deep pull from his drink. I give it a moment.

"Augie, they were covering something up at the base."

I expect a denial, but he nods. "Seems so."

"You're not surprised?"

"That a remote government agency protected by barbed-wire fencing was a cover? No, Nap, I'm not surprised."

"I assume Andy Reeves asked you about the tape," I say.

"Yes."

"And?"

"He said I should make sure you don't release it. He said that it would be tantamount to treason, that it was a matter of national security."

"It has to be connected to Leo and Diana."

He closes his eyes and shakes his head.

"Come on, Augie. They discover this secret, and a week later, they end up dead."

"No," Augie says. "It's not connected. At least not like you say."

"Are you for real? You think this is all a giant coincidence?"

Augie looks down into his drink as though there really is an answer at the bottom of it. "You're a great investigator, Nap. And I don't say that just because I trained you. Your mind . . . you're brilliant in many ways. You see things others can't. But sometimes you need to go back to the basics, to what you definitely know. Stop taking leaps. Look at the facts. Look at what we know for certain."

I wait.

"Number one, Leo and Diana were found dead by railroad tracks miles away from the military base."

"I can explain that."

He raises a hand to stop me. "I'm sure you can. I'm sure you'll tell me that they could have been moved or whatever. But right now, let me just state the facts. No maybes." He raises a finger. "Fact One: Their bodies were found miles from the military base. Fact Two"—a second finger—"the medical examiner concluded that blunt trauma from a moving train caused their deaths, nothing else. Before I continue, are we clear on all this?"

I nod, not because I completely agree—a train strike is devastating and might disguise earlier trauma—but because I want to hear what else he has to say.

"Now let's examine this tape you found. Assuming it is authentic—and I see no reason to think it's not—one week before these deaths, one of the deceased, Leo, saw a helicopter over the base. Your theory, I assume, is that this led to his death. Keep in mind that Diana wasn't with them when they made this video."

"Leo would have told her," I counter.

"No," he said.

"No?"

"Again, stick with the evidence, Nap. If you stick with the evidence, you'll conclude, as I have, that Diana never knew."

"I'm not following," I say.

"It's simple." He meets my eyes. "Did Leo tell *you* about the helicopter?"

I open my mouth and stop. I see where he is going with this. I slowly shake my head.

"How about your girlfriend, Maura? She was on the tape, am I correct?"

"Yes."

"Did Maura tell you?"

"No," I say.

Augie lets that sink in before continuing. "And then we have the toxicology report."

I know what the report said—hallucinogenics, alcohol, and pot in their systems. "What about it?" I ask.

Augie is trying to sound analytical, trying to be "just the facts, ma'am," but his voice is coarse from the pain. "You knew my daughter for a long time."

"Yes."

"You could even say you were friends."

"Yes."

"In fact"—now he sounds a bit like an attorney during a cross-examination—"you set Diana and Leo up."

That's not exactly accurate. I brought them together—I didn't actively set them up—but this hardly seems the time to argue semantics. "What's your point, Augie?"

"All fathers are naïve when it comes to their little girls. I was no different, I guess. I thought the sun rose and set on that girl. Diana played soccer in the fall. She was a cheerleader in the winter. She was an active leader in a dozen extracurricular activities." He leans forward, into the light. "I'm a cop, not a fool. I know none of that means your kid won't do drugs or get into any trouble, but would you say Diana was a big partier?"

I don't really have to think about the answer. "No."

"No," he repeats. "And ask Ellie. Ask her how often Diana did drugs or drank before . . ." He stops himself. His eyes close. "And yet that night, when Leo comes to pick her up, I'm there. I answer the door for him. I shake his hand, and I can see it."

"See what?"

"He's stoned. Not for the first time. I want to say something. I want to stop her from going out the door. But Diana just gives me this pleading look. You know the one—like, 'Don't make a scene, Dad.' So I don't. I let her go."

He's there, as he says this. Shaking hands with you, looking at his daughter, seeing the expression on her face. That what-if, that regret, never leaves him.

"So now that we got the facts out, Nap, you tell me: What's more likely? A big conspiracy involving CIA agents that, I don't know, kidnapped two kids because one of them had filmed a helicopter the week before—if the CIA knew about that, why did they wait a week before they killed him?—dragged them both across town to railroad tracks, and, I guess, pushed them in front of a speeding train? Or is the more likely scenario that a girl went out with a boy who liked to get high and stoned. They partied too hard. They remembered the legend of Jimmy Riccio and together, flying high, tried to jump the track and just fell a little short?"

He looks at me and waits.

"You're leaving a whole lot of stuff out," I say.

"No, Nap, you're putting a whole lot of stuff in."

"We have Rex. We have Hank—"

"Fifteen years later."

"—and you know Maura hid that night. Ellie told you about it. Why didn't you tell me?"

"When should I have told you? You were an eighteen-year-old kid. Should I have told you when you were nineteen? When you graduated from the academy? When you got promoted to county? When should I have told you something as irrelevant as 'your old girlfriend didn't want to go home so she stayed with Ellie'?"

Is he for real? "Maura was scared and hiding," I say, trying not to shout, "from something that happened on the night Leo and Diana were killed."

He shakes his head. "You need to leave this alone. For every-one's sake."

"Yeah, I keep hearing that."

"I love you, Nap. I mean that. I love you . . . no, I won't say like a son. That would be too presumptuous. It would also be an insult to what you had with your dad, a wonderful guy I miss very much, and it would be an insult to my little girl. But I do love you. I tried hard to be a good mentor to you, a good friend."

"You have been that and more."

Augie leans back. His drink is empty. He puts it on the side table. "Neither of us has many people left we care about. I couldn't stand it if something happened . . . You're young, Nap. You're smart. You're kind and you're generous and, shit, I'm starting to sound like one of those online dating profiles."

He smiles now. I smile back.

"You need to move on. Whatever the answer, you're messing with some very dangerous people. They'll hurt you. They'll hurt me. You heard Reeves. He'll hurt anybody you care about. Let's say you're right and I'm wrong. Let's say they saw some-thing and, I don't know, they killed Diana and Leo. Why? To silence them, I guess. And now let's say they waited fifteen years—why did they wait? Again, I don't know—but then they hired a hit man to put two bullets in the back of Rex's head. And they slaughter Hank and conveniently pin it on a viral video. Does all that really sound more logical than my theory about them getting high? I don't know, maybe. But let's say that Reeves and his henchmen are all that horrible and danger-ous and they've killed that many people. Let's say your theory is true, okay?"

I nod.

"Forget you and me, Nap—you don't think they'll go after Ellie to stop us? Or her two girls?"

I picture Leah and Kelsi. I see their smiling faces, hear them, feel their arms wrap around me.

That slows me down. I was heading down this hill at a carefree breakneck pace, but Augie's words force me to pull back on the reins a little. I try to remember what I told myself earlier. Don't act in haste. Think and consider.

"It's late," Augie says. "Nothing more is going to happen tonight. Go to sleep. Let's talk in the morning."

Chapter Twenty-four

I head home, but there is no way I'm going to sleep.

I think about what Augie said, about the possibility of danger to Ellie and the girls, and I'm not sure what to do about that. It is easy to say that I can't be intimidated, but one has to be pragmatic too. What are the odds I'll actually solve the case?

Long shot.

What are the odds not only that I'll learn the truth about Leo and Diana but that I'll also find enough evidence to bring someone up on charges, never mind get a conviction?

Longer shot.

And to the contrary, what are the odds that I or someone close to me suffers terrible consequences because of my blind determination to complete this mission?

The question is practically rhetorical.

Is it worth poking the bear?

I don't know for sure. The wise thing may indeed be to let it go. You're dead, Leo. Whatever I do now, no matter what horror I unearth, that will not change. You will still be dead and gone. Intellectually I know this. And yet.

I open the Internet browser on my laptop. I put in Andy Reeves's name, the state of "NJ," and then I add the word "piano." I get a hit:

Welcome to the Fan Page for PianoManAndy.

Fan page. I click on the link. Yes, Andy Reeves, like almost every performer, has his own website. The home page features a portrait of him in soft focus wearing what looks like a sequined blazer.

World-renowned pianist Andy Reeves is a gifted vocalist, a comedian, and the all-around entertainer nicknamed by those who love him "the Other PianoMan" . . .

Oh boy.

I skim down. Andy "occasionally" does "high-end" private parties such as "weddings, corporate events, birthdays, and bar/bat mitzvahs." A burst in the middle of the page reads:

Want to join the Other PianoMan fan club? Stay in touch via our newsletter!

Below that there is a place to type in my email. I demur.

Down the left side of the page, the buttons read "Home," "Bio," "Photos," "Song Lists," "Schedule" . . .

I click "Schedule." I scan down until I find today. His gig at the Rusty Nail is listed until 6:00 P.M. Beneath that, it shows he'll be playing at a club called Hunk-A-Hunk-A from 10:00 P.M. until midnight.

My phone buzzes. It's a text from Ellie.

You awake?

My thumbs start going: It's only ten. Yes.

Want to go for a quick walk?

Sure. Want me to swing by?

The little dots are moving. Then Ellie's message appears:

I'm already walking. Meet me at the BF lot.

I pull into the empty middle school lot five minutes later. Ellie and Bob don't live far from here. Like most school lots, this one is lit up pretty well, but I don't see her. I park and get out of the car.

"Over here."

There is a classic school playground out on the left. Swings, slides, climbing walls, nets, ladders, monkey bars, all floored by soft mulch. Ellie sits on a swing. She is pushing herself with her feet, but only a little, so the effect is more like a comforting rocking than anything in the swing family.

The cedar smell from the mulch gets stronger as I walk toward her. "You okay?" I ask.

Ellie nods. "I just didn't want to go home yet."

I'm not sure what to say to this, so I settle for a nod.

"I loved playgrounds when I was a kid," Ellie says. "Do you remember the game four square?"

"No," I say.

"Never mind. I'm being silly. I come here a lot, though."

"To this playground?"

She nods. "At night. I'm not sure why."

I take the swing next to her. "I didn't know."

"Yeah, we are learning a lot about each other," Ellie says.

I think about that. "Not really."

"What do you mean?"

"You know everything about me, Ellie. Just because I never told you about beating Trey, well, you knew it was me."

She nods. "I did."

"And the other times. With Roscoe and Brandon and I forget Alicia's boyfriend's name."

"Colin."

"Right."

"So you know everything about me. Everything."

"The implication being that you don't know everything about me?"

I don't reply.

"Fair enough," Ellie says. "I don't tell you everything."

"You don't trust me?"

"You know better."

"So?"

"So I'm allowed my secrets. I shouldn't have told you about Bob because now you'll hate him and think about hurting him."

"A little," I confess.

She smiles. "Don't. You don't get it. He's the same man you admired this morning."

I don't agree, but I don't see any point in voicing that.

Ellie stares up at the night sky. There are a handful of stars out, but it feels like there should be more. "I heard from Maura's mom. The guy in the picture you sent? It's the same man who interrogated her. The pale guy with the whispery voice."

I'm not surprised. "I saw him earlier today."

"Who is he?"

"His name is Andy Reeves." I gesture with my chin toward the Path. "He ran the military base when Leo and Diana were killed."

"You talked to him?"

I nod.

"Did he say anything?"

"He threatened to kill everyone I love."

I just look at her.

"Another person who suggests you let it go," Ellie says.

"Suggests?"

She shrugs.

"But, yes. Joining you and Augie."

"Augie. There's someone else you love."

I nod.

"Are you considering it?"

"What? Dropping the case?"

"Yes."

"I am."

Ellie looks back toward the Path. Her eyes narrow.

"What?" I ask.

"I may reconsider."

"Meaning?"

"I don't think you can drop this now."

"I can if it puts you or the girls at risk."

"No, it's just the opposite."

"I'm not following," I say.

"I know I was the one who said you should let it go. But that was before this creepy guy threatened my kids. Now I don't want to let it go. If we do, he'll always be out there. I'll always be looking over my shoulder."

"If I let it go, he won't bother you."

"Right," Ellie says with a scoff. "Tell that to Rex and Hank."

I could argue that Rex and Hank posed a more direct threat, that they were actual eyewitnesses to that helicopter hovering over the base fifteen years ago, but I don't think it would matter. I get what she's saying. Ellie doesn't want to live in fear. She wants me to take care of it, and she doesn't want to know how.

Ellie pushes with her legs harder now. The swing goes back, and using the momentum, she gracefully jumps off as it comes forward, even triumphantly raising her hands like a gymnast sticking the landing. I care so much about her, and yet for the first time I'm realizing I still don't know her, and that's making me care all the more.

"I won't let anything happen to you," I say.

"I know."

I remember the schedule I'd seen a little earlier on the "Andy the Other PianoMan" website. He'll be at the Hunk-A-Hunk-A Club, whatever that is.

I'll go there and confront him tonight.

"One more thing," Ellie says.

"What?"

"I may have a lead on Beth Lashley's whereabouts. When we were in high school, her parents bought a small organic farm in Far Hills. My cousin Merle has a place down there. I asked her to drive by and just knock on the door. She said she tried, but the gate by the fence was locked."

"Could be nothing."

"Could be. I'll take a little drive tomorrow and let you know."

"Thank you."

"Sure." Ellie lets loose a deep breath and looks over at the school. "Does it seem that long ago when we went to this school?"

I look with her. "A lifetime ago," I say.

Ellie gives that one a small chuckle. "I better head back."

"You want me to drive you?"

"No," she says. "I'd rather walk."

Chapter Twenty-five

Hunk-A-Hunk-A advertises itself as "an upscale revue of male erotic dancers for ladies with class" because no one says "strip joint" anymore. Tonight's featured performer is Dick Shaftwood, which I suspect may be a pseudonym. I find the yellow Ford Mustang tucked in a back corner of the club parking lot. There is no point in going inside, so I park in a spot where I can clearly see the exits and the Mustang. I notice two buses and several large vans in the lot, like maybe tour groups come here.

What I learn from watching the crowd enter and exit is somewhat obvious. Women don't come here alone. I don't see one woman walk in or out by herself, like guys do at their strip clubs. The female clientele here come in groups, usually large ones, all cheering and already at least partially lubed up. Most, if not all, seem to be with bachelorette parties, which explains the buses and large vans. They are being responsible—good, clean, dirty fun with a professional designated driver.

It's getting late. The women departing now are annoyingly hammered—loud, staggering, sloppy, falling over one another, holding one another up—but staying close together in a pack, waiting for any straggler to rejoin the herd before proceeding onward. A few of the male strippers start heading home. Even fully clothed they are not hard to pick out. They all scowl. They all have that stick-up-the-ass, "yo, brah" strut. Most are wearing loose-fitting flannel shirts barely buttoned, their waxed cleavage glistening in the streetlight.

I can't imagine why Hunk-A-Hunk-A would need a piano player, but a quick check of the website on my phone (Hunk-A-Hunk-A has its own app, by the way) shows that they offer "themed events," including some kind of "classy experience" involving dancers in tails moving to old classics on "a Steinway grand piano."

I'm not in the judging business, Leo.

It's just past midnight when Andy Reeves, decked out in a tux, makes his exit. There is no reason to play it coy or cute here. I get out of my car and start toward his. When Reeves sees me, he looks less than pleased.

"What are you doing here, Dumas?"

"Call me by my nom de plume," I say. "Dick Shaftwood."

He doesn't find that funny. "How did you find me?"

"Your newsletter. I'm a card-carrying member of the Other PianoMan Fan Club."

Reeves doesn't find this funny either. He picks up his pace.

"I got nothing to say to you." Then thinking of it: "Unless you brought me the tape."

"I didn't," I say. "But I've kind of had enough, Andy."

"Meaning?"

"Meaning you either talk to me, or I email out that tape right now." I hold out my phone as though my thumb is poised over a send button. It's a bluff. "I start with a friend of mine at the *Washington Post* and move on from there."

Reeves shoots daggers at me with his eyes.

I sigh. "Fine, then." I pretend to get ready to push the send button.

"Wait."

My thumb stays poised and ready.

"If I tell you the truth about the base, do I have your word you'll let this go?"

"Yes," I say.

He takes a step toward me. "I need you to swear on the memory of your brother."

It is a mistake for him to bring you into this, but I do indeed swear. I could voice caveats. I could tell him that if he or his cohorts had something to do with your death, not only would I sing like an oversharing canary, but I would personally be certain to take each and every one of them down.

I don't worry about the swearing. If what he tells me now needs to be revealed, I'll do so with joy and enthusiasm.

"Okay," Andy Reeves says. "Let's go somewhere and talk."

"I'm good right here."

He glances around the lot in full suspicion mode. There are a few stragglers, but this is hardly a hotbed of potential eavesdroppers. Still, he probably spent most of his life working in some kind of clandestine governmental department, CIA or something, so I get the paranoia.

"Let's at least get in my car," Reeves suggests.

I snatch the car key from his hand and slide into the passenger seat. Then he gets into the driver's. We both face forward now. Our view is of an old stockade fence that has seen better days. Several wooden pickets are either missing or cracked, like a vagrant's teeth after too many fistfights.

"I'm waiting," I say.

"We weren't part of the Department of Agriculture," he says.

When he doesn't go on, I say, "Yeah, I kind of figured that."

"Then the rest of this is simple. What happened in that facility is highly classified. You know that now. I'm confirming it. That should be enough."

"And yet it's not," I say.

"We had nothing to do with your brother or Diana Styles."

I give him my best "get to the point" expression. Andy Reeves makes a big deal of considering his next move. He makes me promise yet again to never speak a word of this to anyone, not ever, that he will deny it, that nothing he says leaves this car, you get the drift.

I agree with it all so we can move on.

"You know the time period we are talking about," Andy Reeves begins. "Fifteen years ago. Post-9/11. Iraq War. Al-Qaeda. All of that. You need to put this in that context."

"Okay."

"Do you remember a man named Terry Fremond?"

I search the memory banks. I do. "Rich white kid from a Chicago suburb who got turned into a terrorist. Uncle Sam al-Qaeda, they called him, something like that. He was on the FBI top ten list."

"He still is," Andy Reeves explains. "Fifteen years ago, Fremond set up a terrorist cell when he came back home. They were close to pulling off what may have been the worst event on US soil perhaps in history, another 9/11." Andy Reeves turns and meets my eyes. "Do you recall the official story of what happened to him?"

"He got wind the feds were onto him. Escaped through Canada and made his way back to Syria or Iraq."

"Yes," Andy Reeves says slowly and with great care, "that is the *official* story."

Reeves just keeps staring at me. I think about the orange blur that I assumed was a jumpsuit. I think about the secure location. I think about the need for secrecy. I think about the helicopter coming in at night under the cover of darkness and silence.

"You guys captured him. You brought him to the base."

We had all heard the rumors back then, hadn't we? I remember something else now, Leo—something you told me, but I don't remember when. We had to be in high school. You were fascinated by what the media had then labeled the "war on terror." You told me about them—harsh, dark places overseas where they took enemy combatants to make them talk, not to regular POW camps, but to . . .

"The base," I say out loud. "It was a black site."

Andy Reeves looks back out the front windshield again. "We had black sites in countries like Afghanistan, Lithuania, Thailand, places with code names like the Salt Pit and Bright Light and the Quartz . . ." His voice fades out. "There's one

CIA prison on an island in the Indian Ocean, one used to be a horse-riding school, one was even in a storefront, hiding in plain sight. They were crucial in our fight on terrorism. It was where our military would hold high-value foreign detainees for the purposes of enhanced interrogation."

Enhanced interrogation.

"It made sense keeping them in these foreign countries," Reeves continues. "Most of our enemy combatants were foreigners, so why bring them here? The legal technicalities are complicated, but if you interrogate an enemy combatant off American soil, the laws can be, shall we say, finessed. And you can be for or against enhanced interrogation. That's fine; I don't care. But don't comfort yourself in the lie that it didn't get us good intel or save lives. It did. That's the moral out people give themselves, isn't it? 'I'm against torture,' they say. 'Oh yeah? Suppose beating up a monster who slaughtered thousands would save your child's life—would you do it?' and they can't answer. They can't say, 'Sure, I'll sacrifice my own child for my moral stand,' so they come up with a smug rationalization like, 'It doesn't work anyway.'"

Andy Reeves turns, and his look is as heavy as the ages.

"Torture works. That's the horror of it."

I feel the chill, sitting in this dark car alone with this man, even as he is warming up to the tale. I've seen this before. It is so terrible a secret, so horrible a confession, and yet once you feel free to unburden yourself, once you let go and start talking, the sense of relief makes your mouth go into free fall.

"The problem was an obvious one. Forget overseas. There were—still are—terror cells right here in the United States. More than you can imagine. Most are American citizens, pathetic nihilists who get off on violence and mass destruction. But if we arrest them here in the United States, they have rights and due process and attorneys and all that. They wouldn't talk, and maybe, just maybe, a big attack is imminent."

"So you'd grab a suspect," I say. "You'd stick them on a stealth helicopter, you'd take them to that base, you'd interrogate them."

"Can you imagine a better place for a site like that?"

I say nothing.

"The detainees . . . they never stayed with us long. We used to call the base Purgatory. From there we could decide to let you go to Heaven or send you overseas to Hell."

"And how would you determine that?"

Reeves turns and looks right through me. That's all the answer he is going to give, and that's all the answer I need.

"Now get to the part about my brother," I say.

"There is no part with your brother. That's the end of the story."

"No, my friend, it's not. I now know that he and his friends made a tape of an American citizen being illegally held."

His face darkens. "We saved lives."

"Not my brother's," I say. "Not Diana's."

"We had nothing to do with that. I didn't even know about a tape until you showed it to me."

I try to read his face for the lie, but Andy Reeves is no amateur. Still, I don't see deception there. Did Reeves not know about the tape? How could that be?

I have one last card to play, and I play it.

"If you didn't know about the tape," I say, "why were you looking for Maura?"

"Who?"

This time the lie is easy to spot. I make a face.

"You questioned her mother," I say. "More than that, I think you, what, took her to your little black site? Did something so she'd forget whatever you did to her there?"

"I don't know what you're talking about."

"I showed her your picture, Andy. She confirmed that it was you who interrogated her."

He stares back at the front windshield and slowly shakes his head. "You don't understand a thing."

"Our deal was you come clean," I say. "If you're just going to jerk me around—"

"Open the glove compartment," he says.

"What?"

Andy Reeves sighs. "Just open the glove compartment, okay?"

I reach toward the glove compartment, turning my head for just a second to find the button to open it, but that is enough. His fist—I assume it's his fist, because I never see it—lands square in the spot between my left temple and cheekbone. The impact knocks my head to the right and rattles my teeth. Numbness runs down my cheek and into my neck.

He digs his hand into the glove compartment.

My head is still swimming, but one thought makes its way to the surface.

Gun. He's going for a gun.

His hand is grasping something metallic. Can't make it out, but do I really need to? I get enough of my bearings to grab his wrist with both of my hands. This leaves both of my hands occupied while one of his remains free. He uses that hand now to pummel me with short punches to my ribs.

I don't let go.

He starts turning and twisting his wrist, trying to break free or maybe . . . yes, he's trying maybe to angle the muzzle toward me. I slide one of my hands down far enough to cover his fingers. None are on a trigger. I press down hard now. He can angle the gun, but without a finger on a trigger, he can't hurt.

That's what I'm thinking right now: I have his fingers so he can't shoot me. I'm safe.

And that thinking ends up being tragically wrong.

He twists one more time. For a second I feel the cold metal hit the top of my hand. But only for a second. I see now that it's not a gun. It's too long. It's in the shape of a baton. I hear the crackle of electricity and feel the pain at the same time, the kind of pain that closes down everything else, that makes you recoil to avoid any more of it.

The volts run up my arm, rendering it useless.

Andy Reeves easily pulls his wrist free of my now-nonexistent grip. Then with a gleeful smile, he pushes the device—stun baton, electric cattle prod, I don't know—against my torso.

I start to convulse.

He does it again. My muscles won't work anymore.

He reaches into the backseat and pulls out something else. I can't see what it is. A tire iron, maybe. A baseball bat. I don't know. I'll never know.

He hits me in the head with it once, then again, and then there is nothing.

Chapter Twenty-six

I swim my way to consciousness in the strangest way.

Do you know the dreams where you can't do the smallest of physical tasks? You try to run from danger, but it's like every step is a trudge through wet snow at hip height. I was feeling something like that now. I wanted to move, to run, to escape, but I was frozen in place, like my whole body was encased in heavy lead.

When I blink my eyes open, I'm lying on my back. I see pipes and exposed beams. A ceiling. In an old basement. I try to stay cool, calm, not make any sudden moves.

I try to turn my head to take in my surroundings.

But I can't.

I can't move my head at all. Not half an inch. It feels like there is a vise locking my skull in place. I struggle and try harder. No go. No give at all. I try to sit up. But I'm strapped to some kind of table. My arms are belted against my sides. My legs are wrapped up tight.

I can't move at all. I'm completely helpless.

Reeves's whispery voice says, "You need to tell me where the tape is, Nap."

Conversation won't work here. I know that right away. So without saying a word, I scream for help. I scream as loud as I can. I keep screaming until he jams a gag into my mouth.

"Pointless," he says.

Reeves is performing some kind of task—he's humming as he does it—but I can't move my head to see. I hear the sound of a faucet being turned on, of someone filling a bucket or something. Then the faucet goes off.

"Do you know why Navy SEALs stopped using waterboarding as part of their training?" Reeves asks. When I don't answer—can't answer with the gag in my mouth—he says, "Because the trainee would crack so fast it was bad for morale. CIA recruits lasted an average of fourteen seconds before they begged their instructor to stop."

Andy Reeves stands over me. I look up at his smiling face, and I can see he's enjoying this.

"We would play an entire psychology game with the detainee too—a blindfold, having him escorted in by armed guards. Sometimes we would offer him hope and crush it. Sometimes we would let him know that there was no escape. You play it different ways depending on the subject. But I don't have time for those theatrics tonight, Nap. I feel bad about

Diana, I really do, but that wasn't my fault. So we move on. You're already strapped to the table. You already know this is going to be very bad."

He moves toward my feet. My eyes try to follow, but he's out of sight now. I try not to panic. I hear something cranking, and now I realize that the table I'm on is starting to tilt. I hope maybe I'll slip right off the table, even onto my head, but I'm strapped so tightly, gravity doesn't shift me even a little.

"Inclining your head and raising your feet," he explains, "keeps the throat open and makes filling the nostrils with water easier. You are imagining this is going to be awful. It is going to be much worse."

He moves back into view and pulls the gag from my mouth.

"Are you going to tell me where the tape is?"

"I'll show you," I say.

"No, that won't do."

"You can't get to it on your own."

"That's a lie. I've heard all this before, Detective Dumas. You'll make up a story now. You'll probably make up new stories the first time or two I take you through this process. That's why critics call torture unreliable. You're desperate. You'll say anything for a reprieve. But that won't work with me. I know all the tricks. Eventually you will crack. Eventually you will tell me the truth."

Maybe, but I know one thing for certain: Once he has the tape, he'll kill me. The same as he killed the others. So no matter what, I can't give in.

As if he can read my mind, he says, "You'll tell me, even if it means your death. A soldier who interrogated prisoners in the Philippine-American War once described what you're about to experience this way: 'His suffering must be that of a man who is drowning but cannot drown.'"

Andy Reeves shows me the towel. "Ready?" Then he places it against my entire face, blinding me.

The towel is just lying on my face, not even being held down tightly, but I already feel as though I'm suffocating a little. I try to move my head again, but it still won't budge. My chest starts to hitch.

Calm down, I tell myself.

I try to do that. I try to slow my breathing and prepare. I know that I'll need to hold my breath at some point.

Seconds pass. Nothing happens.

My breathing doesn't become more regular. It stays jangled and uneven. I strain to hear something, anything, but Andy Reeves isn't speaking or moving or doing anything.

More time passes. How long? Thirty seconds, forty seconds?

Maybe this is all a bluff, I start to think. Maybe this is just a psychological game, a way to stress . . .

That's when I hear the splash. A second later, no more, water starts to seep through the towel.

When I feel the wet hit my mouth, I lock my lips and close my eyes and hold my breath.

More water comes in, first a trickle, then heavier.

I feel it start going up my nostrils. I tighten up, keeping my mouth closed.

More water cascades in. I try to move my head, try to tilt my head up or find some way of escaping the onslaught. But I can't move. The water completely fills my nose. I'm starting to panic. I can't hold my breath much longer, and I need to get the water out of my nose and away from my mouth. Only one way. Blow

it out. But the towel is there. Still, I try to exhale now, to push
the water out, and for a second, maybe two, that works. I try to
keep exhaling, try to empty my lungs so as to keep the water at
bay. But there is too much water flowing down, and now the
big problem:

A man can exhale for only so long.

And when you're spent, when the exhale is over—and this is
the awful part—you eventually have to inhale.

That is where I'm at now.

When my exhale comes to an end, water starts pouring back
in, filling up my nostrils and mouth. I can't help myself. I'm
running out of air, and that agony overcomes all else. Holding
my exhale is killing me, and yet I know what awaits. I have to
inhale, have to breathe in, but there is no air. Only water. Lots
of water. The inhale opens the floodgate. The water flows freely
down my nose, into my mouth. No way to stop it. My inhala-
tion drags water through my mouth and down my windpipe.

No air.

My body goes into spasm. I start to buck, try to kick out, try
to flail my head, but I'm strapped down. There is no escape
from the water. There is no relief or letup at all. It just keeps
getting worse.

You don't just *want* it to stop. You don't just *need* it to stop.
It *has* to stop.

It's like I'm being held underwater, but it's worse. I can't
move. I'm locked in concrete. I'm drowning, Leo. Drowning
and suffocating. All rational thought is gone. I can feel a little
part of my sanity start to give way, a permanent rip in my psy-
che, something from which I know I'll never recover.

Every cell in my body is begging for oxygen, for just one

breath. But there is none. I'm gasping and taking in more water. I want to stop, but my gag reflex is unconsciously forcing
me to exhale and inhale. The water floods my throat and
trachea.

Please, God, let me breathe . . .

I'm dying. I know that now. A primitive part of me has given
up, surrendered, wishing death would speed along and get it
over with. But it won't. I flail. I convulse. I suffer.

I hallucinate.

I hallucinate a voice yelling to stop, to get away from him. If
every part of me wasn't starving for air, if every fiber of my
being was concentrating on my need to escape this, I might say
the voice was female. I can actually feel my eyes start to roll
back in my head as I hear the blast from somewhere deep inside
my brain.

And then I see a light.

I'm dying, Leo, dying and hallucinating, and the last thing I
see is the most beautiful face imaginable.

Maura's.

Chapter Twenty-seven

'm unstrapped and rolled to my side.

I suck in air, paralyzed to do anything more than that for a while. I gasp and try not to swallow. Water pours out of my mouth and nostrils, pooling on the floor and diluting the crimson blood oozing out of Andy Reeves's head. I don't care about any of that. I just care about air.

It doesn't take all that long for my strength to start returning. I look up to see who saved me, but maybe I am dead or my brain was starved of oxygen too long. Maybe I'm still being waterboarded and this is some weird state I've reached because the hallucination—no, mirage—is still there.

It's Maura.

"We have to get out of here," she says.

I still can't believe what I'm seeing. "Maura? I . . ."

"Not now, Nap."

And something about her using my name.

I'm trying to put it together, figure the next move, but all that "stay where you are" logic has flown out the window.

"Can you walk?"

I nod. By the time we hit the second step, I'm back in the moment. *One thing at a time,* I tell myself.

Get out of here. We reach the ground floor, and I realize we are in a dilapidated warehouse of some kind. I'm surprised by the silence, but it's probably . . . what time is it? I met up with Reeves at midnight. So it has to be deep into the night or early morning.

"This way," Maura says.

We head outside into the night sky. I notice that my breathing is a little funny, faster than normal, as though I'm still fearful the ability to do so might be taken away from me again. I spot his yellow Mustang in the corner, but Maura—I still can't believe it's Maura—is leading me toward another car. She hits the remote in her left hand. In her right I see the gun.

I get in the passenger side, she the driver's. She starts up and tears in reverse. Two minutes later, we are heading north on the Garden State Parkway. I stare at her profile, and I don't think I have ever seen anything that beautiful.

"Maura . . . ?"

"It can wait, Nap."

"Who killed my brother?"

I see a tear run down that beautiful cheek.

"I think," Maura says, "maybe I did."

Chapter Twenty-eight

We are back in Westbridge. Maura parks the car at the Benjamin Franklin Middle School lot.

"I need you to give me your phone," she says to me.

I'm surprised to find it's still in my pocket. I use my fingerprint to unlock it and hand it to her. Her thumbs dance across the screen.

"What are you doing?"

"You're a cop," she says. "You know that these phones can be traced, right?"

"Yes."

"I'm loading on a sort of VPN antitracker, so it looks like you're in another state."

I didn't know that kind of technology existed, but I'm not surprised. Her thumbs finish the dance. Then she hands me back the phone, opens the car door, gets out. I do the same.

"What are we doing here, Maura?"

"I want to see it again."

"See what?"

But she starts toward the Path and I follow. I try not to stare as she moves, her walk still panther-like, but I can't help it. As we head up into the darkness, she turns around and says, "God, how I've missed you," and then turns back around and keeps walking.

Just like that.

I don't react. I can't react. But every part of me feels ripped open.

I hurry to catch up to her.

The full moon tonight gives off enough light. The shadows cut across our faces as we start up the familiar route. We stay silent, both because the darkness calls for that and because, well, these woods used to be our place. You would think tonight of all nights that would haunt me. You would think that tonight of all nights, walking with Maura, the ghosts would be surrounding me, tapping me on the shoulder, mocking me from behind the rocks and trees.

But they are not.

Tonight I'm not falling back. I don't hear the whispers. The ghosts, oddly enough, stay hidden.

"You know about the videotape," Maura says, part question, mostly statement.

"How long have you been following me?" I ask.

"Two days."

"I know about the tape," I say. "Did you know?"

"I was on it, Nap."

"No, I mean, did you know Hank had it? Or that he gave it to David Rainiv for safekeeping?"

She shakes her head. Up ahead the old fence comes into view. Maura veers off the Path to the right. She bounces a few steps down the hill and stops herself by a tree. I make my way there. We are getting closer to the old base.

She stops and stares at the old fence. I stop and stare at her face.

"I waited here that night. Behind this tree." She looks down at the ground. "I sat right here and watched the fence. I had a joint from your brother. And I had my flask from you." She meets my eyes, and maybe it's not the ghosts, but something smacks me hard in the heart. "You remember that flask?"

I'd gotten it at a garage sale at the old Siegel house. It was old and dented. The color was gunmetal. The faded engraving read: *A Ma Vie de Coer Entier,* which was a fifteenth-century French saying, "You Have My Whole Heart for My Whole Life." I remember asking Mr. Siegel where he'd gotten it, but he couldn't remember. He called over Mrs. Siegel and asked her, but neither of them could even remember owning it. It felt somehow magical and stupid, like a genie's lamp I was supposed to find, and so I bought it for three dollars and I gave it to Maura, who giddily said, "A gift that involves romance *and* alcohol?"

"Am I not the perfect boyfriend?"

"You are," she'd said. And then she threw her arms around me and kissed me hard.

"I remember," I say now. Then: "So you sat by this tree with a joint and a flask. Who else was with you?"

"I was alone."

"What about the Conspiracy Club?"

"You knew about that?"

I give a half shrug.

Maura looks back toward the base. "We weren't supposed to meet that night. I think seeing that copter, making that tape—it freaked some of them out. It was all a game before then. That night made it real. Anyway, I wasn't really part of the"—finger quotes—"'club.' My only real friend was Leo. He had plans with Diana that night. So I came here and sat against this tree. I had my joint and my Jack in the flask."

Maura slides now to the ground and sits just as, I assume, she sat that night. A small smile is on her face. "I was thinking about you. I wished I was at your game. I hated the whole jock thing before you, but I loved to watch you skate."

I don't know what to say to that, so I stay still.

"Anyway, I could only get to the home games, and you guys were playing away that night. Summit, I think."

"Parsippany Hills."

She chuckles. "Figures you'd remember. Anyway it didn't matter. We'd be together in a few hours. I was just getting a little ahead of you here in the woods. The kids call it 'pregaming' now. So I kept drinking, and I remember feeling a little sad."

"Why sad?"

She shakes her head. "It doesn't matter."

"I want to know."

"It'd be over soon."

"What?"

From her spot on the ground she looks up. "You and me."

"Wait, you knew all that when you were just sitting here?"

Maura shakes her head. "You can still be so obtuse, Nap. I had no idea what was about to happen."

"Then—?"

"What I mean is, I knew you and I would never make it. Not for the long haul. We'd finish senior year, maybe last the summer—"

"I loved you."

I just blurt it out, like that. It startles her for a second, but not much longer than that.

"And I loved you, Nap. But you were off to a fancy college and a big life and there wouldn't be room for me and, God, what a cliché, right?" Maura stops, closes her eyes, shakes it off. "There's no reason to revisit this right now."

She's right. I help her ease back on topic. "So you were sitting here drinking and smoking."

"Right. And I'm getting a little wasted. Not terribly. Just tipsy. And I'm staring at this base. It's always so quiet there, but suddenly I hear a noise."

"What kind of noise?"

"I don't know. Men shouting. An engine starting up. So I stand up"—Maura does that now, sliding her back up the tree—"and I figure what the hell. Let's get to the bottom of this once and for all. Be a hero to the whole Conspiracy Club cause. So I start marching toward the fence."

Maura marches toward the base. I stay right with her.

"What did you see?" I ask.

"There were a bunch more of those warning signs. Like a ton circling the base. They were all bright red, remember?"

"Yes."

"Like, 'this is your last chance, go back or die.' We were

always afraid to go past them because they were too close to the fence line. But that night I didn't even slow down. I actually started sprinting."

We are both back there now, on that night, and I almost hesitate at the spot where those red signs used to be. We cross the invisible barrier, heading straight toward the rusted fence. She points to the top of the corner pole.

"There was a camera up there. I remember thinking that they might see me. But I was flying high, not a care in the world. I just kept running and then . . ."

She slows, stops. Her hand comes up to her throat.

"Maura?"

"I was right about here when the lights came on."

"Lights?"

"Spotlights. Huge ones with big beams. They were so bright I had to put my hand up to shade my eyes." She does that now, shading her eyes from an imaginary light. "I couldn't make out a thing. I was sort of frozen there, in the beam, not sure what to do. And then I heard the gunfire."

Maura lowers her hand.

"They were shooting at you?"

"Yeah. I guess."

"What do you mean, you guess?"

"I mean, that's what started it, right?" Maura's voice goes up an octave now. I can hear the fear, the regret. "Me. I ran toward the fence like a stupid kid. I ignored the warning signs. I tripped a wire or they spotted me or something, so they did what they promised on the signs. They started shooting. So, yeah, I guess they were shooting at me."

"What did you do?"

"I turned and ran. I remember hearing a bullet hit a tree right by my head. But, see, eventually I made it out alive. The bullets—they never hit me."

She raises her head and looks me straight in the eyes.

"Leo," I say.

"I kept running, and they kept shooting. And then . . ."

"Then what?"

"I heard a woman scream. I'm sprinting as fast as I can, dodging trees, trying to keep low so I make a smaller target. But I turn when I hear the scream. A woman's scream. I see someone, maybe a man, in silhouette through those bright lights . . . more gunfire blasts . . . then I hear the woman scream again, except this time . . . this time I think I recognize the voice. She screams, 'Leo!' She screams, 'Leo, help,' except the 'help' is cut off by another shot being fired."

I realize I'm holding my breath.

"And now . . . now I hear a man yell for everyone to hold their fire . . . silence . . . dead silence . . . and then maybe, I don't know anymore, but maybe someone yells, 'What have you done . . .' And then someone else yells, 'There was another girl, we have to find her . . .' but I don't hear that for sure, I don't know if it's in my head or for real, because I'm running. I'm running and I'm not stopping . . ."

She looks at me like she needs my help and like I better not offer any.

I don't move. I don't think I can.

"They . . . they just shot them?"

Maura doesn't reply.

Then I say something dumb. "And you just ran away?"

"What?"

"I mean, I get why you ran then—to get away from the danger. But when you were safe, why didn't you call the police?"

"And say what?"

"How about 'Hello, I saw two people shot'?"

Her eyes flick away from me. "Maybe I should have," she says.

"That's not really a good enough answer."

"I was stoned and scared and I freaked out, okay? It's not like I knew they'd been shot dead or something. I didn't see or hear Leo, just Diana. I panicked. You get that, right? So I hid for a while."

"Where?"

"You remember that stone hut behind the town pool?"

I nod.

"I just sat there in the dark. I don't know how long. You can see Hobart Avenue from there. I saw big black cars driving by slowly. Maybe I was just paranoid, but I thought they were looking for me. At some point I decided to go to your house."

This is news to me, but then again, what about tonight isn't? "You went to my house?"

"That was my destination, yeah, but when I reached your street, I saw another big black car parked on the corner. It's past midnight. Two men are sitting in suits watching your house. So I knew. They were covering their bases." She came closer to me. "Pretend now that I call this in to the police. I call and I say I think the guys at the base maybe shot someone. I don't really have any details or anything. But I have to give my name. They'd ask what I was doing near the base. I could lie or I could say I was up there smoking a joint and drinking some

Jack. By the time they'd listen to me, those guys at the base—they'd clean it up. Do you really not see this?"

"So you just ran again," I say.

"Yes."

"To Ellie's."

She nods. "At one point, I said to myself, 'Let's give it a day or two, see what happens.' Maybe they'll forget about me. But of course they don't. I'm watching from behind a rock when they interrogate my mother. And then when I see on the news that they found Leo's and Diana's bodies . . . I mean, I knew. The news didn't say anything about them being shot. They said they were hit by a train on the other side of town. So now what? What could I do? The evidence was gone. Who would ever believe me?"

"I would have," I say. "Why didn't you come to me?"

"Oh, Nap, are you serious?"

"You could have told me, Maura."

"And what would you have done? You, a hotheaded eighteen-year-old boy?" She glares at me for a moment. "If I'd told you, you'd be dead too."

We stand there and let that truth hang in the air.

"Come on," Maura says with a shiver. "Let's get out of here."

Chapter Twenty-nine

When we get back to the car, I say, "I left my car at that club."

"I called it in," Maura says.

"What does that mean?"

"I called the club and gave them the make and license plate and said that I was too drunk to drive. I told them I'd pick it up tomorrow."

She had thought of everything.

"You can't go home, Nap."

I hadn't planned on that anyway. She starts up the car.

"So where are we going?" I ask.

"I have a safe place," she says.

"So since that night"—I don't even know how to put it—
"you've been on the run?"

"Yes."

"So why now, Maura? Why after fifteen years is someone
killing the rest of the Conspiracy Club?"

"I don't know."

"But you were with Rex when he was shot?"

She nods. "I started relaxing the last three, four years. I figured, I mean, why go after me anymore? There was zero evidence. The base was long closed. No one would believe a word
I said. I was low on funds and trying to find a safe way . . . a
safe way to see what was happening. Anyway, I took a risk, but
it was like Rex wanted to keep the past closed as much as I did.
He needed help in his side business."

"Setting up men for drunk driving."

"He had nicer labels for it, but, yes."

We turn off Eisenhower Parkway right near Jim Johnston's
Steak House.

"I saw some CCTV footage from the night Rex was murdered," I say.

"The guy was a stone-cold pro."

"And yet," I say, "you escaped."

"Maybe."

"Meaning?"

"When I saw Rex go down, I figured, they found us, I'm
dead. You know. I was there that night—I was the real target,
I thought—but maybe they knew about the whole Conspiracy
Club. It made sense. So as soon as Rex was shot, I moved
fast. But the guy was already turning the gun on me. I jumped

into the driver's seat, started the car, drove like a bat out of hell . . ."

"But?"

"But like I said. He was a pro." Maura shrugs. "So how come he didn't kill me too?"

"You think he let you go?"

She doesn't know. We park in the back of a dumpy no-tell in East Orange. She isn't staying there. It's an old trick, she explains. She parks at the no-tell, so if the police or whoever spot the car or start a search based on the car, she's not there. She's renting a room about a quarter mile down the road. The car is stolen, she explains. If she senses any danger, she'll just abandon it and steal another.

"Right now I'm changing locations every two days."

We get to her rented room and sit on the bed.

"I want to tell you the rest," Maura says.

As she does, I stare at her. There is no sense of déjà vu. I'm not the teenager who made love with her in the woods. I try not to get lost in her eyes, but in her eyes, it's all there—the history, the what-ifs, the sliding doors. In her eyes I see you, Leo. I see the life I once knew and have always missed.

Maura tells me about where she's been since the night you died. It is hard to hear what her life has been like, but I listen without interrupting. I don't know what I'm feeling anymore. It's like I'm one exposed nerve ending. It's three in the morning when she finishes.

"We need some rest," she says.

I nod. She heads into the bathroom and takes a shower. She comes out in a terry cloth robe with her hair wrapped in a towel. The moonlight hits her in just the right way, and I don't think I've ever seen a more magnificent sight. I head into the bathroom, strip down, shower. When I come out, I have a towel wrapped around my waist. The lights are out except for a low-wattage lamp on the night table. Maura stands there. The towel is gone from her wet hair. She still wears the bathrobe. She looks at me. No pretense anymore. I cross the room fast. We both know it. Neither says it. I take her in my arms and kiss her hard. She kisses me back, her tongue snaking into my mouth. She pulls the towel off me. I yank open her robe.

This is like nothing I have ever experienced before. It is a hunger, a tearing, a ripping, a healing. It is rough and loving. It is gentle, it is harsh. It is a dance, it is an attack. It is ravenous and intense and ferocious and almost unbearably tender.

When it's over, we collapse on the bed, staggered, shattered, like we'll never be exactly the same, and maybe we won't. Eventually she moves so as to lay her head on my chest, her hand on my stomach. We don't speak. We stare at the ceiling until our eyes close.

My last thought before I pass out is a primitive one:

Don't leave me. Don't leave me ever again.

Chapter Thirty

We make love again at dawn.

Maura rolls on top of me. Our eyes meet and stay locked. It's slower this time, more soulful, comfortable, vulnerable. Later, when we are lying back and staring up into the silence, my mobile dings a text. It's from Muse and it's short:

Don't forget. 9AM sharp.

I show it to Maura. "My boss."

"Could be a setup."

I shake my head. "Muse told me about it before I met up with Reeves."

I am still on my back. Maura flips around so that her chin is on my chest. "Do you think they found Andy Reeves yet?"

It is something I've been wondering too. I know how that will play out: Someone notices the yellow car first, maybe they call the cops right then and there, maybe they search the premises. Whatever. They find the body. Did Reeves have ID on him? Probably. If not, they'll figure out his name from the car's license plate, they'll get his schedule, they'll see he worked that night at the Hunk-A-Hunk-A. A club like that will have CCTV cameras in the lot.

I'll be on them.

So will my car. The CCTV will show me getting into Reeves's yellow Ford Mustang with the victim.

I'll be the last person to see him alive.

"We can drive by the scene on the way," I say. "See if the cops are there yet."

Maura rolls off me and stands. I'm about to do the same, but I can't help pausing in something approaching sheer awe to admire her first.

"So why did your boss call this meeting?"

"I'd rather not speculate," I say. "But I don't think it's good."

"Then don't go," she says.

"What do you suggest I do?"

"Run away with me instead."

That could be the greatest suggestion ever made by anyone ever. But I'm not running. Not now, anyway. I shake my head. "We need to see this through."

Her reply is to get dressed. I do the same. We head outside. Maura leads the way back to the parking lot of the no-tell motel.

We scout the area, see no nearby surveillance, and decide to risk it. We get in the same car we used last night and start toward Route 280.

"You remember how to get there?" I ask.

Maura nods. "The warehouse was in Irvington, not far from that graveyard off the parkway."

She takes 280 to the Garden State Parkway and veers off at the next exit, for South Orange Avenue. We pass by an aging strip mall and turn into an industrial area that, like many such areas in New Jersey, has seen better days. Industry leaves; manufacturing plants close. That's just the way it is. Most times, progress comes in and builds something new. But sometimes, like here, the warehouses and factories are simply left to decay and disintegrate into bitter ruins that hint at past glory.

There are no people around, no cars, no activity at all. It looks like the set from some dystopian movie after the bombs hit. We cruise past the yellow Mustang without so much as slowing down.

No one has been here yet. We are safe. For now.

Maura swings the car back onto the parkway. "Where is your meeting?"

"Newark," I tell her. "But I better shower and change first."

She gives me a crooked smile. "I think you look great."

"I look satiated," I say. "There's a difference."

"Fair enough."

"The meeting will be serious." I point at my face. "So I need to figure a way to wipe this grin from my face."

"Go ahead and try."

We both smile like two lovestruck dopes. She puts her hand on mine and keeps it there. "So where to?" she asks.

"The Hunk-A-Hunk-A," I say. "I'll grab my car and take it home."

"Okay."

We enjoy the quiet for a few moments. Then in a soft voice Maura says, "I can't tell you how many times I picked up the phone to call you."

"So why didn't you?"

"Where would it have led, Nap? One year later, five years later, ten years later. If I had called you and told you the truth, where would you be right now?"

"I don't know."

"Me neither. So I'd sit there with the phone in my hand and I'd play it all out again. If I told you, what would you do? Where would you be? I wanted to keep you safe. And if I came home and told the truth, who'd believe me? No one. If someone did— if the police took me seriously—then those guys at the base would have to silence me, right? And then I started thinking about it this way: I was alone in the woods that night. I ran away and hid for years. So maybe the guys at the base would pin Leo and Diana on me. How hard would that be to do?"

I study her profile. Then I say, "What aren't you telling me?"

She puts on the turn signal with a little too much care, puts her hand back on the wheel, keeps her eyes too focused on the road. "It's a little hard to explain."

"Try."

"I was on the road for a long time. Moving, hiding, being on edge. Pretty much my entire adult life. That's the only life I knew. That constant rush. I was so used to it, to running and hiding, I didn't get being relaxed. It wasn't my baseline. In my own way, I'd been okay like that, under threat, trying to survive. But then when I slowed down, when I could see clearly . . ."

"What?"

She shrugs. "It was empty. I had nothing, no one. It felt like maybe that was my fate, you know. I was okay if I kept moving—it hurt more when I thought about what could have been." Her grip on the wheel tightens. "How about you, Nap?"

"How about me what?"

"How has your life been?"

I want to say, *It would have been better if you stayed,* but I don't. Instead I tell her to drop me off two blocks away, so I can walk to the club without anyone seeing her on CCTV. Sure, there is a chance we'll be picked up by another camera in the area, but by then, this will all be played out, whatever way it ends up going.

Before I get out of the car, Maura again shows me the new app I should use to contact her. It's supposedly untraceable, and the messages are permanently deleted five minutes after they arrive. When she's done, she hands me the phone. I reach for the door handle. I'm about to ask her to make me a promise that she won't run, that no matter what happens, she won't just disappear on me again. But that's not me. I kiss her instead. It's a gentle kiss that lingers.

"There are so many things I'm feeling," she says.

"Me too."

"And I want to feel them all. I don't want to be guarded with you."

We both get this connection and openness, don't we? Neither one of us is a kid anymore, and I understand how this potent cocktail of lust and want and danger and nostalgia can warp your perspective. But that's not what is happening to us. I know it. She knows.

"I'm glad you're back," I say, which may rank as the biggest understatement of my life.

Maura kisses me again, harder this time, so that I feel it everywhere. Then she pushes me away, like that old song about the honesty being too much.

"I'll wait for you by that office in Newark," she says.

I get out of the car. Maura drives off. My car is where I left it. Hunk-A-Hunk-A is, of course, closed. There are two other cars in the lot, and I wonder whether they too were claimed to be the result of too much drinking. I need to fill in Augie about Maura's return and Reeves's demise.

As I drive home, I call him on my mobile. When Augie answers, I say, "Muse wants to meet me at nine A.M."

"What about?" Augie asks.

"She wouldn't say. But there are some things I need to tell you first."

"I'm listening."

"Can you meet me at Mike's at quarter to nine?"

Mike's is a coffee shop not far from the county prosecutor's office.

"I'll be there."

Augie hangs up as I pull into my driveway and park. I manage to stumble out of my car when I hear a laugh. I turn and see my neighbor Tammy Walsh.

"Look what the cat dragged in," she says.

I wave to her. "Hey, Tammy."

"Long night?"

"Just some work."

But Tammy smiles as if it's written all over my face. "Yeah, okay, Nap."

I can't help but smile too. "Not buying that?"

"Not in the least," she says. "But good for you."

"Thanks."

Some twenty-four hours, am I right?

I shower and try to get my head back in the game. I pretty much have the truth now, don't I? But I'm still missing something, Leo. What? Or am I overthinking it? The base was hiding a terrible secret—that it was a black site for high-value potential terrorists. Would the government kill to keep that a secret? The answer is so obvious the question is by definition rhetorical. Of course they would. So that night, something set them off. Maybe it was Maura running toward the fence. Maybe they spotted you and Diana first. Either way, they panicked.

Shots were fired.

You and Diana were killed. So what could Reeves and his cohorts do? They couldn't just call the cops and admit what happened. No way. That would expose the entire illegal operation. They also couldn't just make you both disappear. That would lead to too many questions. The cops—and especially Augie—wouldn't rest. No, they needed a good ol'-fashioned cover-up. Everyone knew the legend of those train tracks. I obviously don't know all the details, but my guess is they pulled the bullets from your bodies and then transported you to the tracks. The impact of the train would leave the corpses in a state where no medical examiner would find any clues.

That makes total sense. I have all my answers now, don't I?

Except.

Except fifteen years later, Rex and Hank are murdered.

How does that fit in?

Only two members of the Conspiracy Club are left alive now. Beth, who is hiding. And Maura.

So what does that mean? Don't know, but maybe Augie will have a thought.

Mike's Coffee Shop & Pizzeria somehow manages to look like neither a coffee shop nor a pizzeria. It's in the heart of Newark, on the corner of Broad and William, with a big red awning. Augie sits by the window. He's staring at a guy who is eating pizza before nine in the morning. The slice is so obscenely enormous it makes his full-sized paper plate look like a cocktail napkin. Augie is about to crack wise about that when he sees my face and stops.

"What happened?"

There is no reason to sugarcoat any of this. "Leo and Diana weren't killed by a train," I say. "They were shot."

To his credit, Augie doesn't start with the "What?" "How can you say that?" "There were no bullets found" standard-issue denials. He knows I wouldn't just say something like that.

"Tell me."

I do just that. I tell him about Andy Reeves first. I can see he wants to stop me, wants to argue that none of this means Reeves or his men killed Diana and Leo, that he was water-boarding me because he still wanted to protect the secrecy around that black site. But he doesn't interrupt. Again, he knows me well enough.

Then I get to Maura rescuing me. I skip how Reeves dies for now. I trust Augie with my life, but there is no reason to put him in a spot where he may have to testify to what I'm saying here. Simply put, if I don't say Maura shot Reeves, then Augie can't testify to that if he's under oath.

I keep going. I can see my words are landing on my old mentor like body blows. I want to pause, give him time to breathe and recover, but I know that it will only make it worse and that it would not be what he wants. So I just keep the onslaught going.

I tell Augie about the scream Maura heard.

I tell Augie about the gunfire and then the silence.

Augie sits back when I'm done. He looks out the window and blinks twice.

"So now we know," he says.

I don't say anything. We both sit there. Now that we know the truth, we are waiting for something to feel different. But that guy is still eating his enormous slice of pizza. Cars are still cruising down Broad Street. People are still going to work. Nothing has changed.

You and Diana are both still dead.

"Is it over?" Augie asks.

"Is what over?"

He spreads his arms wide as if to indicate everything.

"It doesn't feel over," I say.

"Meaning?"

"There has to be justice for Leo and Diana."

"I thought you said he was dead."

He. Augie doesn't use Andy Reeves's name. Just in case.

"There were other people at the base that night."

"And you want to catch them all."

"Don't you?"

Augie turns away.

"Someone pulled the trigger," I say. "Probably not Reeves.

Someone picked them up and put them in, I don't know, a car or a truck. Someone pulled the bullets out of their bodies. Someone tossed your daughter's body onto a railroad track and . . ."

Augie is wincing, his eyes closed.

"You were indeed a great mentor, Augie. Which is why I can't move on. You were the one who railed against injustice. You, more than anyone I ever knew, insisted on making sure the bad guys paid a price for what they did. You taught me that if we don't get justice—if no one is punished—we never have balance."

"You punished Andy Reeves," he says.

"That's not enough."

I lean forward now. I had seen Augie knock heads too many times to count. He was the one who helped me take care of my first "Trey," a subhuman slither of scrotum whom I had arrested for sexually assaulting a six-year-old girl, his girlfriend's daughter. It got kicked on a technicality, and he was heading back home—back to that little girl. So Augie and I, we stopped him.

"What aren't you telling me, Augie?"

He drops his head into both hands.

"Augie?"

He rubs his face. When he faces me again, his eyes are red. "You said Maura blames herself for running toward that fence."

"In part, yes."

"She even said maybe it was her fault."

"But it's not."

"But she feels that way, right? Because maybe if she didn't get stoned and run like that . . . that's what she said, right?"

"What's your point?" I ask.

"Do you want to punish Maura?"

I meet his eyes. "What the hell is going on, Augie?"

"Do you?"

"Of course not."

"Even though she might in part be responsible?"

"She isn't."

He leans back. "Maura told you about the big bright lights. All that noise. Made you wonder why no one called it in, right?"

"Right."

"I mean, you know that area. The Meyers lived close by that base. On that cul-de-sac. So did the Carlinos and the Brannums."

"Wait." I see it now. "You guys got a call?"

He looks off. "Dodi Meyer. She said there was something going on at the base. She told us about the lights. She thought . . . she thought maybe some kids broke in and turned on the flood-lights and set off firecrackers."

I feel a small stone form in my chest. "So what did you do, Augie?"

"I was in my office. The dispatcher asked me if I wanted to take the call. It was late. The other patrol car was handling a domestic disturbance. So I said yes."

"What happened?"

"The lights were out by the time I got there. I noticed . . . I noticed a pickup truck by the gate. It was ready to pull out. There was a tarp over the back. I rang the bell at the fence. Andy Reeves came out. It was late at night, but I didn't question why so many people were still at a Department of Agriculture compound. What you said about a black site, that doesn't surprise me. I didn't know exactly what was going on, but I still foolishly trusted my government back then to be doing the right thing. So Andy Reeves comes to the gate. I tell him about us getting a disturbance call."

"What does he say?"

"That a deer jumped into the fence. That's what set off the alarms and lights. He said one of his guards panicked and started shooting. That was the gunfire. He said the guard killed the deer. He pointed to that tarp in the back of the pickup."

"Did you buy that?"

"I don't know. Not really. But the place was classified government stuff. So I let it go."

"What did you do next?"

His voice is coming from a million miles away now. "I went home. My shift was over. I got into bed, and a few hours later . . ." He shrugs away the rest of the thought, but I'm not ready to let it go.

"You got the call about Diana and Leo."

Augie nods. His eyes are wet now.

"And you didn't see a connection?"

He thinks about that. "Maybe I didn't want to see one. That way, like I asked you with Maura, it wasn't my fault. Maybe I was just trying to justify my own mistake, but I never saw much of a link."

My phone goes off. I see the time is 9:10 A.M., even before I read Muse's text:

Where the F are you??!!

I text back: There in a minute.

I rise. His eyes are on the floor.

"You're late for your meeting," he says without looking up. "Go."

I hesitate. In a way, all this explains so much—Augie's reticence over the years, his insistence that it was just two stoned kids doing something stupid, his disconnect. His mind wouldn't let him link the murder of his own daughter to his visit that night to the base because then he'd have to live with the additional guilt of maybe not doing anything about it. As I turn and head for the exit, I wonder about that now. I wonder about dropping this all on him, shattering him anew, whether every night from now on, as he closes his eyes, he's going to see that tarp over the back of a pickup truck and wonder what was underneath it. Or has he already been doing that in some subconscious way? Is the reason he so easily accepted the more obvious explanation for his daughter's death because he couldn't face his own small role in what happened?

My phone rings. It's Muse. "I'm almost there," I tell her.

"What the hell have you done?"

"Why, what's up?"

"Just hurry up."

Chapter Thirty-one

The Essex County Prosecutor's Office is located on Market Street in the simply dubbed Veterans Courthouse. I work here, so I know the building well. This place is always humming—more than a third of the entire state's criminal cases are tried here. As I head inside, I hear an unfamiliar ding coming from my phone and I realize it's that new app Maura installed. I read the message from her:

Drove by again. Cops found yellow Mustang.

This isn't good, of course, but it would still be a while before the course of events I laid out earlier would lead them to me. I have time. Probably. I type back:

Okay. Heading into meeting now.

315

Loren Muse is waiting for me at the door, staring daggers. She is a short woman, and she is flanked on both sides by tall men in suits. The younger of the two is thin and wiry, with hard eyes. The older guy sports a halo of too-long hair circling his bald dome. His protruding gut is giving his shirt buttons a hell of a battle. When we step into the outer office, the older guy says, "I'm Special Agent Rockdale. This is Special Agent Krueger."

FBI. We shake hands. Krueger, of course, tries to give me the dominant squeeze. I frown at him.

With that done, Rockdale turns to Muse and says, "Thank you for your cooperation, ma'am. We would be grateful if you could leave us now."

Muse doesn't like that. "Leave?"

"Yes, ma'am."

"This is my office."

"And the bureau appreciates your cooperation in this manner, but we really need to speak to Detective Dumas alone."

"No," I say.

They turn to me. "Pardon?"

"I would like Prosecutor Muse to attend any questioning."

"You're not suspected of any crime," he says.

"I still want her here."

Rockdale turns back to Muse.

Muse says, "You heard the man."

"Ma'am—"

"Stop calling me ma'am—"

"Prosecutor Muse, my apologies. You received a call from your superior, did you not?"

Through gritted teeth, Muse replies, "I did, yes."

Her superior, I know, is the governor of the state of New Jersey.

"And he did ask that you cooperate and give us jurisdiction on this matter of great national security, did he not?"

My phone vibrates. I sneak a quick peek, and I'm surprised to see it's from Tammy.

> Van of guys searching your house. Wearing FBI windbreakers.

I'm not surprised. They're looking for the original tape. They won't find it in my house. I buried it—where else?—in the woods near the old base.

"The governor did contact me," Muse continues, "but Detective Dumas has now requested counsel—"

"Irrelevant."

"Sorry?"

"This is a matter of national security. What we are about to discuss is highly classified."

Muse looks at me. "Nap?"

I think about it. I think about the issues Augie had raised, about what we should keep secret, about who is to blame for what happened to Leo and how I can get to the bottom of it and end this once and for all.

We are standing in the doorway. Muse's support staff of four are all pretending not to be listening. I look at the two agents. Rockdale is giving me flat eyes. Krueger is clenching and unclenching his fists, glaring at me like I just dropped out of a dog's behind.

I've had it.

So I turn to Muse and say loud enough so that her support staff can hear, "Fifteen years ago, the old Nike control base in Westbridge was an illegal black site incarcerating and interrogating American citizens suspected of colluding with terrorist entities. A bunch of high school kids, including my dead twin brother, taped a Black Hawk helicopter landing there at night. They want the tape from me." I gesture toward the two agents. "Their colleagues are, in fact, searching my house right now. It's not there, by the way."

Krueger's eyes go wide in shock and anger. He jumps toward me, his hand darting out to throttle me. You need to understand, Leo. I'm good with my fists. I've trained hard, and I'm athletic enough. But I imagine, under normal circumstances, this guy is more than up to the task of taking me down. So how to explain what comes next? How to explain that I move fast enough to parry his attack with a forearm? Simple.

He is going for the throat.

The part of me that lets me breathe.

And after last night, after being strapped to the table, something primitive in me will not let that happen. Something both instinctive and maybe supernatural will protect that part of my anatomy no matter what.

The problem is, blocking a blow never ends it. You have to deliver one of your own. I use the heel of my palm to strike his solar plexus. It lands flush. Krueger drops to one knee, the wind knocked out of him. I jump back now, fists raised, in case the other guy wants to join in. He doesn't. He stares at his fallen comrade in shock.

"You just struck a federal officer," Rockdale says to me.

"In self-defense!" Muse shouts. "What the hell is wrong with you guys?"

He gets in her face. "Your man just spouted out classified information, which is illegal, especially when it's a lie."

"How can it be classified," Muse shouts back, "if it's a lie?"

My phone buzzes again, and when I see the message from Ellie, I know I have to get out of here pronto:

FOUND BETH.

"Look," I say, "I'm sorry, okay, let's just all go inside and straighten this out." I go to help Krueger up. He doesn't like it, pushes my hand away, but there is no more fight in him for now. I keep acting all Mr. Peaceful as we head into Muse's office. I have a plan, a ridiculously simple plan, but sometimes those are the best. Once we settle down, once everyone is seated, I stand and say, "I, uh, need two minutes."

Muse says, "What's wrong?"

"Nothing." I try to look a little embarrassed. "I need the bathroom. I'll be right back."

I don't really wait for permission. I'm an adult, right? I head out of Muse's office and down the corridor. No one is following me. Up ahead is the men's room door. I walk past it and hit the staircase. I run down the steps to the ground floor, where I slow into a sort of walk-run.

Less than sixty seconds after leaving Muse's office, I am outside and putting distance between myself and those federal agents.

I call Ellie. "Where's Beth?" I ask.

"On her parents' farm in Far Hills. At least I think it's her. Where are you?"

"Newark."

"I'll text you the address. The ride should take less than an hour."

I hang up. I'm moving fast down Market Street. I turn onto University Avenue and use that new app to call Maura. I worry now that she won't answer, that she's vanished back into the ether, but she picks up right away.

"What's up?" Maura asks.

"Where are you?"

"Double-parked in front of the prosecutor's office on Market Street."

"Head east and make a right on University Avenue. We need to visit an old friend."

Chapter Thirty-two

Once Maura picks me up, I text Muse:

Sorry. I'll explain later.

"So where are we going?" Maura asks.

"To visit Beth."

"You found her?"

"Ellie did."

I put the address Ellie texted me into my navigation app. It tells us the ride will take thirty-eight minutes. We start making our way out of the city and onto Route 78 heading west.

"Do you have a theory on how Beth Lashley fits into all this?" Maura asks.

"They were also there that night." I say. "By the base. Rex, Hank, Beth."

Maura nods. "Makes sense. So we all had a reason to run away."

"Except the others didn't. At least not at first. They finished high school. They went to college. Two of them, Rex and Beth, didn't come back. They weren't exactly hiding, but I think it's clear they wanted no part of Westbridge. Hank, well, he was different. He would walk every day from the old base all the way across town to the railroad tracks. Like he was checking the route. Like he was trying to figure out how Leo and Diana ended up there. I think I get that now. He last saw them get shot by the base, like you."

"I didn't exactly see them get shot."

"I know. But let's say the Conspiracy Club were all there except for you—Leo, Diana, Hank, Beth, Rex. Let's say they saw those spotlights and heard that gunfire and all ran. Maybe Hank and the others saw Leo and Diana get shot. Like you, they're scared out of their minds. The next day, they find out the bodies were found all the way across town on the railroad tracks. That must have confused the hell out of them."

Maura nods. "They probably would have guessed that the guys from the base moved them."

"Right."

"But they stayed in town." Maura veers the car onto the highway. "So we have to assume that Reeves and the guys at the base didn't know about Hank, Rex, and Beth. Maybe only Leo and Diana got close enough to the fence."

That makes sense. "And my guess is, judging by Reeves's reaction, he didn't know about the tape either."

"So they thought I was the only living witness," she says, "until recently."

"Right."

"So what gave them away now? It's been fifteen years."

I think hard about this, and a possible answer comes to me. Looking out of the corners of her eyes, Maura sees it. "What?"

"The viral video."

"What viral video?"

"Hank supposedly exposing himself."

I explain to her about the video of Hank, about how it'd gone viral, how most people thought his murder was some kind of act of vigilantism. When I finish, Maura says, "So you think, what, someone from the base saw the video and maybe recognized Hank from that night?"

I shake my head. "That doesn't make much sense, does it? If they'd seen Hank that night—"

"They would have identified him earlier."

We're still missing something, but I can't help but think it has something to do with that viral video. For fifteen years, the three of them are safe. Then that video of Hank on school grounds goes viral.

It's related.

A brown sign featuring a red-clad equestrian reads WELCOME TO FAR HILLS. This isn't farm country. Not really. This part of Somerset County is for the wealthy rural set, those who want a huge home on a large plot with nary a neighbor in sight. I know a philanthropist out here who has a three-hole golf course on his land. I know other guys who own horses or grow apples for cider or do some other form of what one might label gentlemen's farming.

I look at Maura's face again, and I feel that sense of being overwhelmed. I reach out and take her hand. Maura smiles at me, a smile that hits bone, that makes my blood hum, that jangles my nerves in the best way. She takes my hand, brings it to her lips, kisses the back of it.

"Maura?"

"Yes?"

"If you need to run again, I'll go too."

She puts my hand on her cheek. "I'm not leaving you, Nap. Just so you know. Stay, go, live, die, I'm not leaving you again."

We don't say anything more. We get it. We aren't hormonal teenagers or star-crossed lovers. We are battle-scarred and wary warriors, and so we know what this means. No pretense, no holding back, no games.

Ellie is parked around the corner from Beth's address. We pull up behind her car and step out. Ellie and Maura embrace. They haven't seen each other in person in fifteen years, since Ellie hid Maura in her bedroom after that night in the woods. When they release the hug, we all move toward Ellie's car. Ellie gets in the driver's seat; I take shotgun, Maura goes into the back. We pull up to the closed gate blocking the driveway.

Ellie hits the buzzer by the intercom. No reply. She hits it again. Still nothing.

In the distance I see the white farmhouse. Like every other white farmhouse I've ever seen, it's stunning and nostalgic and you can instantly imagine a simpler, happier life under that roof. I get out of the car and pull on the gate. No go.

There is no way I'm leaving now. I head to the picket fence off the driveway, hoist myself up, and drop down into the yard. I signal to Ellie and Maura to stay put. The farmhouse is probably two hundred yards down the flat driveway. There are no trees or anything like that to hide behind, so I don't bother. I walk down the driveway in plain sight.

When I get closer to the house I can see a Volvo station wagon parked in the garage. I check the license plate. The car is from Michigan. Beth lives in Ann Arbor. You don't have to be much of a detective to figure out the car is likely hers.

I don't ring the doorbell quite yet. If Beth is inside, she knows already that we are here. I start to circle the house, peering in the windows. I start in the back.

When I look through the kitchen window, I see Beth. There is a near-empty bottle of Jameson on the table in front of her. The glass in front of her is half full.

There's a rifle on her lap.

I watch her reach out, lift the glass with a shaking hand, drain it. I study her movements. They are slow and deliberate. Like I said, the bottle is near empty, and now so too is the glass. I debate how to play it, but again I'm not in the mood to stall. I creep over to the back door, raise my foot, and kick it in right above the knob. The wood of the door gives way like a brittle toothpick. I don't hesitate. Using the momentum from the kick, I cover the few feet between the back door and the kitchen table in no more than a second or two.

Beth is slow to react. She's just starting to lift the rifle to aim when I snatch it away from her in classic "taking candy from a baby" style.

She stares up at me for a moment. "Hello, Nap."

"Hello, Beth."

"So get it over with already," she says. "Shoot me."

Chapter Thirty-three

unload the ammo and toss it in one corner, the rifle in the other. I use Maura's app to tell them that everything is fine, to stay where they are. Beth stares at me with defiance. I pull out the chair across from her and join her at the kitchen table.

"Why would I want to shoot you?" I ask.

Beth's looks haven't changed much since high school. I've noticed that the women from my class who are now in their midthirties have grown more attractive with age. I'm not sure why, if it's something about maturity or confidence or something more tangible like a toning of the muscles or a tightening of the skin around the cheekbones. I know only that as I look at Beth now, I have no trouble seeing the girl who played lead violin in the school orchestra or won the biology scholarship at senior award night.

"Revenge," she says. I hear the slur in her voice.

"Revenge for what?"

"To silence us, maybe. Protect the truth. Which is dumb, Nap. For fifteen years we never breathed a word. I would never say anything, swear to God."

I don't know how to play this. Do I tell her to relax, that I'm not here to hurt her? Will that make her open up? Or do I keep her on edge, make her think that the only way to survive this is to talk?

"You have a family," I say.

"Two boys. They're eight and six."

She looks at me now with naked fear in her eyes, like she's sobering up by the second. I don't want that. I just want the truth.

"Tell me what happened that night."

"You really don't know?"

"I really don't know."

"What did Leo tell you?"

"What do you mean?"

"You had a hockey game, right?"

"Right."

"So before you left, what did Leo tell you?"

The question surprises me. I try to go back there now—to earlier that night. I'm in my house. My hockey bag is packed. The amount of equipment you need is ridiculous—skates, stick, elbow pads, shin guards, shoulder pads, gloves, chest protector, neck guard, helmet. Dad finally made a checklist for us to go through because otherwise I'd arrive at the rink and invariably call and say something like, "I forgot my mouth guard."

Where were you, Leo?

What I remember, now that I think about it, is that you weren't in the front foyer with us. When Dad and I would go through his checklist, you were usually there. Then you'd drive me to the school and drop me off at the bus. That was more or less the routine.

Dad and I would go through the checklist. You would drive me to the bus.

But you didn't that night. I can't remember why anymore. But after we finished going through the checklist, Dad asked where you were. I shrugged maybe, I don't know. Then I walked to our room to see if you were there. The light was out, but you were lying on the top bunk.

"You going to drive me?" I asked you.

"Can Dad do it? I just want to lie here for a minute."

So Dad drove me. That's it. Those are the last words we shared. I didn't think twice about it at the time. When people suggested a double suicide, I did wonder about it for a moment maybe—not so much your words, but your solemn mood, lying in that bunk in the dark—but I never put much stock in it. Or if I did, maybe, like Augie with his police visit to the base that night, I pushed it aside. I didn't want your death to be suicide, so I made myself forget about it, I guess. That's how we all are. We pay attention to what works with our narrative. We tend to dismiss that which does not.

"Leo didn't tell me anything," I say now to Beth.

"Nothing about Diana? Nothing about his plans that night?"

"Nothing."

Beth pours some more whiskey into her glass. "Here I thought you two were close."

"What happened, Beth?"

"Why is it so important all of a sudden?"

"Not all of a sudden," I say. "It's always been important."

She lifts the glass and studies her drink.

"What happened, Beth?"

"The truth won't help you, Nap. It will only make it worse."

"I don't care," I say. "Tell me."

And she did.

"I'm the only one left now, aren't I? The rest are dead. I think we all tried to make amends. Rex became a cop. I'm a cardiologist, but I work for the most part for the underserved. I started a clinic to help indigent people with heart problems— preventive care, treatment, medication, surgery when required. People think I'm so caring and selfless, but the truth is, I think I do good because I'm trying to counter what I did that night."

Beth stares at the table for a long moment.

"We are all to blame, but we had a leader. It was his idea. He set the plan in motion. The rest of us, we were too weak to do anything other than go along. That makes us worse in some ways. When we were kids, I always hated the bully. But you know who I hated more?"

I shake my head.

"The kids who stood behind the bully and got off on watching. That was us."

"Who was the leader?" I ask.

She makes a face. "You know."

And I do. You, Leo. You were the leader.

"Leo got wind of the fact that Diana was going to break up with him. Diana was just waiting for that stupid dance to be over, which was a really sucky thing to do. Using Leo like that. God, I sound like a teenager, don't I? Anyway, first Leo was sad, and then he grew livid. You know your brother was getting high a lot, right?"

I give a half nod.

"We all were, I guess. He was the leader in that way too. Personally I think that was what had driven the wedge between Leo and Diana. Leo liked to party; Diana was the cop's daughter who didn't. Whatever, Leo started getting really jacked up. He was pacing back and forth, shouting about how Diana was a bitch, about how we needed to make her pay and all that. You know about the Conspiracy Club, right?"

"Right."

"Me, Leo, Rex, Hank, and Maura. He said the Conspiracy Club would get revenge on Diana. I don't think any of us took it seriously. We were all supposed to meet up at Rex's house, but Maura didn't even show up. Which was weird. Because she's the one who disappeared that night. I always wondered about that—why Maura ran when she wasn't even part of the plan."

Beth lowers her head.

"What was the plan?" I ask.

"We all had a job. Hank got the LSD."

That surprised me. "You guys were taking LSD?"

"No, never before that night. That was part of the plan. Hank knew someone in chemistry class who made him a liquid version. Then Rex's job, well, he provided the house. We would all meet in his basement. I would be the one who got Diana to take the stuff."

"The LSD?"

Beth nods. "Diana would obviously never do it on her own, but she was a big Diet Coke drinker. So my role was to spike her soda. Like I said, we all had our jobs. We were all waiting and ready when Leo went to pick up Diana."

I remember Augie talking about this, about how he thought Leo was high, how he wished like hell he could go back in time and stop Diana from walking out that door.

"So what happened next?" I ask.

"Diana was a little wary when Leo brought her down to Rex's basement. See, that's why I was there too. Another female face. To help her relax. We all promised that there would be no drinking. We started playing Ping-Pong. We watched a movie. And of course, we all drank sodas. Ours was mixed with vodka. Diana's was spiked with whatever LSD concoction Hank had brought. We were all giggling and having such a good time I almost forgot why we were really there. At one point, I remember I looked at Diana and she was nearly passed out. I wondered if I overspiked the drink. I mean, she was really out of it. Anyway, I figured, okay, mission accomplished. It was over."

She stops and looks lost. I try to knock her back on track.

"But it wasn't over."

"No," Beth says, "it wasn't." She looks past me now, over my shoulder, like I'm no longer here and maybe right now neither is she. "I don't know whose idea it was. I think it was Rex's. He worked as a counselor at a sleepaway camp. He used to tell us how the kids would sleep really soundly, so sometimes at night, for a funny prank, they would carry the kid's whole bunk out into the woods and just leave him there. They would hide and start laughing and wait for the kid to wake up and then they'd watch him freak out. Rex would tell us stories about it and they were always so funny. One time, Rex hid under the kid's bed and kept pushing from below until the kid woke up screaming. Another time he put a kid's hand in warm water. That was supposed to make him urinate his bed or something, but instead the kid got up like he was going to the bathroom and walked right into a bush. So Leo said—yeah, it was definitely Leo—he said, 'Let's take Diana out to the woods by the base.'"

Oh no . . .

"Anyway, that's what we did. It's really dark out. We're all dragging Diana up that path. I kept waiting for someone to call it off. But no one did. There's a clearing behind that old rock formation. You know the one. Leo wanted to leave her there because that was their old 'make-out spot.' He kept saying it like that, in a mocking voice. Make-out spot. Because Diana never let him go further, that's what he said. So we dumped Diana there. Just like that. Dumped her like she was so much garbage. I remember Leo looking down at her like . . . like I don't know. Like I thought he was going to rape her or something. But he didn't. He said that we should all go hide and watch what happens. Which we did. Rex was giggling. So was Hank. I think they were just nervous, though, waiting to see how she reacted to the acid. Leo, he just glared at her. I . . . I just wanted it to stop. I wanted to go home. I said, 'Maybe she's had enough.' I remember that I turned to Leo. I said, 'Are you sure you want to do this?' And Leo, he just had the saddest look on his face. It's like . . . it's like he suddenly realized what the hell he was doing. I saw a tear run down his cheek. I said, 'It's okay, Leo, let's take Diana home now.' Leo nodded. He told Hank and Rex to cut it out with the laughing. He stood up. He started walking toward Diana, and then . . ."

Tears are running down her face now.

"And then what?" I ask.

"All hell broke loose," Beth says. "It started with these giant lights. When they hit us, Diana popped up like someone had thrown a bucket of ice water on her. She started screaming and sprinting toward them. Leo ran after her. Rex, Hank, and I just stayed where we were, like we were frozen. I could see Diana's silhouette in the lights. She's still screaming. Louder now. She starts ripping off her clothes. All of them. And then . . . Then I hear gunfire. I see . . . I see Diana go down. Leo turns back toward us. 'Get out of here!' he shouts. And, I mean, he didn't have to tell us twice. We ran. We ran like hell all the way back to Rex's basement. We waited all night in the dark for Leo or . . . I don't know. We all made a pact. We would never ever say anything about tonight. Not ever. We just stayed there, in that basement, as the hours passed, hoping for the best. We didn't know what happened. Not that night, not even the next morning. Maybe Diana was at the hospital, maybe it would be okay. And then . . . then when we heard about Leo and Diana and the train tracks . . . we realized right away what happened. The bastards shot them and covered it up. Hank wanted to say something, go to the police, but Rex and I stopped him. What could we say? That we got the police captain's daughter high on LSD, brought her out to the woods, and these guys ended up shooting her? So we kept our vow. We never spoke of it again. We finished up our senior years. We left town."

Beth continues. She talks about living in fear and hating herself, her bouts of depression, her eating disorders, the guilt and horror of the night, the nightmares, seeing Diana naked, dreaming about it, trying to warn Diana in those dreams, running toward her, trying to grab her before she sprints toward the light. Beth goes on and on and starts to cry and begs for forgiveness and says she deserves all the horrible things that happen to her.

But I'm only half listening now.

Because my mind is spinning and taking me down a path I never wanted to follow. Remember how I said before that we embrace what fits our narrative and ignore what doesn't? I'm trying not to do that now. I'm trying to focus, even though I don't want to. I want to ignore. Beth had warned me. She said I wouldn't want to know the truth. She was right in ways she can't even imagine. Part of me wishes I could go back in time, back to when Reynolds and Bates first knocked on my door, and I would just tell them right away that I didn't know and just let it be. But it's too late now. I can't look away. So one way or the other, no matter what the cost, there will be justice.

Because I know now. I know the truth.

Chapter Thirty-four

Do you have a laptop?" I ask Beth.

My words startle her. She has been going on with her soliloquy uninterrupted for the past five minutes. She rises now and brings a laptop to the table. She turns it on and twirls it around so the screen is facing me. I bring up her web browser and type in the address for the website. I put the email address into the field for user ID and then I guess at the password. I get it right the third go-through. I sift through the private communications, find the one with the matching name. I write down the full name and phone number.

There are dozens of missed calls on my phone—Muse, Augie, Ellie, maybe the FBI. There are plenty of messages too. I get it. The FBI is probably looking for me because of the tape. The cops may have seen the CCTV footage of me in the yellow Mustang at the Hunk-A-Hunk-A.

I ignore it all.

I start making calls of my own. I call the Westbridge Police Station and get lucky. I call down south. I call the name and number I got off the website and identify myself as a police officer. I call Lieutenant Stacy Reynolds out in Pennsylvania.

"I need a favor," I tell her.

Reynolds listens, and when I'm done, she simply says, "Okay, I'll email the video in ten minutes."

"Thank you."

Before Reynolds hangs up, she says, "Do you know now who ordered the hit on Rex?"

I do, but I don't tell her yet. I still might be wrong.

I call Augie. When he answers, he says, "The feds could be monitoring my phone."

"Doesn't matter," I say. "I'm heading back up in a few minutes. I'll talk to them when I get there."

"What's going on?"

I'm not sure what to tell this long-grieving father, but I settle for the truth. There have been too many lies, too many secrets.

"I found Beth Lashley," I say.

"Where?"

"She's hiding at her parents' farm in Far Hills."

"What did she say?"

"Diana . . ." There is a tear in my eye. My God, Leo, what did you do? When I last saw you on that bunk bed, were you stewing over Diana? Were you planning your revenge? Why couldn't you open up to me? You used to tell me everything,

Leo. Why did you pull away from me like that? Or was it me? Was I so caught up in my own stuff—hockey, school, Maura— that I couldn't see your pain or tell you were on a path of self-destruction?

There are so many people to blame. Am I one of them?

"Diana what?" Augie says.

"I'm leaving here in a few minutes," I say. "I think it's better if I tell you in person."

"It's that bad."

Augie isn't asking. He's stating.

I don't reply. I don't trust my voice.

Then Augie says, "I'll be at my place. Get here when you can."

When I see Augie, my heart drops.

I've been waiting here for the past hour. I'm not inexperienced enough to sit by a window like Beth. I found a spot in the living room corner. From here I can see all entryways. No one can sneak up on me.

I know the truth, but I still hope I'm wrong. I hope that I'll just waste my time, that I'll sit in this corner of the farmhouse the rest of the day and through the night, and in the morning I'll realize that I made a mistake, that I messed up someplace, that I was hopelessly albeit wonderfully wrong.

But I'm not wrong. I'm a good detective. I was schooled by the best.

Augie doesn't see me yet.

I aim my gun and flick on the light. Augie turns toward me fast. I try to tell him to freeze, but I can't say it. So I sit there, my gun pointed at him, and hope that he doesn't reach for his. He sees my face. I know. He knows.

"I got onto your dating site," I say.

"How?"

"Your email was the user ID."

He nods, still the mentor. "And the password?"

"Eleven-fourteen-eighty-four," I say. "Diana's birthday."

"Careless of me."

"I went through your communications. There was only one woman named Yvonne. Yvonne Shifrin. Her phone number was there."

"You called her?"

"I did. You only went on one date. For lunch. You were sweet, Yvonne Shifrin said, but there was too much sadness in your eyes."

"Yvonne seemed like a good woman," he says.

"Still, I called the Sea Pine Resort in Hilton Head. Just to make sure. You never booked a room there."

"I could have gotten the hotel wrong."

"You really want to go this way, Augie?"

He shook his head. "Beth told you what they did to Diana?"

"Yes."

"So you understand."

"Did you kill my brother, Augie?"

"I got justice for my daughter."

"Did you kill Leo?"

But Augie isn't going to make it that easy.

"That night I picked up chicken parm from Nellie's. Audrey had a PTA meeting, so it was just Diana and me. I could see something was bothering her. Diana was just picking at her food, and she usually scarfed down Nellie's chicken parm." He tilts his head, remembering. "So I asked her if something was wrong. She said that she wanted to break up with Leo. Just like that. We had that kind of relationship, Nap."

He looks at me. I say nothing.

"I asked Diana when she was going to do it. She said she wasn't sure, but she'd probably wait until after the dance. I . . ." He closed his eyes. "I told her it was up to her, but I didn't think that was fair to Leo. If she didn't like him anymore, she shouldn't string him along. So you see, Nap? Maybe if I had kept my mouth shut, maybe if I had minded my own business . . . I saw your brother when he arrived, all stoned, and me, like an idiot . . . oh God, why did I let her go? Every night I lie in my bed and I ask myself that. Every single night of my miserable, horrible, empty life. I lie there and I replay it and I make all kinds of deals with God about what I'd give, what I'd do, what torments I would suffer, if only we could go back to that night and I could do it over again. God is so cruel sometimes. He blessed me with the most wonderful daughter in the world. I knew that. I knew how fragile it all was. I tried so hard to balance being a strict father with giving my child enough freedom, walking that goddamn tightrope."

He stands there shaking. I keep the gun on him.

"So what did you do, Augie?"

"It was like I told you before. I went to the base on a disturbance call. Andy Reeves brought me inside. I could tell something big had gone down. Everyone was pale. So first Reeves shows me the body in the back of a truck. It's some guy they were holding there. A high-profile American, he explains. The guy had gotten past the fences. They couldn't risk him escaping.

He wasn't supposed to be there, so they were going to get rid of his body, say he ran back to Iraq or something. Reeves told me all this in confidence. But I got it. State secrets. He wanted to make sure he could trust me. I said he could. And then . . . then he said he had something horrible to show me."

Augie's face starts to collapse a little at a time.

"So Reeves walks me out into the woods. Two of his men follow us. Two of his men are already there. Up ahead. He hits the flashlight and there, on the ground, naked . . ."

He looks up, and I can see the rage in his eyes.

". . . and there, next to my daughter's body, sobbing hysterically and holding her hand, is Leo. I'm staring down, completely numb, while Reeves starts explaining it to me. The prisoner in the truck escaped. They turned on the lights. The guys working the guard towers started shooting into the woods. No one is supposed to be out here. It's night. Those warning signs are all over the place. The guards kill the escapee, but accidentally, in the heat of battle, I mean, Diana was screaming like crazy and running right at them, stark naked, so one of the guards, a new guy, he panicked and pulled the trigger. It wasn't his fault, I guess. So there we are, standing there. You'd think I drop to my knees, wouldn't you? My little girl is dead on the ground, and I want to, I want to just fall onto the ground and hold her and sob for hours. But I don't."

Augie looks at me. I don't know what to say, so I don't say anything.

"Leo is still blubbering away. I ask him, calm as I can, what happened. Reeves, he signals for his men to start back to camp. Leo wipes his face with his sleeve. He tells me he and Diana were out in the woods, making out, starting to go further, you know, that kind of thing. Starting to undress. He says when the lights went on, Diana jumped up and panicked. Reeves is standing there listening. I look at him. He shakes his head. He knows what I can see on your brother's face. Leo is lying. 'We got video,' Reeves whispers to me. I help your brother stand. We go inside the base to look at the surveillance tape. First, Reeves shows me a video of your girlfriend. They got her on tape too. Reeves asks me if I know her. I'm too stunned not to answer. I say that's Maura Wells. Then he nods and shows me another tape. I see Diana. She's running and screaming. Her eyes are wide like she's terrified, and she's ripping her clothes off like she's on fire. That's how my little girl spent her last moments alive, Nap. Screaming and terrified. I actually see the bullet hit her chest. She crumples to the ground. And then coming up behind her is Leo. Reeves stops the tape. I turn to Leo. He's cringing now. I say, 'How come your clothes are still on?' He's crying. He starts making up some story about how much they both loved each other. But see, I know: Diana was going to break up with him. I get really quiet now. Like I understand him now. I'm a cop; he's a perp. I'm working him. My heart is falling apart—it's disintegrating in my chest, and I'm just like, 'It's okay, Leo,' just tell me the truth. They're going to do an autopsy. What drugs are in her system? I keep peppering him. He's a kid. It doesn't take long for Leo to crack."

"What did he tell you?"

"It was just a joke, he kept saying. He didn't mean to hurt her. Just a stupid prank. To get back at her."

"What did you do?"

"I looked back at Reeves. He nodded like we both understood each other. Because I did. This was a black site. No way the government was going to let that get out, even if it meant a few civilian deaths. He left the room. Leo was still crying. I told him not to worry, it was going to be okay. I told him what he did was wrong, but really, what would he get via the legal system? Not much. In the end, all he did was slip a girl LSD. No big deal. Unlikely worst-case scenario: They might charge him with manslaughter, go on probation. I told him all this because it was true, and as I did, I took out my gun and pressed it against his forehead and pulled the trigger."

I cringe as though I'm there, Leo, as though I am standing right next to Augie as he kills you in cold blood.

"Reeves comes back in the room. He tells me to go home, that he'll take care of it. But I don't leave. I stay with them. I find my daughter's clothes. I put them on her. I don't want her found naked. We put their bodies in the back of the pickup truck. We drive across town to the train tracks. We get ready. I'm the one who heaves Diana onto those tracks. I watch that big engine steamroll over my beautiful daughter. And I don't blink. I don't flinch. I need it to be horrible. The more horrible, the better. Then I go home. I wait for the call to come in. That's it."

I want to call him names. I want to hurt him. But it all feels so pointless, so utterly wasteful.

"You're a good interrogator," I say, "but Leo didn't tell you the whole truth, did he?"

"No," Augie says. "He protected his friends."

I nod. "I also called Westbridge Police Station. Your rookie cop Jill Stevens answered. It always bothered me that she left Hank's file on your desk and that you didn't follow up. But you did follow up, didn't you?"

"I found Hank by the basketball courts. He was pretty shook up about the whole viral-video thing. I always had a soft spot for him, so I told him he could come stay at my house for the night. We watched the Knicks game on TV. And when it was over, I made up a bed for him in the spare bedroom. He goes into the room and when he sees the photograph of Diana on the bureau, he completely loses it. He starts sobbing and crying and begging me for forgiveness. He keeps saying it was his fault and at first I don't know what to make of it, if he's just having some kind of manic episode, but then he says, 'I should have never gotten that LSD.'"

"So then you knew."

"He kinda caught himself. Like he realized he had said too much. So I had to work him. I had to work him hard. But eventually he told me about that night, about what him and Rex and Beth did. You're not a father, so I don't expect you to get it. But they all killed Diana. They all murdered my little girl. My daughter. My life. The three of them got to live another fifteen years. They got to breathe and laugh and grow into adults, while my baby, my world, rotted in the ground. Do you really not get why I did it?"

I don't want to go there. "You killed Hank first."

"Yes. I hid the body where no one would find it. But then we visited his father. I thought Tom deserved to know what happened to his son. So that's when I strung Hank up. Cut him up so it looked like it was connected to that viral video."

"And before that, you went up to Pennsylvania," I say. Augie was good, thorough. He would have gotten the lay of the land, looked into Rex's life, learned about his scam, used it. I remember Hal the bartender's description of the killer: raggedy beard, long hair, big nose. Maura, who had only met Augie briefly at Diana's last birthday party, described the killer the same way. "You wore a disguise, even changed the way you walked. But when the tapes from the rental car place were analyzed, you matched the height and weight. Also your voice."

"What about my voice?"

The door from the kitchen opens. Maura and Ellie walk through it. I didn't want them to stay, but they insisted. Ellie noted that if the two of them were men, I wouldn't insist they leave. She was right about that. So here they are now.

Maura nods at me. "Same voice."

"Maura says the guy who hit Rex was a pro," I say, because I want this to end. "Yet this pro let her escape. That was my first clue. You knew Maura had nothing to do with what happened to Diana. So you didn't kill her."

That was it. There was really nothing more to say. I could tell him about the other clues that had pointed me toward him—how Augie had known Rex was shot twice in the back of the head even though I never told him, or how Andy Reeves, when he had me strapped down, regretted killing Diana but not a word about Leo. But all of that wasn't important.

"So now what, Nap?" Augie asks.

"You're armed, I presume."

"You gave me this address," he says with a nod. "You know why I came here."

To kill Beth, the last person who had harmed his daughter.

"What I felt for you, Nap—what I feel for you—that's real. We did bond in grief—you, me, your dad. I know that makes no sense, that it almost sounds sick—"

"No, I get it."

"I love you."

My heart is breaking all over again. "And I love you."

Augie's hand starts to go into his pocket.

"Don't," I say.

"I would never shoot you," Augie says.

"I know that," I say. "But don't."

"Let me end this, Nap."

I shake my head. "No, Augie."

I cross the room now, reach into his pocket, take out his gun, and toss it to the side. Part of me doesn't want to stop him. Let it end with a nice suicide. Nice, neat, complete. Rest in peace. Some would say that I get it now, that Augie wrongly taught me to be a vigilante, that just because the legal system doesn't always deliver justice doesn't mean I should take matters into my own hands, that I was wrong to do what I did to Trey the same way Augie was wrong to do what he did to Leo and Hank and Rex. Some would think that I'm stopping him because I want to let the legal system work, that I finally understand that I need to let our laws decide these things, not the passions of certain men.

Or maybe, as I cuff him, I realize that suicide would be the easy way out, that if he killed himself, it was over for him, that forcing an old cop to rot in a prison cell with all those ghosts is a far worse fate than a quick bullet.

Does it matter which is right?

I'm heartbroken, devastated. For a moment I think about the gun in my possession and I think about how easy it would be to join you, Leo. But I only think about it for a moment.

Ellie has already called the police. As they take Augie away, he looks back at me. Maybe he wants to say something, but I don't want to hear it, can't bear to hear it. I've lost Augie. No words will change that. I turn away and walk out the back door.

Maura is standing there, looking off into the fields. I come up behind her.

"There's one more thing I need to tell you," she says.

"It's not important," I say.

"I met up with Diana and Ellie at the school library earlier that day."

I know, of course. Ellie had already told me.

"Diana said she was going to break up with Leo after the dance. I shouldn't have said anything. What was the big deal? I should have kept it to myself."

I had already figured this part out. "You told Leo."

That was how you knew, Leo, wasn't it?

"He got so angry. He talked about getting her back. But I wanted no part of it."

"Which is why you ended up in the woods all alone," I say.

"If I hadn't said anything to him . . . none of this would have happened. It's my fault."

"No," I say, "it's not."

And I mean it. I pull her close and kiss her. We could go on and on with this blame game, Leo, couldn't we? It's her fault because she told you Diana wanted to break up with you, it's my fault because I wasn't there for you, it's Augie's, it's Hank's, it's Rex's, it's Beth's, hell, it's the president of the United States's fault for approving that black site.

But you know what, Leo? I don't care anymore. I'm not really talking to you. You're dead. I love you and I will always miss you, but you've been dead for fifteen years. That's a long enough time to mourn, don't you think? So I'm going to let you go now and grab on to something more substantial. I know the truth now. And maybe, as I gaze upon this strong, beautiful woman in my arms, the truth has finally set me free.

ACKNOWLEDGMENTS

If you read the opening author note, you know I went back to my childhood. The reminiscences on the *Livingston—60s and 70s* Facebook page were invaluable, but I especially need to thank Don Bender, a patient man and an expert on all things involving New Jersey's old missile sites. Other people to thank, in no particular order: Anne-Sophie Brieux, Anne Armstrong-Coben, MD, Roger Hanos, Linda Fairstein, Christine Ball, Jamie Knapp, Carrie Swetonic, Diane Discepolo, Lisa Erbach Vance, John Parsley, and a few people I'm forgetting, but because they are generous and wonderful, they'll forgive me.

I also want to acknowledge Franco Cadeddu, Simon Fraser, Ann Hannon, Jeff Kaufman, Beth Lashley, Cory Mistysyn, Andy Reeves, Yvonne Shifrin, Marsha Stein, and Tom Stroud. These people (or their loved ones) made generous contributions to charities of my choosing in return for having their names appear in the novel. If you would like to participate in the future, visit www.HarlanCoben.com for details.

ABOUT THE AUTHOR

Harlan Coben was the first ever author to win all three major crime awards in the US. He is now a global bestseller with his mix of powerful stand-alone thrillers and Myron Bolitar crime novels. He has appeared in the bestseller lists of *The Times*, the *New York Times*, *Le Monde*, *Wall Street Journal* and the *Los Angeles Times*.

Also available from Harlan Coben

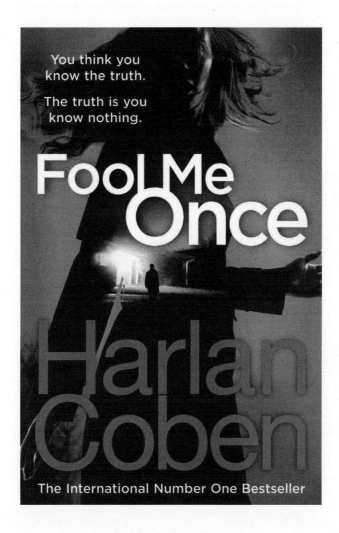

OUT NOW

Also available
from Harlan Coben

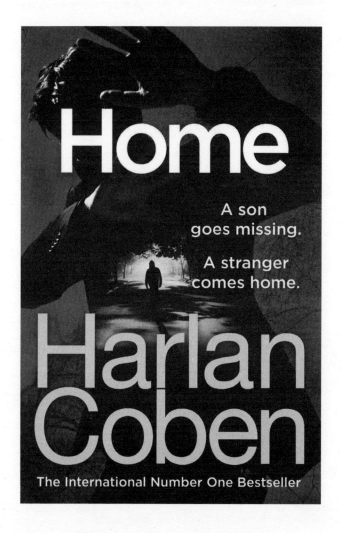

OUT NOW

Harlan Coben

Find out more online:

WWW. harlancoben.com

 @HarlanCoben

 @harlancobenbooks